Pierrette's anger won out over her curiosity and shock. It was up to her to act before the Templars unleashed some new evil. She wrapped her scarf around her mouth and nose, threw a smoke bomb, and jumped into the chaos.

Someone shouted, "Alive, you idiots! Take her alive!"

She shot at the attackers, and hit one, but something was wrong. There was blood on her right hand now – no, all the way down her right arm. A wound above the collarbone; it was bleeding. A lot.

She toppled, slipping in her own blood, and banged her knee and shoulder hard on the packed dirt floor. Two sets of arms were around her.

At least the smoke was clearing; at least she could breathe a little. Then she looked up, into a face she knew from her nightmares.

MORE ASSASSIN'S CREED® FROM ACONYTE

Assassin's Creed: The Magus Conspiracy by Kate Heartfield

Assassin's Creed: The Ming Storm by Yan Leisheng
Assassin's Creed: The Desert Threat by Yan Leisheng

Assassin's Creed Valhalla: Geirmund's Saga by Matthew J Kirby
Assassin's Creed Valhalla: Sword of the White Horse by Elsa Sjunneson

BY THE SAME AUTHOR

The Course of True Love
Armed in Her Fashion/The Chatelaine
Alice Payne Arrives
Alice Payne Rides
The Embroidered Book
Assassin's Creed: The Magus Conspiracy
The Valkyrie

ASSASSIN'S CREED

THE ENGINE OF HISTORY

The RESURRECTION PLOT

KATE HEARTFIELD

ACONYTE

UBISOFT

First published by Aconyte Books in 2023.

ISBN 978 1 83908 235 1

Ebook ISBN 978 1 83908 236 8

Cover art by Bastien Jez

Distributed in North America by Simon & Schuster Inc, New York, USA
Printed in the United States of America
9 8 7 6 5 4 3 2 1

ACONYTE BOOKS

An imprint of Asmodee Entertainment Ltd

Mercury House, Shipstones Business Centre

North Gate, Nottingham NG7 7FN, UK

aconytebooks.com // twitter.com/aconytebooks

For everyone who has ever stayed up
too late for one more mission

CHAPTER ONE

Pierrette Arnaud sat on the edge of a four-story roof and pulled her cloak tightly around her, so the blue ballgown beneath wouldn't draw attention. Beside her, Safiya El-Nadi was dressed in her usual dark shawl that fell in a peak over the forehead, a thin gold cylinder between her eyes holding the black crocheted veil that hit at her waist. Much less conspicuous, at least in this part of Cairo.

The women were two small additions to a skyscape of square roofs and twisting domes, lattice windows and fluted columns, stonework and plaster. Their feet dangled from the roof of a gable. A good vantage point.

Safiya had kept company with Pierrette on the walk from the house they shared near one of the old city gates. From the beginning, Pierrette felt they were being followed. She trusted her instincts, but if there *was* someone following, she couldn't see them. Perhaps she had reached the moment in her life as an Assassin when ghosts would dog her steps. It would only be fair; she had created enough of them.

Nonetheless, she had signaled to Safiya to change course, so they'd come to the street where Safiya's husband, Gamal Sabry, was selling books today. It was a street they knew well, and they'd both climbed lightly up onto the roofs in a narrow alley. In the coffee shop opposite their rooftop, a half-dozen men smoked long pipes under an awning, and chatted with Gamal, who had spread the books from his cart onto a carpeted table. Gamal liked to say that bookselling was merely an excellent way for an Assassin to monitor the streets of Cairo, but he couldn't hide his passion for the job.

Gamal caught the women's eyes, his turban tilting slightly as he looked up.

The street was busy, with water carriers and vendors calling out, and women passing through on donkeys, servants at their side. Gamal took an English copy of Darwin's *On the Origin of Species* off his table to show it to a customer. Pierrette recognized it from the golden triangles on the green spine. She'd perused the books on Gamal's cart many times.

"I see no followers," Safiya said.

The shadows were long. The sun was beginning to set. She had to be at the Opera House soon. Still, something kept her where she was.

"Do you want to go over the plan again?" Safiya asked patiently. "You seem nervous."

Pierrette was thirty-seven years old, a skilled Assassin, and a veteran circus performer. She did not think of herself as a person who got nervous. The reason she'd come to Egypt in the first place was that she'd been frustrated by the unwillingness of the British Assassins to take risks. She was here to fight. She was grateful to have a task she believed in.

Nonetheless, she couldn't deny her unease. Safiya seemed to sense it too; she had spoken in French, although she usually spoke in Arabic to help Pierrette practice.

"I suppose I am. It's been a long time since I've been in fine company," Pierrette said, tucking a silk bow beneath her cloak. Truth be told, she was looking forward to the chance to wear a beautiful new dress. "And I've never met the khedive."

She was looking forward to that, too. Khedive Ismail Pasha, viceroy of Egypt, technically answered to the Ottoman Sultan, but he had ambitions of his own. Not only was he intent on rebuilding half of Cairo, but he had covered Egypt in railway lines and presided over the ten-year construction of the Suez Canal. Tonight, weeks of celebrations would begin, as the canal was nearly ready to open. The khedive would entertain his guests, including heads of state, at a reception and opera. And Pierrette would be among them.

"He will be dazzled by you," Safiya said staunchly. "Who wouldn't be? Besides, he wants your expertise for his new circus and hippodrome."

"That's just the line we used to get my invitation. The khedive has many people to advise him on entertainments."

"I wouldn't be so sure. He had to send away his Armenian impresario in the spring, don't forget."

"I haven't forgotten. And I still don't think that story makes sense. Why did the man leave Cairo freely, with money in his pocket, if he tried to plant a bomb in the khedive's theater box? It doesn't add up. There is too much happening in this city that we don't understand."

It was not for lack of trying, she knew. Cairo's Assassins kept careful watch on their ancient enemies, the Templars.

There was always a strong Templar presence in the city, since that Order was obsessed with finding artifacts, so it had a spy on every archeological dig site. After the bomb was found in the theater, the Assassins' minds had gone right away to the Templar-orchestrated assassination of Abraham Lincoln, four years ago. But there was no evidence connecting the Templars to the attempt on the khedive's life. All monarchs had to deal with such threats, after all.

"The khedive has guards to protect him. Your job tonight is to face a much more terrible danger," Safiya said. She leaned toward Pierrette and said with mock horror: "An American businessman."

That got a smile from Pierrette. She wiped her hands and prepared to leave their perch when a flash of purple and gold caught her eye. On the table across the street, Gamal had placed a book upright so that its gorgeous, embossed cover faced them. The Bulaq Press edition of the *Book of Gnosis* by Ibrahim Hakkı Erzurumi.

It was a striking and unusual edition, which was why it was their agreed symbol. It meant danger.

Safiya had noticed it too. Moving as little as possible, they swept their gazes over the streets below. Nothing unusual in the street between them and the coffee shop. Gamal was casually chatting, but there was no doubt his signal was deliberate. Over to the left, in the alley between buildings, stood a man in European dress. He was doing a good impression of waiting for someone, but what he was actually doing was listening. Listening to Pierrette and Safiya. Pierrette's eyes narrowed.

Safiya pointed toward the man – a signal that this one was hers – and rose silently to her feet. She leaped over the edge of the roof, her cloak floating for a moment. There was a sound like a sack falling off a wagon, then a sound like a wagon wheel in need of grease. While Safiya dealt with the spy, Pierrette checked their surroundings. She glanced at the coffee shop opposite and grinned. No one had noticed anything, because Gamal's well-trained donkey was conveniently braying and customers and tradesmen alike all offered help to the apparently frustrated and apologetic bookseller.

Pierrette ran to each corner of the roof, searching for accomplices. The streets and alleys seemed clear of anyone suspicious. She and Safiya and Gamal knew the names and faces of every water carrier, beggar, food vendor, itinerant priest, scholar or listless lover in the neighborhood. There was no one else out of place.

Taking her time so as not to rip the beautiful dress, which really had cost quite a lot, Pierrette climbed down into the alley where Safiya whispered her final words over the man she'd just killed. It didn't seem likely he'd hear them. He'd died from a single blow from above, Safiya's knife in the back of his neck between his vertebrae.

Safiya straightened up. "A Templar lackey. I've seen his face before. May he find mercy."

If the Templars were following her, they must have got wind of the fact that Pierrette had an invitation to the opera tonight. How much did they know about her plans?

All the same, she felt strangely light, now that her instincts had been confirmed. Let them come. If they wanted a battle, they would find her willing.

CHAPTER TWO

Safiya and Pierrette dragged the spy's body into a recessed doorway. Night was falling and once it was fully dark Gamal and Safiya would use the book cart to take the body to the necropolis, where, by tradition, both Templars and Assassins left their dead to be claimed. Safiya motioned Pierrette on and stayed to keep watch in the meantime.

Pierrette left Old Cairo, walking toward the setting sun. Calls to prayer rang out as she reached the new neighborhoods, where the streets were wide and the buildings low. Behind her, lanterns carried by people as they walked or rode gave the impression of fireflies from a distance.

Ahead of her, a line of gas lamps lit the new district of Azbakeya below the purple sky. Pierrette knew this area well because Gamal often came here, as did other booksellers. He would spread his books out on the wall that surrounded the Azbakeya Garden. In the daytime, the garden was filled with children feeding the ducks, and families in little boats on the ponds. On this night, it was busy with people on their way to the new opera house, a short walk from the hotels clustered around the garden.

The khedive had invited heads of state to witness the upcoming opening of the Suez Canal to traffic. A feat of engineering ten years in the making, the canal would allow ships to pass directly from the Mediterranean Sea to the Red Sea, instead of going around Africa. Pierrette had always believed that human efforts could reshape the world, and it was exciting to be here at this moment when humans were dividing the continents of Africa and Asia. Some of the illustrious visitors would not arrive in Egypt for another week or two, but tonight's guest of honor would be Empress Eugenie of France.

Pierrette's job was to make sure that one particular guest at the opera never got a chance to speak with the empress: Albert Hawkins.

Amira Benyamina, a Master Assassin and a member of Cairo's Council, ran a radical newspaper, which helped her find information and plant sources. Yesterday, she'd intercepted a telegram that suggested a Templar called Albert Hawkins was going to take advantage of the empress's presence at the opera to conduct some business with her. Amira used to live in Paris, and her connections there had told her that the Templars had been trying to influence Eugenie for years, hoping to use her to sway French policy.

The Cairo Council had decided the moment had come to take out Albert Hawkins before he could do any more damage. Killing a Templar was always a considered decision; it risked bringing attention from the police, and retribution from the Order. But Hawkins had to die.

Since he'd come to Egypt a few years ago, Hawkins had

been trying to undermine the khedive's efforts to chart Egypt's own course. The khedive seemed genuinely interested in establishing greater freedom for all, whatever the Ottoman bureaucrats said about it. He had put an end to forced labor, despite French insistence that it was necessary to finish work on the Suez Canal.

Albert Hawkins had made it hard for the khedive to stand on principle; it was an open secret that Hawkins had built an unfinished railway to an uninhabited area near the new canal, using unauthorized forced labor to do it. A project designed to take speculators' money, and make the khedive look like he had no control in Egypt.

There was no doubt about it: Albert Hawkins was a blight on the world. The Assassins were trying to make Egypt a bulwark against corruption and coercion, and Hawkins stood in the way of that, by undermining the khedive and his goals. With him dead, the khedive would have more breathing room and the Templars in Egypt would have one less connection to their American and European interests. Pierrette didn't know what conversation Hawkins hoped to have with Empress Eugenie tonight, but it would not be good for the people of Egypt or the people of France.

Pierrette had seen no signs of another Templar follower since she parted from Safiya, and no longer felt uneasy. When no one was looking, she pulled off her old cloak and stowed it behind a loose rock in the garden wall, one of the Cairo Assassins' many drop spots. Her old cloak had been suitable when she was trying not to attract attention in the streets, but going into the opera it would have the opposite effect.

Pierrette walked differently in her blue dress. The style gave her a pleasing ease of movement; it was sleeveless, save for the golden epaulettes. She tugged her white gloves up over her elbow, adjusting the gold cuff that disguised the spring device for her Hidden Blade.

The new Opera Square was filled with people, milling past the great equestrian statue, past the palm trees in perfect symmetry, to the Opera House. Beyond the illuminated Opera House, the city rose on its hills, a shadow against the night.

She slipped in among the richly dressed people coming out of the Azbakeya Garden, a slow tide through the columns on either side of the Opera House doors. People of every description: young and old, every shade of skin, conversations in several languages and accents. The only commonality was that they all had an invitation to the opera, and money to dress for it.

Most guests went into the large room where there was food and drink before the performance. Pierrette kept climbing to the third floor. Albert Hawkins would be at the khedive's private reception, waiting for a chance to greet the empress, who was expected to make a late entrance. Hawkins' plan would be to speak with her at the entr'acte, but he would be dead by then.

At a door flanked by two guards, she gave her name. They admitted her to a long room, warm with light from great crystal chandeliers over tables filled with food and flowers. About twenty people stood in a few clusters.

To the right, a doorway led to the box seats in the auditorium (she'd studied the building plans). Opposite that, dark windows overlooked the rooftop terrace. There was red bunting around the walls, and a large photograph of the sultan at one end of the room.

At the other end, the actual ruler of Egypt: the khedive, in the flesh. There was no mistaking him. A stocky man, with thick eyebrows, wearing a dark suit with a red fez. There were three security officers near him – good.

One of the half-dozen people talking to the khedive was just as familiar to Pierrette from the photographs she'd studied. Albert Hawkins was in his thirties, with dark curls tamed with pomade above a boyish face. He didn't look like a robber baron; he looked as though he had dressed up as a rich man for a costume party. His suit fit poorly, and he was holding an ornate silver cane. Affectation certainly, but also, likely, a weapon. Appearances could be deceiving.

And so could Albert Hawkins. By that innocent half-smile as he listened to the conversation, you'd never know he had left a trail of cheated investors across the American West (and at least three wives with children).

He'd come to Egypt a few years ago and established himself as a man with useful expertise. He knew about cotton production – the source of Egypt's wealth in the khedive's early years, when the American Civil War had made Egypt the world's top supplier. He claimed military and logistics expertise from his service in the Confederate Army, which was how he convinced the khedive to let him build his railway from Alexandria to an uninhabited spot midway down the canal in the first place. After all, soon the canal would be lined with new settlements, he argued.

He'd been just as persuasive with the local people, convincing them they'd be sorry if they refused to work for him. When the khedive told him to stop, Hawkins had protested that he had no other way of completing the line. He demanded an exorbitant payment from the khedive – whose coffers were depleting now that the United States was back in the cotton trade – or the right to carry on forcing people to work for him.

Unsurprisingly, this was the subject of conversation as Pierrette joined the group of people talking with the khedive. Every Assassin had their own way of hiding in plain sight, and this was Pierrette's. She'd long been comfortable moving between classes and worlds, from circus sawdust to upper-class mahogany. She was a performer and could play the role expected. In some rooms, her reputation as a retired circus performer, traveler and equestrienne would not have given her much cachet, but here, it did: state-of-the-art cultural entertainment was as much a part of building the new Egypt as the canal was.

An older French woman was saying to the khedive, "But I thought Egypt had an ancient tradition of requiring public labor for public works. Don't you call it the corvée?"

The khedive replied in perfect French, "I beg your pardon, madame, but *you* call it the corvée. It is a French word, and no wonder, since it existed there until recently as well. We have abolished it in Egypt, and your emperor made sure it cost us dearly to do so."

"*Our* emperor?" The French woman looked aghast.

"He demanded that we pay thirty-eight million francs to the Suez Canal Company, to compensate them for the lack of forced labor. But you see, we are building a country here, madame, not merely a canal."

"And now you invite the French empress to see your canal open," said Hawkins, in American-accented French. "To see your victory?"

The khedive cocked his head. "I invite a good friend to witness a historic day. And to see *Rigoletto* performed, of course! I had hoped to have commissioned a new opera from Signor Verdi, but it is not ready yet. Artists cannot be rushed."

"Much like canals," said Hawkins. He was quick, even in his halting French.

While everyone smiled at Hawkins's joke, he scanned their faces. His gaze landed on Pierrette, and the khedive saw, and turned to look at her.

"I present Mademoiselle Pierrette Arnaud," said the aide standing beside him.

The khedive took her hand and smiled. "Ah, the equestrienne! I hope you will consider coming to talk to me about circuses. I would be grateful for your advice about my new hippodrome."

Safiya had been right. The khedive did seem interested in her expertise. But perhaps he was just polite.

"I have not performed for years," she said, a little wistfully. Her work as an Assassin was crucial. She did believe that serving the light required some people to work in the dark. But sometimes, she missed the days when all that mattered was the beauty she created, when she could show off her skills, when she could bring light to the eyes of every person in a crowd.

"But you once performed all over Europe," the khedive replied. Clearly, he'd done his research. "Do you find that tastes vary by city?"

"Every city is different, but the best hippodromes do not worry about tastes or fashions. All these modern troupes with their performing cockatoos and goats and elephants – they don't treat the animals well, and it's a sad and smelly affair. Real horse people, though, treat their horses better than humans, and they'll work marvels, if given the chance to improve their craft instead of trying to find work all the time. If I were managing a hippodrome, Your Highness, I would pay the best equestrian performers and keep them there year-round. Soon, you'll have an attraction that will draw people to the city, instead of a mere copy of what every other city has."

He contemplated her. "If you were managing a hippodrome, you say."

She felt herself blush. How could she make it clear she was not looking for a job? She glanced aside as she thought and realized that Hawkins had left the group.

He was, in fact, gone from the room entirely.

This was her moment.

If time had permitted, the council might have developed a plan to kill Hawkins in a quieter location: a suborned cab driver, a dark alley. But they'd only intercepted the telegram yesterday, and besides, as Pierrette had argued, it might be easier to catch him off guard at a public event. He was known for going out on terraces and balconies to smoke and conduct business; the Assassins had sent Hawkins a telegram purporting to be from a dealer of enslaved Sudanese people, asking to meet on the terrace before the empress arrived. The plan was in motion.

She made a quick excuse about the heat and, brushing aside the khedive's concern, strode out through the terrace doors. It was empty.

Cursing herself for becoming distracted and missing which way the man had gone, she went back through the reception room, moving swiftly through the crowd. She flung open a door, then another, then she nearly gasped at the sight of the auditorium. Four levels of boxes formed a horseshoe, of which she was in the middle, three levels up. Below, there were chairs on the floor level, and a great stage, with a curtain bearing the portraits of the khedive and of his guest of honor, Empress Eugenie. The auditorium was empty – no.

There was a figure in the box nearest the stage and one level down: by the richness of the chairs and flanking curtain, the royal box. He leaned forward slightly, into the light, and she glimpsed Albert Hawkins's curls.

Pierrette stepped back into the shadows. What was he doing in the khedive's seat? She remembered the bomb in the theater in the spring – if it was a bomb being planted now, where would Hawkins have obtained it? The guards would have searched the building. No, there must be some other reason. Hawkins was an arrogant, narcissistic risk-taker. He probably wanted to see what it felt like, to sit in the royal box. Maybe it had tickled him to plan an assignation there; the slaver and the empress might not be the only people he planned to talk to tonight.

Her unease from earlier in the day had returned. But she had him, now, in an empty auditorium. Too far for the throwing knife in her boot, and she couldn't risk missing by an inch and giving him a chance to make a noise.

Back out into the curving corridor that connected the entrances to all the boxes. She ran lightly to where it ended, before the royal boxes, which must have had their own entrance. She moved into the last box, planning to drop from there to the second level, right next to the royal box.

Instead, she saw Hawkins climbing up towards the third level, hanging from the railing over the royal box, a few feet to her right and a little below her.

Pierrette winced and stepped backwards into the shadow, so she could just see part of his jacket tails moving as he climbed. The box above the royal one was covered top to bottom in a tight lattice that screened it from view. It was for the khedive's wives, who lived in seclusion. Hawkins clung to the lattice screen, and seemed to have found a way to open it at the end closest to the stage. She leaned forward just enough to see him swing the screen fully open and slip inside and out of view.

Why would Hawkins want to go into the wives' box? It didn't make any sense.

She went to the edge of her box, climbed over, and dropped, hanging by her fingernails from the railing, inching her way below him as he retied the screen in position. She was tempted to thrust her blade upward right then, but blood drops in the orchestra pit would raise questions. After listening for his breath, she moved.

Left hand up to the lattice, pull. Right hand on the lattice, pull. It creaked and a small part of her brain wondered whether it would hold her weight, but she didn't need it to hold for long. She was looking into his startled eyes when she released her Hidden Blade and thrust it through a hole in the lattice, right into his windpipe.

There was no one in the auditorium to hear those horrible soft sounds. He grabbed at her fingers weakly, then collapsed in a heap. Damn. She'd been hoping he'd fall backwards, for blood cleanup purposes. She pulled herself over to the edge of the screen, unfastened it, and slipped into the box.

The blood, luckily, was mostly confined to his white waistcoat. As the light left his eyes, Pierrette put one hand on his shoulder; it was her job now to ease the passing of even this odious man. A necessary passing, sanctioned and commissioned by a council, not a murder out of passion or self-interest. Unlike her teacher, Simeon, she did not agonize about the philosophy. And she had never been religious. But she felt that a human, at the end, should not pass alone, even if their only company was their killer.

She pulled a white handkerchief out of her reticule, on which she had embroidered her own initials, P.A., intertwined with those of her target, A.H., in simple stitches, the work of an hour this morning. She let the handkerchief rest briefly on his bloody throat, and then tucked it back where it came from. A sign she'd carried out her assignment.

Not that it had gone to plan. She had a conveniently situated wagon beneath the rooftop terrace from which she'd planned to toss the body of Albert Hawkins. Here, she only had a blood-covered corpse and nowhere to carry it. And an audience outside, eager for the opera to begin.

The box was framed with heavy red curtains, pulled to the side. They seemed entirely decorative; there was no reason for anyone to pull them, especially given that the wives' box was already obscured from view. From here, they'd be able to hear the opera, and to see basic movements, but they'd miss a lot as much on the other side of the lattice was blurry. Why had Hawkins climbed up here, when he could just as easily have left the royal box on the second floor, the way he came?

As she shoved his body, sitting up, behind the red curtain, it dawned on her. The wives were in seclusion; that meant they would enter the Opera House separately. And a separate entrance was, from another point of view, a separate exit.

Hawkins had been trying to leave the Opera House, without being seen.

She tucked the curtain around his legs – that would have to do, and heaven help her if one of the royal wives found a corpse during the performance – and opened the edge of the lattice again. She peered out: the auditorium was still empty. But she could hear the murmur of many voices approaching. From behind the stage, she could hear other voices rising in scales, and a violin being tuned.

She dropped, hung on the railing, and swung into the royal box on the level below. Everything seemed normal. It was empty. Just in case, she looked under the khedive's red-upholstered chair.

There was a small rack for umbrellas and canes that ran under the chairs, and lying on that rack was Hawkins' silver cane.

Why had he left it? An oversight? Had he been in a rush?

She picked it up. An ordinary-looking metal cane, thick, with a straight silver handle coming off at an angle. It was heavy, but that was what he got for not using wood or bamboo like everyone else. An odd thing caught her eye: a section of about a hand-span below the handle seemed to open up. It was held closed by two screws. She unscrewed them, opened the section.

A bit of clockwork, like the back of a pocket watch. Wires. A smaller metal tube inside the top – no, not a tube. The muzzle of a small gun?

She didn't understand how a cane could be a bomb, but what else could it be? Whatever it was, Hawkins had wanted to get away from it in a hurry.

Pierrette went to the railing, cane still in hand, prepared to run through the auditorium, to warn someone. But there was a crush of people at the door, and a rush of sound as their conversations filled the giant space. She looked up at the levels of boxes. People were filling them too.

Breathe.

The khedive would be the last to take his seat, with the empress. Hawkins would have known that, and set the timer to allow himself to escape. How long would it take to evacuate eight hundred people, even once she could make herself understood? What sort of panic would it cause? Would there be injuries in the rush to get out?

No, there was only one thing to be done. Find the exit Hawkins had meant to use, and get the cane out. Now.

She hooked the cane onto the sash of her dress, gingerly, and climbed up again to the women's box. Then, with the cane in one hand, she opened the door and ran down a narrow corridor to a stairway. And nearly into the retinue of fine women in airy veils and beautiful jewelry, their servants yelling at Pierrette. Luckily, she was not well known at the palace, so if all went well and everybody lived, it was unlikely anyone would connect her name with the rude woman in the blue dress, and raise questions about what Pierrette Arnaud had been up to. And if they did, so be it. She didn't have time to be discreet. She could only push her way through, apologizing, hoping no one looked behind the curtain. If they made it that far.

Then she rushed through the little crowd of women and out a small door, into the street. It was full of vendors and people walking and taking the air, hoping for a glimpse of royalty.

Pierrette ran through Opera Square, into the garden, the cane bouncing against her dress.

A few silhouettes here or there, but away from the gaslight the park was empty and dark. She slowed her pace and made for the slight curve she could just make out ahead: a footbridge over a pond.

As she threw the cane and it splashed into the water, Pierrette stood for a second at the top of the bridge and felt like a child playing a game, placing bets on when the stick would float to the other side. But it sank immediately. She walked away as quickly as her lungs would let her, over to the garden wall.

Minutes passed. She caught her breath. Distant music swirled in the Opera House; the empress must have arrived, and the performance had begun. Maybe it was all for nothing. What other explanation could there be for a cane with clockwork and wires inside? Perhaps many explanations. It could be any sort of device. She regretted not making Albert Hawkins talk before he died.

She walked over to the loose stone in the wall and retrieved her cloak. Time to tell Gamal and Safiya that the job was done – and to ask for their help in removing the body after the performance.

Pierrette took one step toward the old city when, behind her, with a great rumble, bang and a spray of water, the bomb went off.

CHAPTER THREE

In Gamal and Safiya's house, Pierrette occupied the uppermost room, on its own floor, which caught the breeze. Her married friends took the middle floor. The bottom floor was divided into two sitting rooms and a kitchen. Pierrette loved the smaller sitting room best. The walls were decorated with framed aphorisms in beautiful Arabic calligraphy, and the shelves held Gamal's personal book collection, which never seemed to shrink despite his skill at selling them.

It was unusual for a married couple to eat or talk together with a female guest in Cairo, but Assassins were unconventional people, and besides, Safiya said, Pierrette was practically family. It was also a house without servants. Gamal and Safiya would not endanger them.

So, the morning after the assassination, there was no one to disturb. They sat on cushions around a low table and Gamal examined Pierrette's drawing of Hawkins's cane.

He pointed to the arrangement of gears she'd sketched. "I'm surprised that clockwork had the strength to pull the wire.

But it must have. I think you're right that there was a small pistol – with a hair trigger – in the cane's handle. It pointed toward a blasting cap, and the clockwork would create a delay so Hawkins could get to safety."

Pierrette rubbed her temple. None of them had got any sleep, after an inconvenient early-hours trip back to the Opera House to dispose of Hawkins's body. Luckily, none of the wives had shifted the curtain during the performance. Pierrette grimaced. How gruesome to think of it sitting there hidden behind the curtain while the wives listened to that sublime music. And the Assassins had just barely got into the box before the cleaners, requiring a diversion and an arduous journey carrying the body through the corridors while avoiding said workers. So this morning, her head was foggy.

"I've seen drawings of the device that Confederate soldier used a few years ago, what they called the 'horological torpedo,'" Safiya said. "It used a clockwork mechanism. But that was so much bigger – twelve pounds of gunpowder. I don't see how one could fit that much gunpowder into a cane."

"Because it wasn't gunpowder," Gamal said grimly. "It was dynamite."

Safiya and Pierrette winced. They'd heard about the new explosive, made from nitroglycerine soaked into wood pulp or some other absorbent material. But they hadn't come across it yet.

"A single stick of dynamite might not create sufficient damage on its own," Gamal explained, "but maybe there was more than one stick, and gunpowder or something else added. Besides, the metal cane's containing effect would have amplified the blast, meaning one wouldn't need much explosive material.

It's ingenious, really. Of course, we'll never know whether the bomb would have achieved its purpose."

He looked almost wistful. The Assassins didn't use bombs often, because of the likelihood of injuring innocent people. But they studied their enemies.

Safiya said, "Right under the khedive's chair like that, I don't think it could have failed. And think of the shrapnel. Pierrette, you saved more than one life last night, I'm sure of it."

Pierrette reflected on what might have been. It made no sense for the Templars to kill Empress Eugenie, after working here and in Paris to influence her. Perhaps that influence had failed. Or perhaps the plan had been to call the empress away at the last minute with an urgent telegram or something of the kind, saving her by apparent luck from yet another bombing. The first bombing the empress had escaped seemed to make her and her husband even more authoritarian, so Pierrette suspected that was the explanation. The Templars liked what they thought of as "strong governments", so long as those governments could be controlled by Templars, and they always could. It was all part of the Templar ambition to create their utopia, in which no individual's plans could interfere.

The khedive, though, was an obvious target. He bristled against Ottoman control and stood up to European empires. The Templars would not take this defeat as final.

She pulled her shawl tighter. "We should send word to the khedive's security forces, warn them to be vigilant. The Templars won't stop here."

Gamal twisted the signet ring, a habit he had when he was thinking. "We thought the man who followed you that night had learned of your plan to kill Hawkins. But now I wonder whether they were simply monitoring us to make sure we stayed out of Hawkins's way. Maybe other Assassins in Cairo had followers last night. We'd better go see Amira."

On their way to Amira's newspaper office, Pierrette thought about the first time she had saved Empress Eugenie from a bomb. That time, like this one, the empress had no idea that she had a woman named Pierrette to thank.

The first time, Pierrette had diverted one of the bombs destined for the empress and her husband, Napoleon III, outside another opera house, in Paris. She hadn't done it out of any feeling of duty to the royal pair, but to protect others, and to fulfill a promise to a friend. That night, she hadn't been the only person trying to prevent bloodshed. Simeon Price, the first Assassin she'd met, was there too. After that night, Simeon took Pierrette on as a student. For the next four years, they'd chased Simeon's own teacher and Assassin traitor, Oscar Kane, until they finally cornered him in Bath and put an end to his efforts to obtain a terrible weapon.

With Kane dead, Simeon had been eager to leave London. He'd become a minor celebrity there after his court martial, and Simeon did not enjoy celebrity. Pierrette stayed. She had friends there: the Aurora Troupe of circus performers. More than friends – her chosen family.

So Simeon had gone his way, and Pierrette had gone hers.

However, Simeon's letters always arrived from a different place. The last one had been from a village in the south of Russia. He seemed happy enough, but it was always hard to tell with Simeon.

And Pierrette, newly inducted into the British Assassins, had plenty to keep her busy, at first. She was thrilled to find that as she gained skills and experience, the Council of Assassins would provide her with weapons, armor and respect. She was sent to assassinate targets, and there were plenty of them. While she and Simeon had been focused on stopping Kane, they hadn't realized how quickly the Templars were spinning their webs throughout London's financial and commercial corridors.

Over the next five years, Pierrette watched with frustration as the British Assassins lost more ground. The council became more cautious with every setback. Ethan Frye, one of the most respected British Assassins, was a wise man and an excellent teacher, but he seemed to be as distracted by other problems as she and Simeon had once been. His teenage children were younger than Pierrette, and though she trained and chatted with his daughter Evie sometimes, she felt lonely. She started seeking missions farther afield, so that she'd be able to do as she liked.

One day, she'd gone to see the Assassin George Westhouse in Crawley, frustrated that it had been months since she'd had anything to do.

"The struggle is long," George had said, with a kind smile.

He was a dozen years older than Pierrette and came from a background similar to Simeon's. Simeon had started life working in a pub, and George in a mill, both on the outskirts of London. They were both practical and private men. Maybe that's why she'd gone to him, hoping that he'd be a replacement for her old friend. But that smile had snapped something in her spirit.

"The struggle is long, but does it have to be eternal? I want to win. When do we *win*, George?"

The smile faded. "You spent a decade of your life fighting an enemy who turned out to be an Assassin who lost his way. Even if we destroyed the Templar organization, don't you think there will always be those who seek control of humanity, whether or not they call themselves Templars?"

"Yes, of course, but that doesn't mean we let them gather their strength. We can change this world. I know we can. It just takes courage."

He'd pursed his lips. "Courage is not something the Brotherhood lacks."

She'd protested that wasn't what she meant, but he'd only held up his hand. He'd said, "You came to the Brotherhood in an unorthodox way, Pierrette, and with an unorthodox teacher. Simeon was barely an Assassin himself when he taught you. And his own grounding in the history and philosophy of the Brotherhood came from a tainted source. Perhaps we haven't done right by you. This isn't a game to be won or lost, Pierrette. And it's not a performance."

Her face had flushed. How dare he sneer at her background, when her circus friends had risked their lives for the Assassin cause?

She and George had agreed it might be best for Pierrette to leave England for a while. George suggested she go to Egypt, to learn about the roots of the Brotherhood, its artifacts and ancient secrets. To learn the history of the long struggle.

Pierrette had been happy to get away, and to her delight, she'd found that the Egyptian Assassins were powerful, and not reluctant to target high-ranking Templars. And Amira was there; she had taught Simeon and had been a friend to Pierrette.

Then a miracle happened. In the two years that Pierrette had been away from England, something had shifted. Ethan Frye's two children had gone off to London on their own and broken the Templars' hold, without instructions or permission. She still couldn't quite believe it. Maybe the tide was turning. Maybe the Assassins were ready to do whatever was necessary to take down the Templars, despite the risks. She favored bold action as she had seen the cost of hesitation too many times. Whether on the back of a horse or in a street fight, one always had to commit fully or fall.

While the Assassins grew braver in England, in Egypt they were already bold. Still, even in Cairo they kept to the shadows.

At sixty, or close to it, Amira Benyamina still wore the wide trousers and tailored waistcoats she had favored when Pierrette first met her in Paris, and her silver curls did their best to escape a thick braid coiled around her head. She took the three Assassins into her office at *Le soleil de l'Egypte*, the French-language newspaper she ran, and shut the door.

Pierrette handed her the blood-stained handkerchief bearing Hawkins's initials.

"I hear the city owes you a debt," Amira said. "Not to mention Empress Eugenie. For the second time!"

Pierrette smiled. "I was just remembering that. But I wonder whether she was really in any danger. The Templars seem to see her as an asset and an ally. Maybe they meant to rescue her, scare her, while conveniently taking out the khedive."

"And countless others," Amira said.

Gamal filled her in on the bomb design, and they learned that there had indeed been Templar tails following several Cairo Assassins last night, all of them Assassins who might well have tried to get a ticket to the opera performance for one reason or another.

"I wonder if we misjudged Albert Hawkins from the start," Amira mused. "He seemed a typical mountebank. I never dreamed he had the courage to carry out a bombing under the noses of palace security, or the sang-froid to murder scores of people. A terrible crime, even by Templar standards. I know they tell themselves that any cost is worth it so long as it furthers their aims, but even so, some Templars would hesitate to bomb an opera house full of people. I'll try to get more information on Albert Hawkins. It seems he was more powerful in the Order than we knew, unless he went rogue."

Safiya nodded. "I've been thinking about his railroad to nowhere."

"A project for bilking speculators," Gamal said.

"But what if it served another purpose?" his wife responded. "I can understand why the khedive would have said yes to one more railway, even one that ends in an empty spot, because the khedive is convinced that the canal will soon be lined with new cities. But why would Hawkins have chosen that spot in particular? If he was only interested in making the khedive allow forced labor, he would have wanted a contract to someplace essential, like Helwan or Fayum. So why was he striking out for empty desert?"

Amira pondered the question. "Maybe it isn't so empty. I agree it's worth investigating. I can tie up the loose ends here in the city. Are the three of you willing to go out and have a look at the spot his railroad was heading?"

"When should we go?" Pierrette asked, feeling tendrils of excitement.

"Tonight, if you can," Amira said. "Rest first, and travel by darkness. I'll have some camels ready, with everything you'll need."

Action, with no arguments, no delays. Pierrette sighed happily. "You have no idea how refreshing it is to be in Egypt."

Chapter Four

They left the city in the evening, walking through the parts of Cairo without street lighting. The three of them looked similar and nondescript, in hooded coats over trousers, high boots, scarfs over their mouths and noses, and daggers at their waists. Gamal, who had an unerring sense of direction even in the dark, leading them northeast.

For more than an hour, they walked in the sort of silence that can only be shared by three Assassins on a journey.

Soon, the great obelisk of Heliopolis loomed ahead of them in the darkness. And there was the man Amira had arranged to meet them: he had three camels, laden with packs of food and water.

Pierrette had only ridden a camel twice. She found it tiring as her body was so used to horses that sitting differently, on a creature with different responses, was a constant drain on her thoughts.

The evening turned pleasantly cool, a perfect early November night. They continued northeast, into open desert, avoiding the roads. On previous camel rides in the desert, Pierrette had been astonished at the view from the high seat, the sense of moving through the wideness of the world. But it was so dark that she could only see a few feet around them, the animals stepping around tumbled stones.

The silence was broken only by the occasional low rumble from a camel, or an update from Gamal on where they were. Shortly after dawn, they came across a railway track. It ran northwest to southeast, from Alexandria toward the canal, and this was its nearest point to Cairo.

"This is Hawkins's railroad," Gamal said. "We follow it southeast. But first, breakfast."

He checked his pocket watch, and Safiya and Pierrette shared a little smile.

Gamal was an excellent orienteer – he said it came from years poring over old books of maps – and he liked to play a game in which he'd make some ridiculously precise estimation and then prove it right. He'd once argued that cutting through a particular alley would be a faster route from one city gate to another and raced the fastest runner among the Cairo Assassins to prove it. He'd never lay a wager but enjoyed the looks on his colleagues' faces when he managed some feat.

Pierrette's smile widened as she asked, "How long will it take us, Gamal?"

"About fifteen hours."

"*About*?" Safiya teased. "What is this *about*?"

"Fine." He grinned. "Fifteen and a quarter hours."

As the day warmed, they continued to follow the tracks straight through the open desert. The land rose in hills or drifts, so they guided the camels down the tracks. As Safiya pointed out, it was not as though a train was running on Hawkins's line to nowhere. They kept a brisk pace. All the same, the long day was punctuated only by breaks to eat, drink, pray or (in Pierrette's case) keep watch, and let the camels rest.

Shortly after sunset, the railway track ended abruptly, running into the sand, or so it appeared by the way the drifts covered its final steel inches. They dismounted, and Pierrette swung a small lantern around the area, illuminating signs that people had been working here not long before: a broken one-wheeled cart, a few twisted pieces of metal, and a camel skeleton. It had a ghostly feeling, this work interrupted, as though some disaster had intervened. But it had only been Hawkins's greed. When the khedive had ordered a stop to his use of forced labor, Hawkins had paused the project.

They rested before the final push, on to the track's proposed terminus. Gamal said they were not far from the canal now.

Gamal had not forced them to end their breaks on any specific schedule, and Pierrette wondered whether his predictions would hold. When at last he halted, and said, "This is the place," she knew he'd got it right. He would have said something if he'd been wrong.

"And was it fifteen and one-quarter hours?" Safiya asked.

"Fifteen hours, fourteen minutes," he said. "Let me check the elevation of that hill, but I'm sure this is the spot."

There was nothing to mark it, and there were certainly no signs of Templars anywhere. They'd timed their arrival for nighttime on purpose, so that they could approach any enemies under cover of darkness. They stood motionless and listened but heard nothing. They walked a wide circle but saw nothing.

"A false path," Pierrette said at last. Her voice sounded small and strange in all that nothingness.

"Maybe, and maybe not," Safiya said. "We'll see what the morning shows us. The camels need a proper rest, anyway."

The camels were already kneeling. The three Assassins piled the packs on the ground. Gamal and Pierrette sat with their backs against them. Safiya paced, taking first watch. She was often on watch, because her eyesight and her powers of observation were among the best of the Cairo Assassins, and she could sense an enemy in a crowd before Gamal or Pierrette had even become suspicious. So it fell to Safiya to stay awake, while Pierrette tried to sleep.

Pierrette had never liked darkness. Simeon had set her all sorts of challenges to get her used to it, but she hated them all. "I am not a lurker by nature," she'd said to him one day.

He'd laughed. "And I am. I admit it. But it's something you must learn to tolerate, Pierrette. It's what we do: we work in the darkness to serve the light."

"I don't think that's meant to be *literal*," she'd said, with confidence born of enthusiasm.

To her surprise, Simeon had flushed, and looked away. He'd said something about how he wasn't qualified to be teaching her, that he hadn't learned enough yet himself.

Now the surrounding darkness seemed infinite. It was disorienting to see nothing beyond a few feet, knowing there was open land all around them. She trusted Safiya to keep watch, but she couldn't stop herself from opening her eyes, convinced that she'd heard something with every breath of wind.

She had just drifted into an unsettled dream, when Safiya

stopped walking. In the stillness, Pierrette opened her eyes, and she sensed, from a change in his breathing, that Gamal had opened his too. They remained motionless and silent. A camel grumbled; that would give them away. But give them away to whom? Safiya must not be certain there was an enemy out there, or she would have acted by now.

Then Pierrette saw what had alerted Safiya. She could just make out something different about a patch of darkness, not movement but a sense of greater stillness. Of presence. An animal, maybe? Pierrette didn't think so. Slowly and silently, she put her hand to the knife at her belt. She could throw it right into the intruder, but she hesitated. This was, so frequently, the Assassin's dilemma. It was critical to act before one's enemy, but never if it meant harming an innocent. Between the suspicion and the action was when Assassins died.

Someone in the darkness spoke, and every Assassin leapt to their feet, knife in hand, before they registered the English words: "Pierrette, I have no doubt your knife flies as fast as it ever did, but I am older and slower than I used to be, so just this once I concede the argument."

"Simeon!" she shouted, dropped her knife, and ran to wrap her arms around her mentor.

Simeon Price at forty-three was hardly decrepit, though Pierrette would tease him anyway. As first daylight broke, she got a better look at his face. He had a day or two of stubble, which was gray in patches, broken by a small white scar that hadn't been there before.

"What on Earth are you doing in Egypt?" she demanded. "Did Amira tell you where to find us?"

He smiled wearily. "The answer to the first question is long. As for the second, I didn't even know you were here. I haven't been to Cairo. I came from the north."

Pierrette introduced him to Gamal and Safiya. Simeon looked relieved that they spoke English. Although he could have managed fine in French, he spoke no Arabic, and he looked tired enough to be grateful to stay in his mother tongue.

"I should have known there would be other Assassins looking for these Templars," he said. "I debated going straight to Cairo to let the Brotherhood know. But I didn't want to lose their trail. I didn't even have time to send a telegram."

He sounded exhausted and opened his flask to drink water. Safiya passed him their basket with bread and bean patties.

"So there *are* Templars nearby?" Gamal asked.

Simeon nodded. "If you'd kept on for about half a mile, you'd have come to a scattering of limestone hills and one of those hills contains a hidden cave. I only found it because I was following a group south from Port Said."

"What sort of group?" Gamal asked.

"Twelve people who traveled from Constantinople on a private ship. At Port Said, they took on new servants and traveled overland by caravan. I followed on foot." He hesitated, looked at each of them, and then said, "Their leader is Armen Kazan."

That got a reaction even from Safiya, who was still walking the perimeter of their little camp, watching for enemies. She paused and stared, and Gamal shook his head in wonder.

Armen Kazan was one of the most infamous and elusive Templars in Europe. He was an art dealer who bought art he considered dangerous, so no one could ever see it. There were two theories about what he did with the art: some suspected a private collection, others a bonfire.

When Kazan switched from collecting art to collecting artists, the Brotherhood grew alarmed. He published a small, private book of aphorisms, ostensibly written by hidden mystics. He inducted artists and socialites into something halfway between a club and a cult, and he took their money and ambition, and had them ostracized if they turned against him.

Kazan owned remote, well-guarded estates in three different countries. Three Assassins who were sent after him were found with their throats cut, and two ended up convinced of his divine genius and turned their coats. For the past several years, the Brotherhood had had no solid evidence of his whereabouts, and some believed he was dead.

"Are you sure it's Kazan? How?" Pierrette asked.

"I'm sure. I was about to dispatch Kazan's guards and go inside myself, but I took cover to wait for the guard on patrol. That's when I heard something from out here – one of your camels, I think."

Pierrette glared good-naturedly at the nearest camel, who glared back, unbothered.

"I thought perhaps it was another band of Templars. But I couldn't be sure. In the darkness, I got very close before I saw it was you."

Gamal frowned. "You said you were trying to get inside the cave. Why? Is it more than just a stronghold?"

Simeon shook his head. "I don't know." He rubbed his temple. "I believe they have the Ankh with them."

Pierrette sensed Gamal and Safiya wondering whether Pierrette's high opinion of her old mentor had been colored by nostalgia. He wouldn't be the first Assassin to be led astray by his own pet theories, or Templar misinformation, or both.

One reason George Westhouse had sent her to Egypt was that he wanted her to understand the sources of Templar power. The Templars were obsessed with Pieces of Eden, artifacts left behind by ancient godlike beings. These objects had strange powers, allowing their wielders to control and manipulate. That's why the Templars were so fascinated; they thought these artifacts would help them rule humanity.

Some artifacts were well attested, their whereabouts known. Some were even in the hands of Assassins. Others were mere stories, garbled and contradictory. According to one such story, the goddess Isis used the Ankh to resurrect her husband. The Ankh, a piece of stone in the shape of the ancient Egyptian symbol for life, supposedly held the power to reanimate a corpse temporarily. Some said it carried the memories of the dead.

As far as Pierrette was concerned, all of this might as well be a fairy story.

"The Ankh!" Gamal said at last. "Are you sure? Have you seen it?"

"I haven't seen it, no. I have good information about its recent whereabouts, and their actions, this rush to Egypt, suggest they at least believe they have the Ankh."

"But why bring it back to Egypt?" Pierrette asked.

"Maybe they need some information here to confirm its authenticity," Simeon suggested.

"Or maybe they are returning looted artifacts," joked Safiya drily. "Perhaps they could have a word with the Louvre and the British Museum."

"I'll be happy to take the Ankh from them," Gamal said with a smile. Then his expression changed. "If they truly have the Ankh, and it truly works as people say it does, then they must plan to resurrect someone, sooner or later. I wonder: who is buried in that cave?"

Pierrette shuddered. Gamal had a scholar's curiosity. While Pierrette was curious about the Ankh too, if she had her way she'd drop all these magical artifacts at the bottom of the sea. In her years as an acrobat, she had learned to respect the laws of nature and the workings of the human perception, and to use them for her own ends. She was happy to meet any Templar, any time, with a knife in her hand. But devices that changed the laws of nature, that even took control of people's minds, if the stories were true – that made her truly afraid in a way nothing in the ordinary world around her could.

Even the weapon the Magus – Simeon's old Master – had tried to build had simply been a machine, based on her friend Ada's designs. A machine can be broken. But with seemingly magical powers in their arsenal, the Templars might do things Pierrette couldn't even imagine. And she had a very good imagination.

"Whatever they plan to do, I expect they'll do it in the dark," Simeon said. "So I have to be in position by sunset tomorrow, somewhere inside that cave, so I can find out what they're doing with the Ankh."

"We'll join you," Pierrette said.

Simeon started to object, but Gamal interrupted him. "We set out from Cairo to find the end of a railway that seemed to go nowhere. The council has given us permission to engage the Templars if we found them. We would lose too much time

Assassin's Creed

watching and waiting. And with four of us, perhaps we can do more than gather information. Perhaps we can take the Ankh away from them, if that's what they have."

Simeon smiled. "All right. I can't say I'm sorry to have found you. There are a dozen Templars in that cave. I didn't know they were building a railroad to this place. How odd. Maybe they won't act until it's finished."

"Or they got impatient and chose another mode of transport," Pierrette said. "Whatever this place is, it seems important to them, since they brought the so-called Ankh to it."

Safiya stood at a distance, peering toward the hill. "You know, I think I see something, a glimmer. It's hard to explain. It might be another entrance on this side of the hill. There's no one guarding it."

Simeon glanced at Pierrette, as if to confirm that Safiya had the gift of eagle vision. Pierrette nodded. She didn't fully understand how Safiya's heightened perception worked, but she had seen it in action many times, and trusted it.

Gamal spoke suddenly, reciting from memory. "Oh Openers of Roads! Oh Guides of Paths to the Soul made in the abode of Osiris! Open ye the roads, level ye the paths to Osiris with yourselves." He smiled at their expressions. "It's from the ancient texts they used to bury in tombs. The Book of the Dead, some people call it. An English translation came my way last year."

Simeon rubbed his hands through his dusty hair. "All right then, openers of roads. If there is another way into this cave, we'd better find it."

CHAPTER FIVE

The sight of Pierrette working with respected colleagues in a land far from home filled Simeon with pride, although he took no credit for it. She had always been brave and smart, and he'd always felt that the best he could do as her teacher was simply to keep her alive.

After he left her behind in England, he had searched for others who might need guidance, as he once had. In Russia, Simeon had watched a group of young people who wanted to build a better world – and tear down the old one. He joined their ranks, helped with their pamphlets and meetings. He kept an eye out for any mention of violence. Simeon's old teacher, Oscar Kane, was dead and no longer able to manipulate freedom fighters into half-baked assassination schemes, but others in the world would benefit from such mistakes. And sometimes, people made errors without the need for outside manipulation.

Not that Simeon opposed violence as a tool for liberation. Far from it. He had dedicated his life to serving the light by working in the darkness, and he had an entire case full of calling cards stained with blood. But he never wanted to watch another principled and courageous person throw their own life away – and endanger their cause – by going off half-cocked. He helped them make better plans. And he carefully recruited some of the Russian radicals into the Brotherhood of Assassins, where they could learn the skills and discipline to make a real difference.

But most of the time, the recruits refused, lost interest, or made other choices. One of the central paradoxes of the Brotherhood was that it required obedience, even as it lauded personal responsibility. The young people Simeon befriended were impatient. The promise of brotherhood wasn't enough to temper their anger. How could Simeon blame them? There was plenty to be angry and impatient about. Tsar Alexander II was not the brutal tyrant his father had been, but his fear of real reforms was even more maddening because of it.

One of the young students, Dimitry, had a plan. Simeon tried, and failed, to reach him. Dimitry tried, and failed, to shoot the tsar. He was hanged. Two dozen of his friends were sent to prison, hard labor, or exile in Siberia.

Simeon had spent the last two years doing what he could for those men, seeking clemency for their sentences, or finding small ways to reduce their hardship. As for Dimitry himself, Simeon had tried to carry out his last request. It had come to Simeon in the mail the day after Dimitry was arrested.

Like many of the radicals in Russian cities, Dimitry was born into a landowning family. While Simeon toured the small towns to make sure that various cousins were cared for and not hounded by secret police, he happened upon the trail of the Ankh. The possibility that the Templars could have acquired an unpredictable new weapon was too alarming to ignore.

"You're supposed to be sleeping, not brooding," said Pierrette.

He smiled and opened his eyes, blinking in the desert light. She was looking out at the sand and sharpening her knife. She spoke English, as she always did with him; his French was good, but her English was better.

"How do you know I wasn't sleeping?"

"Because you weren't snoring."

"I do not snore. I'm an Assassin."

She shrugged. "Michel Moulin used to do a wonderful imitation of it. Sort of a whistling sound. I could never do it justice."

He sat up. "You can't be serious. The Assassins of Paris used to make fun of my snoring, which I don't do anyway, and this is the first I'm hearing of it?"

Now she smiled, and he wondered whether she'd invented the whole thing. Of course, there had been many times he'd napped in the Assassin headquarters beneath a Paris train station, in between tasks. No, she was making it up. Breaking the tension of the situation and reminding him they were old friends, that they had each other's backs.

"So what were you brooding about?" she asked.

He hardly knew where to begin. "The Ankh, for one thing."

"Yes, I've been wondering about that. Since you came alone to Egypt in a hurry, I assume no council sent you."

"No council even knows. I wasn't sure there was anything to tell, until it was too late to seek help. I was in a small town in Russia, and I met an out-of-work opera singer. He had attached himself to a middle-aged Russian woman, a member of a minor noble house named Helena Blavatsky. They were desperate for money. She fancies herself to be some sort of clairvoyant or mystic."

Pierrette looked at him sharply. "Like Armen Kazan."

"Something of the sort. Who can say whether she's wrong? She was certainly shrewd. She learned I had returned a stolen heirloom to a family that was down on its luck – it's a long story – and she offered to help me find things, using her connection to the spirit realm. She assumed I'd take payment from the owners, and give her a cut."

Simeon paused, remembering the woman's steady hand as she rolled a cigarette, the smell of the Turkish tobacco as the smoke joined the steam from the nearby samovar.

"As a first gesture and proof of her talents," he continued, "she offered to sell me an Egyptian cross, lost for generations. The symbol of eternal life. She mentioned another interested client, which I assumed at first was an invention to pique my interest. I didn't pay much attention. Europe has been awash in Egyptian objects, real and fake, since Napoleon's day. And I had no interest in buying or selling any of them, of course."

The mention of artifacts or archaeology always reminded him of his mentor, Oscar Kane. He'd rivaled the Templars in his desire for powerful objects, whether newly invented or left behind by the ancients.

"What made you suspect it was the real Ankh, then?"

"Because the next day, she was terrified when I brought it up. White as a sheet, her hands shaking. Insisting that the object had turned out to be a worthless fake, and anyway, she didn't have it anymore. I was curious about the other interested seller. It took me months, but the trail led me to Armen Kazan."

"But nobody's been able to find him for years!"

"Well, I did, but just as he was embarking for Port Said. I was on the damned boat before I was sure it was him."

Pierrette suddenly looked up and past him. He turned to see Gamal and Safiya walking back to them, a grin on Gamal's face. "We've found a way into the cave," she said.

The entrance Safiya found was half a mile from the cave entrance where Simeon had last seen the Templars. It might have been something totally unconnected, but Safiya was confident it was a tunnel leading toward the Templar cave. It was, she said, the back door.

It took the four of them some time to clear the door of sand enough to open. Luckily, it swung inwards.

There was depth to that darkness, and a stirring on the stale air.

They carried packs with weapons, smoke bombs, water, and food. Pierrette held the group's "dark lantern". Simeon had seen police with similar devices: a brass cylinder with oil and wick in the base, and a large glass eye facing front. A shutter could be rotated to stop the light, while vents on the top kept the flame alive.

She held it high, and it illuminated paint on the walls, a straight-hewn corridor stretching onward.

"This is no mere tunnel," Simeon whispered. "If this truly is connected to the cave where the Templars went in, it's a sophisticated complex."

Simeon propped a piece of wood in the door to prevent a sandstorm from blocking it. It wouldn't prevent anyone from deliberately locking them in, but they had no reason to suspect the Templars knew they were here.

Gamal, several steps ahead, let out a whistle. "This is – I don't know what this place is. But it may be worth trying to find out. If we know why the Templars came here, that may help us understand what they're doing, and why they must do it here of all places. Some sort of ceremony?"

"Of course it has to be in a dusty old tomb," Pierrette said morosely. "You aren't noticing anything strange, are you, Safiya? Traps or hidden rooms?"

"Nothing so far," Safiya said. "I see what you see."

The paintings on the walls flickered in the torchlight, in earthy yellows, reds and blues.

"How old is this place?" Simeon asked.

Gamal ran his fingers over a line of hieroglyphs. "I think this image shows the pharaoh Hatshepsut, which would make it, what, fifteen hundred years before the Common Era? Yes, here is her cartouche."

"Her?" Simeon asked. "This is a woman?" The image above looked like any other masculine figure: ochre-skinned, standing astride, with a stylized rectangular beard and a tall crown. One hand held a mace or a scepter.

"Yes, this is Hatshepsut, or the symbolic image of Hatshepsut, anyway," Gamal said. "Once she took the throne, she depicted herself as male." He paused for a moment. "I don't believe her tomb has been found, but this doesn't feel like a tomb, somehow. That entrance – rather plain. And built into a natural hill like this? No, I think this is something else. Look at these scenes – these are battles."

The paintings showed people, smaller and less detailed than the figure of Hatshepsut. Bows drawn, flails and maces smashing into bodies. There were rows of horses too, their nostrils flared.

For the first time in a long time, Simeon heard Oscar Kane lecturing in his head. Seven years after he'd dipped his calling card in Kane's last blood, Simeon could remember those lessons with the numbness of perspective, and could consider Kane's words for what they were: the views of an intelligent but fatally arrogant man. For better or for worse, he had introduced Simeon to the Brotherhood, and much of what he had taught him still had value.

One day, soon after Simeon met him in Vienna, Kane had told him that the Templars were the only people who could ever truly understand Assassins, and vice versa.

"We exist outside history, in a manner of speaking," Kane had said. "We have our own traditions and knowledge, even our own weapons, clothing and culture. If you were to meet an Assassin from five centuries ago, you could understand each other. Your way of seeing the world would be the same. Like the Templars, we Assassins grow in strength and knowledge, but we are not creatures of our time, not the way other people are."

But as Simeon walked deeper into the dark corridor lined with the images of battles long ago, he felt very much a visitor to this part of history.

"Look," whispered Gamal, forgetting in his excitement that none of the rest of them could read the hieroglyphs. "Now it makes sense. This battle was against the Hyksos." Smiling at their confusion, Gamal explained, "The Hyksos are what historians call the rulers of a small kingdom in this part of Egypt. I thought the Hyksos were all vanquished before her time, but this engraving says that Hatshepsut fought a battle here and eradicated one of their communities." He looked forward, down the corridor. "Some historians say the Hyksos introduced horses to Egypt, which might explain… that."

From that point, both sides of the corridor were lined with panels, each depicting a life-sized horse, engraved and painted. These were more detailed and realistic than the horses arrayed in battle, but they were still stylized, all in the same posture.

It was as though the horses were flanking them, Simeon thought, as they walked onward. Or accompanying them. To where? They must be getting close to the Templar stronghold. They should be on their guard and he should caution Gamal, in particular, who was so excited.

But Pierrette and her lantern were already around a corner. Simeon caught up and saw the others standing at the threshold of an open archway. "There's some sort of a chamber here," Pierrette whispered, and slipped inside, with Safiya and Gamal following.

Simeon came next, his hand on his knife.

But inside, there was no sign of danger. Just a small chamber, barely big enough for the four of them to stand inside. Each of the four walls held a doorway, and beside the doorway, a figure. One was bright yellow, wearing a woman's dress, with an odd spiky headdress, holding an ankh as casually as a purse. Opposite her was a male figure in bright green, wrapped in white, holding a flail and a hook. Between them stood a figure with a falcon head, wearing a crown.

"That ankh," Pierrette said. "It's not *our* Ankh, is it?"

Gamal replied, "It might be. It's a very common symbol of life and immortality, and gods are often depicted holding it. This is the whole family on this wall. That's Isis and Osiris, with their son Horus between them."

"Dwelling here in total darkness," said Safiya.

It was so quiet that Simeon felt he could hear the darkness whispering.

They turned. On the final wall, behind them where they had come in, was another figure. This one had a red human body, but a black animal's head, with a long, curved snout and two rectangular horns rising above an eye that fixed Simeon in its gaze.

"Fascinating," breathed Gamal. "I believe the Hyksos were Set worshippers. This room must represent the victory of Isis and her husband and son over Set, maybe as a symbol of the victory of Hatshepsut over the people who once lived in these hills."

Kane had made Simeon learn the names and stories of those who had gone down in history as gods. He knew Set had killed Osiris, and that a grieving Isis had used the Ankh to resurrect Osiris for long enough to conceive a son who would take revenge on Set.

"That's Set?" Simeon asked, pointing. "But what sort of animal is he supposed to be?"

"No one knows!" Gamal grinned. "He's represented by an animal that may be extinct, or may be a composite of other things, or may be imaginary, or..." he paused.

"Or?" Pierrette prodded.

"What I think is that the Set-animal is not a visual representation, but a symbolic one. The same way that Hatshepsut's image looks nothing like she did – we know this from her earlier statues, before she took the throne. Perhaps the Set-animal looks strange simply because the artists want us to understand there is something strange about it. Set is an animal that we know nothing about. But whatever that animal is, it might have looked nothing like that. Art in ancient times was about the way things *are*, not the way things look."

Simeon glared back at that great eye. It seemed to watch him, but he could feel the eye of Horus behind him, watching back, and somehow that made him feel better.

"Set is the lord of chaos and violence," Gamal said. "The Hyksos were his worshippers, or at least, that's what has come down to us all these centuries later. I believe this place is here to commemorate the victory of Hatshepsut over them, the way that Isis had her victory over Set. Putting chaos and violence into the earth. Locking the door on it."

Pierrette cut in. "We've lingered here long enough. We should move on."

She had always been impatient.

"It's important to understand things," Gamal chided her.

"And it's important to get to the Templars before they use the Ankh to do something terrible," she retorted. "And before they realize we're here and ambush us. Or bar the exits and leave us here to die of starvation, still squabbling."

"If we act without knowing the full context, we'll fail. Remember, at the Opera House, you said yourself, you got lucky. We should have been better prepared."

"There was no way to know," Pierrette said, tightly.

Safiya chuckled. "That is the European refrain, isn't it? There was no way to know."

Something had shifted in the room, between them all. Simeon could feel it, like a presence. He was irritated with Pierrette, more than was justified by her impatience, and he wasn't sure why.

"I'll go on alone," Pierrette said, holding their only lantern. She was about to leave them in darkness. She was going to put them all in danger, by rushing onward as she always did.

Safiya seemed to sense Simeon's feelings and turned to him, nodded once.

"Let him see as you see, Safiya," said Gamal, in the voice of a teacher and a guide, the voice that Simeon had waited his whole life to hear. "Let him hear as you hear, let him stand as you stand."

"I will come forth and stand on my feet," Simeon replied. He looked at Pierrette, and saw her as she truly was, a great storm of chaos. "I will take responsibility. It's only right that I should be the one to protect the world from you."

She spat, "You did not make me, and the one who made you is dead."

Years of frustration with Pierrette, and with himself, weighed on him. He had indeed made her what she was: a killer like him, but worse, because she was still as impetuous and arrogant as when she'd burst into his life. He should have known that people couldn't change, that she could never learn the discretion and patience it took to be an Assassin. He saw it clearly now at last. Simeon tried to smile at her, to show that her failings weren't her fault. "I have lost many young people in many lands. I have failed to save them from themselves. What does it matter if I lose one more?"

"I am Set among the Gods," responded Pierrette. "I do not die."

As if in answer, Safiya wailed, "I see Osiris. I have seen my quiet Lord. Osiris is placed in his place, as the living Lord of Heaven. He has been preserved. Hail, Osiris! Lead on, Horus!"

The Lord of Light was coming. Simeon understood this, though he didn't know how. He felt that he had been waiting for someone to come and illuminate everything his whole life. But he had been afraid of that illumination, of what it would show, of how exposed he would be. He had not been ready. Now he was. Tears filled Simeon's eyes as he waited for the strength to do what he must do. He took a step toward Set – toward Pierrette – and suddenly he was blinded, the lantern in his face. He knocked it away, she bolted, and by the time his eyes opened, it was utterly black in the room.

And he knew he was alone.

"Gamal?" he asked, uncertain, as though the name was somehow wrong. "Safiya?" He stepped closer to the wall, groped his way to one opening. "Pierrette?"

He could hear footsteps, but from which corridor? Everything echoed strangely. His stomach lurched, and he felt the memory of anger like a sudden hangover – why had he been so angry? What had he said to Pierrette? Something to send her running. What the hell was wrong with him? What had just happened to him, to them all?

He staggered into the nearest corridor in total darkness. With one hand, he felt his way along the wall, tracing the engraved forms of long-dead horses, galloping into oblivion.

Chapter Six

Exhilaration drove Pierrette onward, the light she bore illuminating painted horses like a magic lantern. She couldn't hear anyone following, but she ran anyway, from sheer joy and rage. It was a relief to have everything out in the open. The truth was, she had never really fit into the Brotherhood. She was an Assassin by coincidence because she and Simeon had once shared a common enemy. In the years since, the only thing the Brotherhood had done was try to hold her back.

Something about that room had affected them, that was clear. But if it took a strange Egyptian spell to draw the truth out, so be it. Let them call her dangerous, reckless, selfish, arrogant – these were just words for greatness. She had seen many performers rise to the top, and not a one of them had been nice. Pierrette was not nice either. She was *ready*.

Somewhere nearby were a dozen Templars with a device that could, supposedly, raise the dead. For how long? Pierrette imagined mummies leaving their sarcophagi, reaching for her from the shadows. She imagined long-forgotten gods whispering ancient knowledge to the Templars, teaching them how to subjugate humanity. Perhaps Pierrette wouldn't even know when the Templars used the Ankh. Perhaps they would gain control over her mind, and she'd never even realize it. That was the most frightening prospect of all.

She shivered, thinking of the room at the crossroads. The resentment she'd felt was fading. And with it, the blessed rage that roared so loudly all her other thoughts were mercifully quiet.

The corridor ended, but there were seven doors on either side, each one with a series of hieroglyphs above: animals and shapes. Some kind of understanding whispered to her. But she couldn't quite catch what it was saying.

She chose one door in the middle and walked a few more lengths of corridors lined with horses. How she missed riding, especially her old horse, Attila, who'd died in a comfortable stable a few years ago. One more tie severed with her old circus life.

Another set of doors made her stop short. A maze. Pierrette touched a fingertip to the soot on the vents on her lantern and marked the side of the door she chose.

After she did this three times, she found herself back in a corridor that had a soot-mark by one door. She'd gone in a loop.

Her beautiful anger had drained away, and she just felt sick and lost. It was a wonder there were no skeletons of the lost in these corridors; perhaps there would soon be at least one.

There must be a way through. The hieroglyphs over the doors… Gamal would know how to read them. But where was he? He might be choosing between doors somewhere too, but he didn't have a lantern, and the hieroglyphs were too high to be felt. He must have some matches on him, surely? Would that be enough to help him through?

If only they hadn't all turned on her, they'd be together now. She felt a little of the resentment returning, waiting to be nurtured into flame. She resisted. Somewhere Gamal would be working on the problem, lantern or no lantern. That was what they did, after all, she thought with a bitter smile. They worked in the darkness to serve the light.

The Lord of Light. That was what someone had said – who? It was hazy now. In that crossroads room, with the paintings on the walls, everything had seemed so clear.

It was easy to retrace her steps to the crossroads room. Anger and energy surged through her limbs as she walked through that door, and she glared at the image of Osiris, so smug, so certain. He held the answers to everything.

She could not do this alone. She needed the courage and strength of purpose she had gained from Set, the lord of storms, deserts, and lost causes. But she also needed to light her path forward. She steeled herself and ignored the call of Set on her left, and walked forward toward Osiris. Toward Gamal. Her friend, her companion, with his flashing eyes and quick smile and a book about everything.

Yes, Gamal, who had spoken with the voice of Osiris so easily, so quickly. Leaving her channeling Set, the outcast, the criminal. Why shouldn't the Lord of Light have spoken through her? If she only knew what Gamal knew.

She approached the Osiris painting, holding her lantern aloft. Somewhere, distantly, she heard footsteps.

"Lord of Light," she whispered. A supplication, an accusation, a plea.

And suddenly, she understood exactly how to get through the doors.

Pierrette strode like a priestess through the corridors and chose her path without stopping. The hieroglyphs were names. She held the knowledge of both Set and Osiris. She was a brotherhood of one.

"She goes in with exultation; she comes out in peace," she said, in a voice not quite her own, speaking words she didn't understand. "She is neither stopped nor turned away. She goes in as she wishes, she comes out as she likes. She is justified."

At the first set of doors, she knew which set of hieroglyphs to choose, and it wasn't the one she had chosen before. "The Second Hall. The name written on it is Destruction." Another corridor, another choice. "The name written on it is Great Stopper of the Vain."

She walked forward into a plain corridor, feeling less sure of herself, as if the guidance of the gods had left her. Her lantern spilled light into an opening, another crossroads, but this one wasn't marked. She could hear voices ahead, many voices chanting together.

Pierrette froze. Any sound, any shifting shadow, could give her away. And if her enemies became aware of her, here where she could easily be trapped, she was as good as dead.

The Templars, at last. It was no wonder they'd made a door for themselves at this end, the deepest part of the tunnel complex. They hadn't wanted to go through the maze; maybe they had known there was something in the crossroads room that would scatter them. Just as it had scattered Pierrette and her friends.

It was up to her now to stop them.

She walked forward, toward the voices, and came to one last

choice. To the left, the tunnel ended, with light silhouetting two figures.

Pierrette swore silently and ducked back the way she came and shuttered her lantern with a flick of her finger. She fought her instincts and made herself wait. Standing where they were, against the light, the guards would be easy targets for two thrown knives. But she only threw right-handed and throwing two knives at once, accurately enough to kill instantly, was beyond even her. The moment she killed the first, the other might yell and alert the rest of the Templars, who were presumably in the lighted room beyond.

No, better to make them come to her. The old trick: make a sound, force them to investigate.

She was about to knock on the wall when someone came at her from the dark side of the crossroads.

He was big, whoever he was. He pinned her arms against the wall, her Hidden Blade pointing uselessly at the ceiling, his body pressed against hers so that she couldn't move her legs. She still had the lantern in her right hand and wiggled her fingers just enough to flick open the shutter.

The light pointed directly at his face illuminated a stranger – the Templars must have posted guards in more than one part of the tunnel. He blinked against the light, flinching just enough that Pierrette was able to wrench her right arm free and whack him in the head with the brass lantern hard enough that he went down.

That brought the other two running.

Somehow, the brass lantern, now lying sideways and bloody on the tunnel floor, hadn't gone out. She drew her knife. Another breath, maybe two and then – they were upon her.

Simeon had always been right about one thing: the closer you were to your enemies, the more certain the kill. With her left hand, she skewered a woman through the neck with one knife, while she slashed at a man's neck with the other. It wasn't deep enough; he tried to scream, but it came out as a gurgle, as she plunged the knife under his ribs. She let the woman drop, and covered the man's mouth with her hand as he slumped and died.

Her breath was loud in the silent tunnel. She waited, her knife in her hand. The first guard had pinned her, when he might have killed her. They probably had orders to take any intruders alive, to find out what they knew, or how they got in. That was a useful piece of information.

Pierrette crept toward the light. The tunnel opened at the top of an amphitheater, with the same series of life-sized horses painted all around the walls, lit by the flickering light of dozens of lanterns. The room could have housed three times as many Templars as those arrayed on the stone benches inside. Pierrette counted twelve, including three standing in the middle around a stone slab. On that slab, lying in a recess that seemed made for it, was the Ankh, its carved stone surface catching light and shadow.

The man speaking in a high, clear voice was facing her direction, so she stayed well back from the brink, in the shadows of the tunnel. At any point, he might glance up and notice her – or notice an absence of guards. But he seemed to be almost in a trance. Armen Kazan; it could be no one else. He was younger than Pierrette, with long dark hair bound loosely behind him, and Templar armbands bearing the red cross the only feature on his black pants and jacket. She found it difficult not to stare at him, not to listen to him.

Kazan said, "The moment is coming that will shift the balance. What was lost will return. The breath of life. It begins with one and more will follow."

It begins with one what? The Ankh was rumored to animate corpses temporarily and store memories in some way. Pierrette still half expected to see a mummy or sarcophagus. But there was nothing of the kind, unless it was hidden under that slab.

The slab started to shake.

Pierrette's anger won out over her curiosity and shock. Over and over, the Templars had demonstrated their eagerness to use anything they could to control and manipulate the rest of humanity. Before the Frye twins had wrenched an artifact from him and ended his malignant existence, the Templar Grand Master Crawford Starrick had inflicted a hallucinogenic drug on ordinary Londoners. Pierrette had listened to the British Council when they'd said not to act too quickly against the Templars of London; thank goodness the Frye twins hadn't.

Now it was up to her to act, before the Templars unleashed some other evil.

She wrapped her scarf around her mouth and nose, sheathed her knife at her waist, opened her pack, and drew her revolver and a smoke bomb. She noted where everyone in the room was standing. They were all watching Kazan, seemingly rapt, but otherwise acting normally. If there was magic in this place, it didn't seem to be doing anything noticeable to the Templars. Then she crept to the brink where the corridor led to the amphitheater.

Her bullet went straight into the middle of Armen Kazan's chest as he was mid-lecture, and his voice ended in a strangle as he toppled backwards.

In the commotion, she shot the woman standing nearest him. Then she threw a smoke bomb and jumped into the chaos.

The best thing about being in a fight with no allies was that she didn't have to think about who she was fighting. Knife now in her right hand, revolver in her left, she stabbed and shot at everything that moved as the smoke settled. As they closed in around her, she used the butt of the gun, and wrenched limbs.

A loud crack to her right, and a chunk of stone went flying. A bullet, and close.

There was a stinging just above her right collarbone. She put her left hand there, and it came away bloody.

Shapes loomed in front of her. She had to get above the smoke, to breathe, to see where her enemies were. She jumped up onto the slab.

The slab still rattled as though there was an earthquake. There was the Ankh – it looked bigger close up. Should she wrench it out of the slab? No – not yet – there were half a dozen Templars running down the steps toward her, guns drawn.

Someone shouted, "Alive, you idiots! Take her alive!"

All right, if they didn't want her to die here, she had that in common with them. She shot at the attackers, and hit one, but something was wrong. There was blood on her right hand now – no, all the way down her right arm. Her heart was racing, and she felt strangely cold. Her wound above the collarbone; it was bleeding. A lot.

She toppled off the slab, slipping in her own blood, and banged her knee and shoulder hard on the packed dirt floor. Two sets of arms were around her.

At least the smoke was clearing; at least she could breathe a little.

She looked up into the face she knew from her nightmares.

Art Hennighan had lost what remained of his hair, in the years since he'd helped Konstanze von Visler imprison and torture Pierrette. It had been his job to beat her, his job to bring her food and water afterward. She knew the scar on his face; she knew the light in his eyes. The twist of his mouth, as he smiled in recognition.

A man with a white mustache standing beside Hennighan said, "The Assassins are even more diminished than we realized, if they send one woman to attack us here."

Her head spun. "One woman who killed eight of you. I would not call that diminished."

"It does not matter how many of us you kill," said the mustachioed man, the fury on his face turning to triumph. He coughed for a moment; the smoke had got to his throat too. His eyes were red. "The Templar Order is not its people. The Order is a system and a plan. When you kill a Templar, nothing but the body dies. But when you die – which will be shortly – everything you love dies with you, because the Assassins love nothing beyond themselves. Nothing is true, you say. So nothing, for you, is eternal."

"Go to hell," she said, her voice barely above a croak. "And may it be eternal."

A brilliant light came out of the Ankh, and she fell backwards, deeper into the grip of whoever was holding her arms. Behind the bald man, something projected upwards from the slab: an image made of light. The image of the Ankh, but in midair. It illuminated Hennighan's bald head, and he turned to see it.

"Put her in chains," said the mustachioed man, rapt. "It's beginning."

The blue light from the Ankh was blinding, and Pierrette couldn't shield her eyes. Someone shackled her wrists and ankles. She managed to get to a kneeling position, turning her head from the light until her vision could adjust. She had time to wonder why the Templars had chains with them. Maybe they always had chains with them.

They all gasped, and she turned back to the light to see why. Nothing she did made her vision any clearer. She must be losing blood from her wounds. On the wall beyond, a painting of a horse seemed to change. Its outlines were more nuanced, more lifelike. Instead of an engraving, it seemed now to stand out from the wall like a relief, or a sculpture – but it was impossibly gaunt, almost skeletal.

A series of shots rang in the amphitheater, a dozen, more. Several people screamed. Hennighan drew a gun and fired it, and then raced past Pierrette, and she was conscious that the two people who'd shackled her no longer stood behind her. She tried to get the strength to stand, but all she could manage was to turn and see Gamal leaning against one of the stone benches, his hand clasped to his upper arm, blood running through his fingers.

And there was Simeon, locked in a wrestle with Hennighan, who had his gun pressed against Simeon's windpipe. It was a dirty, desperate fight, and all Pierrette could do was watch, straining at her shackles, struggling to stand. If she could run at Hennighan, startle him, that might be enough.

A whinny like the memory of a nightmare, and a sound like thunder breaking, and something large flew into Pierrette's field of vision. It knocked the two men to the ground, and then the horse – for it was a horse, flesh and bone, but moving strangely, too quickly – galloped right at Pierrette and she fell backward as it went over her. The hooves missed her by inches. Bile rose in her throat and the world shifted to black and white, with the blackness creeping in at the edges inexorably.

The last thing she heard that made any sense was Simeon's voice, saying to no one at all, "A bloody *horse*?"

CHAPTER SEVEN

A bloody horse. All that effort, all that secrecy, so the Templars could pull a horse's bones out of the wall, put flesh on it, give it life?

Simeon's head was ringing. The horse hadn't made contact when it leaped past him, but the stone floor certainly had. Flat on the ground with blood running into his eyes, he scrambled to his hands and knees in time to see Hennighan get up and run in the same direction the horse had taken: out of the amphitheater, into the narrow passage the Templars had used as an entrance into this godforsaken place.

Simeon scanned the bodies, looking for a twitch of a finger, a gleam in an eye, any sign of danger. Then he saw Pierrette. Caked in blood, lying in an unnatural way at the base of the stone where the Ankh had rested.

Safiya knelt at her side, tearing strips off her cloak and bandaging Pierrette. "He took the Ankh!" she yelled hoarsely.

The recess on the top of the stone was empty. Hennighan, damn him. Once more, they were left with nothing.

Pierrette's face was blank; she wasn't conscious. No, no, no. He wanted to wake up, to find this but a nightmare.

"Go!" Safiya cried to him. "I'll take care of her. Go, or it's all for nothing!"

Pierrette would be saying the same, if she could. He picked up his revolver where it lay on the floor and ran.

The entrance on this side was not closed off. After a few turns in a plain, rock-hewn tunnel, he saw daylight streaming in, and the massive horse that had knocked him down. The horse reared, screaming, a rope around its neck. Hennighan held the rope, bracing himself on a rough rock stairway.

Why in God's name did they want this horse so badly? Hennighan had a pack on his back. The Ankh must be inside it.

Simeon aimed, trying to remember how many shots he had left. Only one way to find out.

The revolver clicked. Nothing.

Hennighan, still occupied with trying to stop the horse from bucking, didn't even notice. Simeon might be able to get close enough to use a knife. He crept forward in the tight corridor.

A shot from behind him rang through the tunnel. Simeon whirled to see Gamal, holding a smoking gun.

The echo of the shot resolved into hoofbeats, and he looked back toward the entrance, expecting to see Hennighan on the ground.

But what he saw was Hennighan, tangled in the rope, being dragged behind the horse as it galloped out into the light.

"Oh my God," Simeon breathed. "Come on. He has the Ankh." He looked back at Gamal, saw blood running down his arm. "Are you all right?"

"Just a scratch," Gamal said.

They ran through the tunnel, blinking in the clear light of early morning. They must have spent longer in the maze than they realized. Simeon's stomach was empty, which was a blessing, given how dizzy he felt.

"He must have tied himself to that rope, the fool," Gamal said, huffing beside him as they bolted across the desert. They could see the horse disappearing ahead, and a cloud of sand rising behind it, obscuring Hennighan.

"If he just wanted a horse to ride, he could have walked over to the caravan they took to get here," Simeon panted.

By one accord, they slowed to a walk, holding their sides.

"How far is that caravan?" Gamal asked.

Simeon understood his meaning. "A half hour walk. I suppose they didn't want the servants seeing their business. To get there, deal with the guards, saddle the horses ... I think we should follow on foot. Surely the horse will get spooked or exhausted soon."

They plodded onward. The trail was in front of them: the marks of the hooves in the sand obscured by the wake of the dragged body.

There was little blood. It was hard to say whether Gamal's bullet had hit Hennighan, or merely spooked the horse, if a resurrected horse could be spooked.

Then they heard a shot in the distance, and they both stopped, their guns drawn. It seemed to echo from all directions. Simeon could read Gamal's worry on his face; was it from the cave? Had Safiya been ambushed? But they had to keep going, hoping Safiya and Pierrette could get to safety.

"You know this Templar?" Gamal asked, anger and anxiety in his voice.

Simeon remembered the day in London when he had been surprised by Pierrette, up on a rooftop. The bruises on her face. Bruises given to her by Hennighan, following the orders of Countess Konstanze von Visler.

"He's a brute," Simeon said bitterly. "But not a fool." The countess would not have worked with a fool.

Back in the cave complex, Pierrette was lying in blood. Alive? God, if she was not, Hennighan would not be the only Templar to know Simeon's revenge.

Gamal stopped suddenly, and Simeon saw why a second after. The wake caused by the dragged body ended, with only a spatter of blood on the sand.

Then, unbelievably, the trail changed: a man's footprints next to the hoofprints of the horse.

"The horse is walking now," Gamal said. "Walking lame, I'd say."

"Hennighan managed to shoot the horse to cripple it," Simeon guessed. "That was the shot we heard. Then he got up, after being dragged all this way, and walked beside it. Unbelievable. Stubborn son of a bitch, isn't he?"

"I guess my bullet missed him, back in the tunnel."

"Damn it. Why won't the bastard die?"

They followed the prints and drops of blood, their pace faster now. They could catch up with an exhausted man leading an injured horse. It was just a matter of time and persistence. And Simeon was nothing if not persistent.

He was wondering how much they should ration the water in their flasks when they came up to the top of a drift and saw the Suez Canal before them. Blue water, impossibly straight, cutting through the sand and scrub.

There was not a single ship to be seen on it; the canal had

not yet opened to traffic. But there was a rope tied to a post, at the water's edge. A rope that might have tied a boat.

The trail of blood and hoofprints ended there.

Simeon had never been so exhausted. The sun was high by the time he and Gamal returned to the cave. Hennighan and his resurrected horse were gone, north or south on the canal, or across it into Sinai. And he'd taken the Ankh with him.

They met Safiya at the Templars' entrance to the cave complex, leading two camels.

Simeon didn't like the grim look on her face. He dashed into the tunnel, ran to the amphitheater. Pierrette was lying on a pile of clothing Safiya must have taken from the dead Templars, and she looked more comfortable, with her wounds clean and bandaged. But her own clothes were caked with blood, and her face was white. She was half-conscious, muttering something unintelligible.

"She needs a doctor," Simeon said.

"Yes," Safiya said. "The fastest way to get her one is to go back to Cairo. Let's get her onto a camel and I'll hold her while we ride. The other camel will take the packs."

"I'll take her," Simeon said, knowing he spoke out of emotion and not reason, and not caring. He had left her once already today, and he didn't want to leave her again.

"I know the way, and I can see enemies at a distance," Safiya retorted. "Besides, I'm smaller, and can fit her easily on the saddle in front of me. We need someone to stay here in case Hennighan returns with the Ankh, or in case there's another group of Templars on the way. I'll send someone to relieve you both as soon as I can."

Simeon reluctantly agreed, but it was hard watching them go, with Pierrette slumped against Safiya and the camel walking so slowly. He willed her to live, taking hope from the knowledge that Pierrette was stubborn. So stubborn that she'd run into a room full of Templars, alone.

But he knew there had been something more at work, something uncanny about that room with the painted gods in it. Pierrette had been herself and not, the same way Simeon had been himself and not. He hated to recall it and didn't know what he would say to Pierrette about it, if he was lucky enough to get the chance.

Gamal seemed desperate to talk about it, as though they could exorcise the experience that way.

As they pulled a Templar body past the great stone block in the middle of the amphitheater, Gamal paused to adjust the bandage around his arm. He put a hand onto the block, near the ankh-shaped depression, empty now.

"I wonder whether that room with the paintings of Isis, Horus, Osiris and Set would have the same impact on us now," Gamal said.

"What do you mean?" Simeon asked, warily.

"The Ankh was in position, in the room, when we were in the tunnels. This stone was clearly carved to hold it; it fit inside perfectly. It's a part of this complex. And the Ankh, from the stories I've heard, is said to hold the memories of the dead."

"I'm not sure the Templars even know that room with the paintings exists, or at least any details about it. They came in at this end, and set their guards here."

"But it could have been an effect of the Ankh they don't know about."

Simeon sighed. "Perhaps. Who knows what the thing does?"

"I'd like to," Gamal said thoughtfully. "I'd like to study it. It reminds me of a publisher in Paris who has been making images out of sounds. He uses a vibrating membrane, a boar bristle and lampblack on a glass plate. I wonder if what we experienced could be some sort of record or imprint – not of sound, perhaps, but of the psyche. As if that room were something like a photographic plate. And when the Ankh was in position, that was like a light, shining on the plate."

Simeon grimaced as he remembered the blue glare from the Ankh, and the words that he'd spoken in his own mind, words that seemed now to belong to a stranger: *Lord of Light.*

Gamal, recognizing that Simeon was not keen to talk, picked up the arms of the Templar they'd been carrying before they stopped: a young, slim man neither of them recognized. A man who had believed in a cause. They carried him out in silence and buried him with the others. It was hard work, but even Templars deserved a decent burial. And neither of them relished the idea of spending the night in a cavern full of bodies, after the day they'd had.

But there were ghosts here all the same, he thought. The ghosts of his mistakes, of Pierrette's frustration.

He appreciated Gamal's silence, as they walked back into the amphitheater. Gamal cleaned the packed sand from under his fingernail with a knife. A practical man, but a philosopher, nonetheless. And the Brotherhood did need to understand the artifacts that the Templars sought.

Hardly believing he was saying it, Simeon offered to go back to the crossroads room to test Gamal's theory.

This time, they carried two lanterns taken from the Templars and marked their passage with bits of charcoal. This time, the room held no power. The four gods were mere paintings, and Simeon felt no strange words forming in his mind, no strange emotions toward Gamal. Maybe it was because there were only two of them, but Gamal seemed pleased that there was nothing to contradict his theory about the power of the Ankh.

It didn't explain, though, why the Templars had brought the Ankh here. Had they truly intended to resurrect a horse? Or was that only the beginning of their plan? As he followed Gamal back through the corridors, Simeon stopped and ran his hand over one of the painted horses on the wall. Life-sized.

He gouged a bit of painted plaster out with the tip of his knife. Gamal winced but didn't object. Not even an inch below the surface, the scraping sound changed, and he held the lantern up.

Bone.

"They're all skeletons," Gamal whispered, holding his own lantern high and gazing down the corridor at the painted horses on the walls. "All of them bones."

Maybe the Templars had intended to resurrect more of the horses, or all of them, before they were interrupted. But surely Templars could buy horses anywhere. Maybe the horse was a test of the Ankh's power?

They passed a chilly and uncomfortable night in the amphitheater, taking turns on watch. Every so often, Simeon thought he heard something, but whenever he stilled to listen, there was nothing. Luckily, he was so exhausted from fighting, chasing Hennighan, and burying bodies, that he slept, and even after morning came, they did little but rest.

It was well into the evening of their second day on watch

when a group of Assassins arrived from Cairo to relieve them. Gamal greeted them warmly, but they were strangers to Simeon. They listened carefully as Simeon and Gamal showed them the entrance to the tunnels and the horses on the walls.

"We'll guard it well," said the Master Assassin among them, a member of the Cairo Council named Mustafa Hussein. He looked at Simeon and smiled. "You don't seem reassured, Mr Price."

Simeon shook his head. "I don't think I ever will be again. Not unless we bury this godforsaken place in something stronger than sand."

Chapter Eight

Simeon practically fell onto the mat Safiya offered him in a small screened-off part of their house back in Cairo, and woke up sweaty and starving some hours later. He pushed the hair out of his face and went into the main room.

To his great relief, Pierrette sat on a low couch, talking with a woman Simeon knew well: Amira Benyamina. She had inducted Simeon into the Brotherhood, years ago in France, and he always felt better about the world when she was around.

Amira rose and embraced Simeon, despite his protestations that he still wore half the desert.

"You can have a bath, tea, and food, in whatever order you like," she said with a smile.

"If you can stand my company for a few minutes, I'll have the news first." He looked cautiously at Pierrette, whose small smile didn't light her face.

Safiya came into the room with a tray bearing four steaming glasses.

At that, Pierrette laughed. "One of these days, I will learn the secret of your infallible instinct for the number of glasses of tea required. I half suspect you put your eagle vision to use, somehow."

Safiya rolled her eyes above her veil and sat. "The only secret is being willing to have extra tea that may go to waste."

"And has that ever happened?" Amira asked.

"I will accept it on the day that it does."

Simeon sat across from Pierrette, relieved that the laughter had broken the worry on her face. She was pale, wrapped in a blanket.

"Has the doctor been?" he asked.

Pierrette nodded. "The wound is shallow, but I lost some blood. I have strict orders to eat plenty of good food and drink a lot of water."

"And to rest," Safiya added, admonishing.

"I have been resting for two days. I have drunk enough broth to drown a pharaoh's army. I have been a model patient."

Simeon had never been at a loss for something to say to Pierrette. Their conversations had always come so easily, even when they were annoyed with each other. Especially then. Their silences, too, had been the silences of family. But now, he wasn't sure what to say. What words could dispel the memory that they'd seen each other as enemies in that horrible room?

It was tradition for a newly inducted Assassin to take a leap of faith from a great height, using their skills to protect themselves from the fall. Simeon's leap had not been the traditional one. Not for him the moment of soaring on the wind, the ebullience of knowing he would survive. No, Amira had made him dive instead. She knew he feared deep water, that it reminded him of the day his troop ship had gone down, drowning most of the soldiers and sailors on it. So she'd taken him to the gardens of Versailles, to a long stretch of water. Out in a rowboat. She'd made him dive right down to the bottom, to grasp the sand, to come up empty-handed.

She had looked at him then the way she looked at him now, having faith in him even if he didn't have faith in himself.

"You have all done the Brotherhood a great service," Amira said. "Armen Kazan is dead, and can't do any more damage. Simeon, good work finding the Ankh."

"But it's lost again," Simeon grumbled. "Hennighan has it."

"Yes. I find that interesting. Art Hennighan has never been powerful in the Templar Order. I thought he was little more than a servant to Konstanze von Visler. Was she in the cave?"

Simeon and Pierrette both said, "No."

"Very interesting. And now he has the Ankh. He may have the horse, too."

"Is the horse important?" Safiya asked.

Amira shrugged. "I don't know. We'll send out scouts in all directions, and see if they get any word. In the meantime, it strikes me that these were European Templars, carrying out a plan they hatched in Europe. Hennighan may still be working for the countess. I haven't heard anything about her whereabouts in a long time." She paused for a moment, thinking. "I believe the most useful thing for you to do, Simeon, is to follow that thread. I suggest starting in Paris. No one knows the comings and goings of the Templars of Europe better than Michel Moulin. Pierrette, you might join him, if you're well enough. Paris is your home, and you and Simeon have always worked well together."

Pierrette frowned. "But you've said yourself, Amira, that Cairo needs more people. Keeping guard on that cave will be a terrible drain on resources. God, I wish we could simply fill the place with dynamite and light a fuse." She paused and raised an eyebrow. "I don't suppose we can."

"It may come to that," Amira said gravely. "But we can't ignore the fact that it's an ancient place. Who knows what bones lie there? And we don't understand its power yet. I'm as anxious as you are about it, Pierrette, but the fact is that the surest way to stop the Templars from returning there to use the Ankh is to take the Ankh from them."

Simeon was about to say that yes, of course he would go to Paris, when Gamal entered, holding a piece of paper.

"There's a telegram for Pierrette," he said.

Several Assassins pulled knives out of their belts as she struggled to open the envelope, and then they all burst out laughing. It was like a breeze blowing away the lingering fog from the crossroads room. Pierrette took the knife Safiya offered her and sliced the envelope open.

The Assassins, like the Templars, had private telegraph lines, to avoid interception. But over great distances, both orders had to use public infrastructure, as neither of them had oceanic cable. This was a message from England, so it would have gone to an operator in Egypt in code. There was talk of making telegrams more efficient with automatic printing, which the Assassins wanted because it would reduce the intermediaries. And there was talk of making them easier to read by inserting characters or full words between sentences, which Assassins didn't want, because it was harder for their enemies to break the code when it was one unbroken line of text. There were a few things Assassins did better than Templars, despite the wealth and technology of the Templar Order, and deciphering was one of them.

It took Pierrette a few minutes to decode the message, scribbling with a pencil on the envelope.

Then her smile fell.

Simeon braced himself to hear about a death. Since the message was for Pierrette, it would likely be one of their friends in England. Not an Assassin, or Amira would know first. Maybe a member of the Aurora troupe.

But it wasn't about a recent death at all.

She handed him the telegram, her hand shaking. Simeon hesitated, taken aback and strangely touched that her first thought was to share it with him.

He read:

L Siddall exhumed please come E Frye

CHAPTER NINE

Pierrette got little sleep on the train to Alexandria and the ship to Southampton. She cursed every moment wasted in travel. Most of all, she cursed the Pierrette of seven years before, too sloppy and sentimental to destroy the notebook that had belonged to her friend, Ada Lovelace. She'd known it was dangerous. She'd kept it safe from the Magus for years, before and after they learned that the Magus was Oscar Kane, Simeon's mentor. She had snatched it away from Countess von Visler's grasp. Among its notes, calculations and designs, the notebook contained plans for a terrible weapon that the Magus had never made work as he intended, though his lesser attempts were evil enough.

It had been the decision of a moment, while Pierrette was mourning her old friend Lizzie Siddall. A painter, a model, a muse. An unhappy woman, who'd gone to her death in a laudanum haze. Her troubles had not been Ada's troubles, but they'd both been women in their thirties who had more to give than the world had been ready to receive. Maybe it was that similarity that had given Pierrette the rash notion to hide the notebook in Lizzie's coffin, under her red hair. A tribute, a farewell.

She should have destroyed it. But it was the only thing she had left of Ada's. And she was still used to making decisions alone in those days; she had not learned to have faith in the Brotherhood. Besides, who could have thought the Templars would exhume Lizzie, after all these years? No one had known the book was there. Only Pierrette and Simeon. And eventually, the British Assassin Ethan Frye, in those first years of Pierrette being an official member of the Brotherhood at last. She'd wanted to lay her actions bare, like laying a sword before a sovereign. To say: here I am, here is what I have done, here is the material you can use. Somehow, that had felt necessary, to make sure her comrades knew what they were getting. Whatever she knew, they would know.

It had been a long time since she'd thought about the notebook. Surely it must be rotted by now? Unreadable? She shuddered. Ethan Frye had died the year before. But he must have told his daughter about the notebook. Or perhaps he'd kept records or a diary of his own. One way or another, Evie knew. And a good thing she did.

Pierrette finally dozed on the final leg of the journey, the train to London, and woke up dazed and foggy, with a muttonchop-cheeked man watching her with lazy curiosity. Her legs ached, and she was chilly beneath her shawl.

Waterloo Station was full of people, sunlight slanting through the glass roof, smells of hot pies, coal smoke and newsprint. Pierrette suddenly wished Simeon had come with her, although she'd insisted he go on to Paris and track down what information he could about Hennighan and the Ankh expedition.

Then she saw a young woman with brown hair and a practical, tailored jacket, leaning against a railing, watching her. Evie Frye strode toward her with a wide grin and let herself be embraced.

Pierrette held her by the shoulders and looked at her face, taking in every freckle. Evie was fifteen years younger than her, which made her twenty-two now. Evie stepped back, and stood in the midst of the train station as though she owned it, glancing and taking note of everything.

"I'm the one coming home, but you're the conquering hero," Pierrette said. "I swear, London feels different. It doesn't smell different, though."

Evie laughed. "A lot has changed since you left."

"Yes, I've heard that you and Henry Green are very close," Pierrette teased.

"I don't mean that," Evie said, blushing.

"I know. You and your brother are to be congratulated, too. It's astonishing what you've done. To rid a city of its Templar yoke like that – you and Jacob working alone – I hope the British Council recognizes what a triumph you've pulled off."

"I'm afraid London isn't entirely out of danger yet. Shall we go somewhere quiet?"

The exhumation. Pierrette could hardly believe anyone had done such a thing. "Is Rossetti still living in the house he took in Chelsea, after Lizzie died?"

Evie nodded.

"Then let's get a cab and go there," Pierrette said firmly. "You can fill me in on the way."

•••

The cab was just going past the Houses of Parliament when Evie told her that Rossetti himself had ordered Lizzie's coffin exhumed, about a month ago.

"But why would he do such a thing?"

Evie grimaced. "The rumor is that he wanted to retrieve a book that was in with her. Poems, people say, but they're just assuming that because Rossetti writes poems. As soon as I heard about it, I knew it had to be the notebook my father told me about. I don't think he ever imagined it would be exhumed, but he made sure I was aware of everything that had happened over the last few years, in case anything caused ripples he couldn't foresee."

Pierrette wanted to fall through the bottom of the hansom cab into a deep, dark hole.

"This will cause more than a ripple," she groaned. "Ada's notes and designs. If it's in Templar hands, who knows what machines and weapons they might build. Do you have any idea where the book is now?"

Evie shook her head. "We've been looking – I've told the other Assassins, of course. But Jacob and Henry both have other projects at the moment, and we're preparing to go to India…"

"Of course," Pierrette said, wondering if she could possibly feel worse.

"There are still so few of us, and while we have allies, none are close enough to Rossetti to learn the truth. But you used to share rooms with Rossetti and his wife. You must know him well."

She had once. But as the cab stopped outside of 16 Cheyne Walk, Pierrette was unsure. She'd never been to this house, even though Gabriel Rossetti had moved here soon after Lizzie's death back in 1862. Pierrette had been busy, and Gabriel was grieving. She'd seen him a few times at salons and parties, but they hadn't had a proper conversation.

She turned to Evie. "I think it might be best–"

"Go on without me. You can find me at this address." Evie handed her a card. "And thank you, Pierrette, for coming home. We'll find the book, and we'll find who's behind this."

The housekeeper took Pierrette's calling card with indifference and let her into a sitting room with curtains covering the windows.

The smell was suffocating, as though someone had bottled the London Zoo. Somewhere, a bird chirped. For a moment, Pierrette thought it was the bullfinch that Lizzie had kept, years ago, but no, of course it wasn't.

The walls were packed with paintings and some of them bore Lizzie's face, or Lizzie's face as Gabriel had perceived it. Several mirrors hung angled from chains; the effect was dizzying. But then again, Pierrette had lost a lot of blood, a fortnight before. She became dizzy easily.

She made for a place to sit down, on a settee upholstered with bottle-green velvet, when the departing housekeeper drawled, "Not there. You'll be bitten."

"I beg your pardon?"

But the housekeeper had gone. Pierrette bent to examine the settee and stood back up again with a start. Behind the cushion were two small eyes.

"My family of dormice," Gabriel said at the door. "They make their home there. If you sit a little to one side, it ought to be fine."

In the dim room, the shape of him was so familiar: the impatient posture, the prominent forehead, the slightly wild hair, the dark beard.

She approached him and shook his hand. "Gabriel, thank you for seeing me. I'm sorry for appearing out of nowhere like this."

"Oh, women appear out of nowhere in this house all the time," he said, walking over to a side table. "It's haunted, you see. Will you take whisky?"

She was tempted, just to have something near her nose to dispel the stench of animals. But whisky was expensive to waste, and she wanted her wits about her, especially with comments like that coming from Gabriel. "Not just now, thank you."

"I will take a glass because I am in mourning. A glass of whisky in this house is like a black armband in another."

"Mourning," she repeated, not quite a question.

"Yes." He looked at her steadily, took a sip. "I had a wombat. It didn't live long."

"A wombat. And dormice?"

Something scuttled nearby.

"And a raccoon," he added. "Peacocks, several owls, a pair of dogs, some parrots, a raven, a marmot or two. I had an armadillo, but he hasn't been seen in some time. The wombat, though. That was a real blow."

"You are a collector," she said, in a tone that was colder and more accusing than she meant it to be.

"A collector of moments. I had thought all our moments together were complete, Pierrette. It has been a long time."

"It has indeed."

"And Simeon. Is he... where is he?"

"Paris, at the moment."

She felt faint, and took her chances next to the dormice. "Gabriel, I heard something strange about Lizzie – that someone had raised her coffin."

He downed the rest of the whisky and put down the glass. "Some friends of mine were good enough to do it. It had to be done, Pierrette."

"Why, in heaven's name?"

"It's my eyes. I can't see properly anymore. I can't see things at a distance. I can't see things close up. I can't see in the darkness and I can't see in the light. Nothing looks quite as it should. The colors. How can I trust the colors?"

"I'm sorry to hear that," she said, trying to be patient.

"So I'm no good as a painter anymore."

Some of the images on the walls were of Jane Morris, his friend's wife, she noticed. And women she didn't recognize. They looked recent. She said nothing.

Gabriel continued, "I needed to put out a book of writing. But my best work was in... in there, with her. I couldn't write anything new because I kept thinking about those poems, the ones I could never get back. I had to be free of them. I had to get them back."

She stood, watching carefully for animals on the patterned carpet, and went over to him. "Gabriel, so it was a book of poems you took out, then? Your own poems?"

He looked confused. "Yes, of course. Come and see. It's over here."

He walked into an adjoining room, to an oak desk where a book lay open on a vertical stand. She stopped when she realized what it was. It was discolored, and there was a hole that began on one edge. She forced herself to take a step forward and saw a page of Gabriel's loose handwriting. The ink was barely faded.

"There was just this one book, then?" she asked, her voice almost a whisper.

"Yes, of course, I only put one book in. I only had one to give! I was never prolific, more's the pity."

She turned back to him. "But what I mean is that nothing else came out of the coffin?"

His brows lowered. "Why are you here, Pierrette?"

She swallowed and decided to use as much of the truth as she could. "When I heard about the exhumation, I wondered whether anyone had... organized it. These friends of yours, the ones who carried it out."

"I won't have them impugned," he said fiercely. "I won't have them spoken against. It is not a civilized business, but art is not civilized. My friends understand that."

She nodded, feeling dizzy again. It was just as dark in this room as it had been in the other, and there was a smell here of wood polish. At least the housekeeper was doing something. It must be a difficult house to keep.

"I don't mean to speak a word against your friends. It was more, well, I was concerned that whoever suggested it might have had some reason to impugn *you*. To stir up scandal. I see now I was wrong. It was all your own idea."

"Yes. Well, not entirely my idea, but I saw the necessity of it."

She proceeded in her interrogation carefully. "You had to be persuaded, I don't doubt. You would have wanted to make sure there was no other way, before considering such a thing."

"Yes, it's the sort of thing one doesn't consider."

"Until someone mentions it, and then–"

"Oh, not even then," Gabriel said with a little laugh. "When Howell first mentioned it, I was aghast. But eventually I saw that it was the obvious solution to my problem. I am a man haunted by my own work. There was no other way forward."

Howell. She turned over her name in her mind. It was familiar. She and Simeon had looked up a Charles Augustus Howell, once, when they'd been chasing the Magus. But they'd found nothing solid. Those days in Paris, soon after the bombing, with the smell of smoke and blood still in her nostrils. Searching safehouses in dark alleys, reading letters and police reports and newspapers, making connections between names and places, and trying to see whether the Templars had a hand in any of it. There were so many names that never led anywhere; people who weren't Templars or Assassins, who had some relationship to the bombers but who seemed to be nothing more than suppliers of material, or ideological hangers-on who had never been privy to the real plans. Howell had been one of the latter, she recalled now, an English sympathizer whose letters were among some of Orsini's things.

"There was a Charles Augustus Howell connected to that business with Felice Orsini in 1858," she said slowly.

"Oh, Howell is connected to everything and everyone," Gabriel said. "One of John Ruskin's people. Who isn't? Why, it was Ruskin who connected you with Lizzie and me, in the old days, when you were always with Ada Lovelace. Well, Howell was Ruskin's secretary or something of that nature, for a time. Now Howell helps me with business matters. He is level-headed, that one. Which was why he saw what needed to be done."

Pierrette would need to find Howell, but if she tried to approach him through Rossetti, that might give everything away.

"Of course," she said, with what started as a deliberate attempt at a kind smile, and suddenly became one, all on its own. She pitied Gabriel, who grieved more than just his wombat, who managed to be terrified and cocksure all at once. She did not envy him his house of beasts and spirits.

CHAPTER TEN

That evening, Pierrette was inside another townhouse, embracing her old friend, Anne, the daughter of Ada Lovelace.

"It's Anne Blunt now," she said, her eyes twinkling in a face framed by neat black curls. "I was married in the spring."

"Married at last! I was beginning to think you had your heart set on being an inveterate spinster, like me," Pierrette teased.

"Yes, well, I couldn't resist Wilfrid."

"Is he that handsome?"

"He's... well, he has eyes that see right through into one's soul. My grandmother would have been horrified to see me make the same mistake she did, marrying a poet."

"I should like to meet him," Pierrette said.

"Oh, he's working for the diplomatic service, and it keeps him away from the house, although I joke he does it to escape my violin playing. But I know he'll want to meet you and hear all about Cairo. I want to hear about it, too."

It was heartening to see Anne so happy, even if it did seem a feverish, nervous sort of happiness. Her brother Byron

Ockham – named after their famous grandfather, the poet – had died at twenty-six, mere months after helping Pierrette and Simeon put an end to the Magus. Pierrette had wondered whether his death might have been related to effects of the wounds he'd sustained in the fight, but she'd said nothing about that in the letter she'd written to Simeon, telling him the sad news about his friend. And she'd said nothing about it to Anne, who had been so protective of Byron. Byron had been the oldest, but he wanted nothing to do with the family fortune, working on the docks in anonymity, taking a new surname from his title, Viscount Ockham.

His death had followed so closely on Lizzie's that Pierrette had worn the same black dress to both funerals.

"I would love nothing better than to have a good long chat, but I'm afraid I'm here on urgent business," Pierrette said. "I need a society introduction. Charles Augustus Howell. Do you know him?"

"Yes. He's a friend of Ruskin's. And Rossetti's, I believe. He seems to get involved in people's business affairs, and has a talent for talking and for making deals."

"He seems to have convinced Rossetti to exhume Lizzie's coffin."

Anne grimaced. "So that rumor is true, then. Terrible. Did he really do it for the sake of a book?"

Pierrette hesitated. She'd already put this family through so much. But Anne deserved to know the truth. "He did take a book of his own poems out. But Anne, there was another book in the coffin. Your mother's notebook. I know it was there because I put it there myself. There are several people who would be very interested in obtaining that notebook. Your mother considered it dangerous, which was why she entrusted it to me."

A cloud passed over Anne's face. "Why, in God's name, would you have put it into a coffin?"

"Believe me, that's a question I've been asking myself. I was in a position where I needed to hide it quickly, and putting it there seemed final. It may be dangerous in the wrong hands, and Howell doesn't seem trustworthy to me. You know that your mother made notes about all kinds of machines and inventions, including some that could be used in weapons. I have to make it right. All I need is an introduction, so I can go see Howell and find out what he knows. I don't want him to be suspicious, you see, so I need some reason to call on him, and some mutual friend's good word to put him at ease."

Anne shook her head. "I'll do better than that. Come here tomorrow evening at this time, and Howell will be here."

"Anne, you don't have to do that. I must warn you that if he gets suspicious, if he's stubborn, there could be violence."

"I insist. If there is anything I can do to protect my mother's legacy, I will."

Pierrette paused. "All right. Should we have a story prepared, for why you're introducing us?"

"That part is simple. The man is a more dedicated gambler than my mother was. But his game is whist, so we'll need a fourth."

It would not have surprised any observer that Anne Blunt won the first rubber of whist the following night, taking the first two games before her opponents could catch their breath.

She had her mother's facility with numbers. Ordinary players could recall whether or not the aces and face cards had been played, but Anne remembered every card. She was not the kind of player who would lay down a six of clubs, hoping the seven would not appear.

Her partner at the table, Charles Augustus Howell, had the sort of face that looked pleased with itself in all circumstances; an effect of the tiny rectangular mustache or the cockscomb of shiny brown curls, perhaps. He was especially pleased that night.

It was also not surprising that Pierrette and her partner were losing. Pierrette was too bold, risking everything. Her partner, on the other hand, was confident and calculating, which might have worked with a different pairing. Evie Frye took a long time to think about every play, setting up long strings of possible outcomes that were, inevitably, stymied when Pierrette took an unwise risk that Evie could not have predicted.

Howell's good spirits couldn't be dampened by being banished to the smoking room alone when he took out his pipe. He was surprised, though, when Pierrette quietly opened the door and took a cigarette out of a silver case.

"You don't mind, do you, Mr Howell?" she asked, her eyes red. "I find it steadies the nerves."

"Think nothing of it," Howell said gallantly, lighting a long match and holding it out for her. "I'm not a man to criticize anyone else's vices. Rotten luck in that rubber. The next one will be better."

"I hope so." Pierrette's voice broke. "I have a confession to make. I accepted Lady Anne's invitation this evening in hopes of making enough to pay my landlady. That's the worst of it, having friends who come from money, isn't it? They will never understand. Oh, I don't mean to presume–"

"Not at all, not at all. I agree. I've had to make my living by my wits myself. And sometimes, by the cards."

Pierrette nodded, taking a long draw on her cigarette, and speaking more steadily, as if grateful for the sympathetic ear. "I used to be in the circus. We had a tent for card playing sometimes. But I'm ashamed to say that we cheated."

Howell smiled. "I think anyone who plays cards in a tent in the circus ought to expect to be cheated. Not at all the same as a game among gentlemen and ladies, is it?"

"Not at all," Pierrette said, warmly. "Do you know, we had a code?" She stepped closer to him. "When we wanted our partner to lead diamonds, we'd touch the earlobe, like so. The hollow of the neck for hearts, and clubs was a scratch of the hand, and what was spades? Oh yes, I remember now. Scratch the chin for spades."

"How ingenious!" Howell said indulgently. "Was that the entire code?"

"If one of us asked what trump was, pretending to forget, you see, that was a sign we held high trump cards."

He nodded, suddenly serious. "If you want my opinion, there is not enough fairness in this world, Mademoiselle Arnaud. I don't think there is anything wrong with evening the odds a little from time to time. You're in need of a win tonight. Let's suggest a change of partners, shall we? I might bring you a little luck."

"I'll need more than a little," she said, her face falling again.

So, for the second rubber, Howell sat opposite Pierrette, and Evie and Anne were partners. They won handily. Anne Blunt, truly Ada's daughter, raised the bet.

Howell led the aces of hearts and clubs, taking both tricks. Then he considered his next play. Pierrette smiled at him, and casually fiddled with her cheap earring.

He led the seven of diamonds.

Pierrette cringed apologetically as she laid her ten of diamonds over Anne's king.

But the next diamond hand, she retook with a trump heart, and she gave him a look that suggested maybe she'd had a longer strategy.

Half the time, her clues led to success, and half the time, they didn't. Once, she asked what was trump, and later, when he frowned to see that she had no trump in her hand, she blurted out, "Oh, I really did forget what trump was. I'm sorry about that."

And he blushed, while Anne moved the pointer on the brass marker.

They lost the rubber badly. Howell was red in the face.

Anne said, "A man's luck can change, Howell."

He stared at her, fish-mouthed.

"My friends here need information, and I know that's something you have. I propose a trade. Leave here with all the money you came with, and you don't even have to cheat for it."

His eyes narrowed. "You've swindled me. I'll take my money whether you–"

As he reached for the pile of sovereigns, Evie pointed a gun at his forehead.

He looked around, sweating, baffled. "What is this madness?"

Pierrette leaned forward. "Tell us why you convinced Gabriel to dig up Lizzie's coffin."

Howell was not stupid; he caught the use of first names and looked at Pierrette with interest. Then he said, "He was in a low state, thought his best work was behind him."

"Out of kindness and concern, then?" Evie asked drily.

"If you can't believe that I wanted to help my friend in his career, I will say that I act on his behalf in certain business matters. His melancholy was bad for that business. I am an art dealer. Among other things."

Evie, her voice a quiet growl, asked, "Is one of those things a Templar?"

That startled him more than the gun had. Anne frowned slightly in confusion but said nothing.

Howell stayed silent for a long time, then: "I am aware of the Order, and I have dealings with it. I retain my independence."

Pierrette suspected that meant the Order found him useful but unworthy of membership. That might make him resentful. "What use could a man like Crawford Starrick have had for someone like you?"

"I am not a servant of Crawford Starrick's or anyone else's. John Elliotson was a close personal friend."

Evie's face was unreadable, but the hand that held the gun was steady. "The doctor who ran Lambeth Asylum?"

"The same. His death last year was a lamentable accident. A significant loss for our city."

"Yes, lamentable," Evie said. "He used cadavers in his work, didn't he? He must have known some resurrection men. Perhaps even employed some."

"Anyone can dig up a grave. The key is getting to know the people who put them into the ground. They can ensure the graves are not too deep. But there is a strange surfeit of honor among undertakers. It takes time to get to know the ones who can be worked with. I look for the gossips. The bent, resentful old men. And in the course of conversation with such a man, I learned there were two books in the coffin with Lizzie Siddall."

"Two books?" Pierrette asked, keeping her voice even. "Rossetti's poems, and what else?"

He shrugged. "An artist's model lives an eccentric sort of life, and Lizzie and Gabriel didn't marry until shortly before her death. I would not have been surprised to learn she had other men who felt moved to place some memento into the grave with her. I thought Rossetti might be interested in this information, and interested, perhaps, in keeping it quiet."

"In other words," said Anne Blunt, "you thought there might be money in it for you."

Howell glanced at Pierrette. "We all have to make our way in the world."

Pierrette asked, "And did you mention this second book to anyone?"

He paused, then shrugged. "To John Elliotson. He was very grateful to me for finding a useful ally in the undertaker, and as payment, he offered to help me with the exhumation. Insisted upon it. He said there would be money to be had, not only from Rossetti, but from the other lover, whoever he might be. He might pay to make sure Rossetti didn't learn about him. Rossetti's somewhat unbalanced state of mind is well known. A state of mind that Elliotson had been, well, encouraging. He treated Rossetti for a time."

If John Elliotson hadn't already been killed by Jacob Frye, Pierrette might have gone to find him herself. Could he have been motivated only by money? Elliotson was a Templar and if he had known about the second book, he might have told someone else in the Order before he died.

"But it was you who convinced Rossetti to exhume his wife," Pierrette said.

Howell looked uncomfortable. "He was reluctant, at first. It was more than a year ago that I first mentioned it to him. By the time Rossetti gave his permission, Elliotson had died. But I didn't have any trouble in obtaining the necessary paperwork."

Of course not.

"So you exhumed the coffin and found both books. What then?"

At that, he dried up, looking embarrassed. Evie moved the barrel of the gun right to his forehead, and Howell raised both hands, protesting, "You won't believe me, but it's the truth, so help me God."

"God won't help you," Evie said. "So you might as well try your luck with us."

He winced, but said, "There were several of us at the graveside: friends of Rossetti, all of us. There was a doctor – not Elliotson. Another man. All were sworn to secrecy. We set both books aside on a folding table for the doctor to disinfect. And then–"

"And then?" Anne prodded.

Howell wrung his hands. "It was a foggy night. Nearly morning by that time. We saw a strange thing – it looked like a woman, all in white."

"Mourners don't usually wear white in England," Anne said.

"No, they do not. This was no mourner. It looked… well, I don't have to tell you what it looked like, at that hour, to a group of men who had just pulled the lid off a coffin and reached into the red hair of the corpse inside. A group of men who had fortified themselves more than a little with brandy and other things, before the business began. I don't know if I can trust my memory. I followed it, to speak to it."

"It?" Evie asked, her eyebrows high. "You're saying the woman was an apparition?"

"All I know is that she vanished as suddenly as she appeared. And the next time we looked at the table, there was only one book on it." He laughed, nervously. "None of us have spoken a word about it to each other since. I combed the area afterwards, once the sun was up and the mist cleared, but I found nothing."

Pierrette asked, "Were there any women in your group? Or any women who knew about the plan?"

He shook his head.

"What did she look like, this woman? What age? What color of skin and hair?"

"She was veiled, and all in white. That's all I know."

She was tempted to ask him whether he knew Countess von Visler, but what good would it do if he said yes? What would it tell her that her instincts weren't screaming already? Howell had told Elliotson, and Elliotson, before he died, had told the countess.

She nodded to Evie, who pulled the gun away from his temple. Pierrette could see the calculations she was making. Howell was not a Templar, but he was no innocent.

Pierrette decided for her, mainly because she could see Anne's face. She had asked a lot of Anne already; she wouldn't force her to witness an execution in her drawing room.

"This carpet looks very expensive," Pierrette said coolly. "We arc going to lct you live. We are even going to let you leave with the money you came with. Unlike you, we have scruples about cheating at the card table. But if you breathe a word about this conversation to anyone, you will not live long to regret it."

He stood abruptly, shakily, and put his sovereigns into a little purse and tucked that into his coat pocket.

As he hurried to the door, Pierrette followed him.

"There's one thing you've forgotten, Mr Howell."

He turned to her with fear on his face. "I swear, I told you everything I know."

She turned her hand over and tapped her wrist.

Flushed and angry, he pulled a card out from under his sleeve and handed it to her. It was warm and slightly damp. The ace of spades – the suit that had been trump in the last hand, which he'd dealt.

"You ought to be careful what you keep in your sleeves, Mr Howell."

Emboldened by the lack of a gun to his head and the proximity of the door, he spat back, "And you ought to be careful about what you choose to resurrect."

CHAPTER ELEVEN

Simeon sat on the lid of a coalbin and read his newspaper. There were more pleasant places in Paris to spend an hour on a July afternoon than the yard of a glass factory, downwind from the La Villette abattoir. But he had business here, on the outskirts of the city. Business for which he was willing to wait.

Waiting was his chief occupation these days, or so it felt. Eight months he'd been in Paris, and he felt no closer to finding what he'd come for. He hadn't found Art Hennighan.

A horse dealer reported a sighting of him in Yenbo, in Arabia, from a horse dealer, but when the Cairo Assassins sent a scout there, there was no trace of him.

As for his movements before the Ankh expedition, the Paris Assassins had determined that Hennighan had indeed come to Paris about a year before, without Konstanze von Visler. As for the countess herself, Michel's sources said she seemed to have fallen off the Templar landscape. Rumor had it she was occupied with her own pet projects, and when those projects weren't appreciated sufficiently by the rest of the Order, she retreated into solitude. It must have galled her not to be involved with the Ankh, Simeon thought; she had a fascination with all ancient artifacts, especially the powerful Pieces of Eden.

Her companies, though, were doing a brisk business. She owned half the rail lines in Europe, and her company had been one of Hawkins's suppliers. Her locomotive company made the fastest trains in the world. She also owned a telegraph company, and the mining operations that had created her wealth in the first place.

All of which added up to questions without answers, when it came to the Ankh.

Pierrette was convinced that the countess was back in London, or had been recently. She had written him a breathless letter about an apparition in a cemetery. Whether this apparition was the countess, someone else, or a figment conjured by brandy, the fact was that Ada's notebook was gone. All those years keeping it out of malicious hands, only for it to re-enter their lives in the most terrible way. And Pierrette was, as usual, putting herself at ever greater risk, trying to find answers.

Simeon hadn't been in Paris for years. He soon learned there was an uneasy impasse between the Templars and Assassins of Paris, who were evenly matched. Each held sway in certain areas of the city. Michel Moulin, his old friend and now head of the Paris Assassins, was helping find out what he could, but he wasn't willing to risk open war. Simeon didn't blame him, but he jumped at the chance when Michel gave him a Templar target – one who used to work closely with Art Hennighan. It served both their purposes: Virgile Donat might be able to tell Simeon something about Hennighan, and Donat was increasingly flouting the fragile balance of power. Donat ran a glass factory in the nineteenth arrondissement, squarely in Assassin territory. Besides, he was odious enough, and the source of enough scandal and annoyance, that the Templars might be happy to let his death go unanswered.

Simeon turned a page of the newspaper, aware that a man was approaching from the factory doors. He waited until the man was close, then let the paper drop enough to give him a supercilious look.

A guard, in a rumpled uniform with brass buttons. He was young, with shiny brown hair combed from a deep side part, and a thick mustache.

"You've been reading that newspaper for a long time," the guard said.

"There's a lot of news."

The guard coughed. "Move along. You can't stay here."

Simeon folded the newspaper and crossed his legs. "How much do they pay you? Fifty centimes an hour? Difficult to support a family on that. Twelve hours a day, just to make rent and food."

The guard coughed. "Are you offering me a job, sir?"

That took Simeon aback; the only sort of job he might offer ought to be clear from his hooded cloak, the scars on his knuckles.

"I'm offering you a chance to consider what you owe your employer, for wages such as those. Let's see. This factory is owned by Virgile Donat, isn't it?"

Uncertainty flickered across the man's face.

Simeon picked up the newspaper. "I've read a great deal about Monsieur Donat, as it happens. A successful man.

Friends in high places. And he is loyal to his friends, isn't he? So loyal that he fired every worker who didn't vote for his friend in the legislative election last year. So loyal that he has been known to procure anything his friends desire for their parties. Or anyone. I wonder whether the children of Paris have a new name for the bogeyman."

The guard's face reddened. "I'm not going to ask you again to move along."

"You most certainly will not. Because fifty centimes an hour is barely enough to buy soup. Is it enough to make up for the list of crimes your employer has committed?" Simeon paused, and said seriously, "Is it enough for you to give your life for him?"

They stared at each other for a moment.

Then Simeon opened his copy of *Le Siècle* and listened to the sound of the guard walking away. He smiled slightly.

He had meant it when he told the guard there was a lot of news in the paper. There were strikes throughout France, and the government was sending in the army to crush workers in several towns. He turned the page. Speculation about the possibility of war with Prussia. Napoleon III had been nervous about Prussia's growing power for years, and many of his advisors were trying to make war look both inevitable and good.

Simeon, who had been a soldier, knew it was neither.

One of the loudest voices urging war was the emperor's wife, Eugenie. A target of Templar influence, and at least one Templar bombing, although Simeon agreed with Pierrette that it was likely she would have been rescued at the last moment. Simeon was starting to wonder whether Pierrette had been right to save her life. Twice.

He checked his pocket watch. Ten minutes to five.

Footsteps, and this time they weren't the guard's. And they weren't coming through the muddy factory yard, but on the cobbled road just around the corner from where Simeon sat. Virgile Donat, leaving his office, later than usual but still well before five.

Simeon turned the page of his newspaper, loudly.

A ragpicker or a beggar might have escaped Donat's notice, but a man waiting for someone outside his factory was a threat. It meant someone was stealing from him – or at least stealing time from his workers, whether this was a romantic assignation or a fight.

The footsteps paused, then continued dully into the mud of the yard. "What's your business here?" Donat shouted.

Simeon folded the newspaper and held it in front of him with his right hand. He waited until Donat was standing close enough to grab the newspaper.

Then, Simeon thrust a knife right through the newspaper and into Donat's gut.

It went against his training and instincts to kill the man in a slow and noisy way, but Simeon didn't want this killing to bear the hallmarks of a skilled Assassin. He was killing this man on behalf of the people of Paris, so it should look as though any of the people of Paris might have done it. Someone would report the body to the police, or someone might panic and dump it into the Seine to be fished out with the others that appeared on any given day at the Paris morgue. He did not think the sight would cause much sorrow to the workers who'd be leaving their shift in three hours.

And it gave him a chance to question Donat.

"Tell me where Art Hennighan is, and I'll give you mercy."

Donat coughed and sputtered, trying to get a grip on his own gun. Simon reached forward, pulled out the gun, tossed it behind him.

"You can put an end to the pain now. You don't deserve mercy, but we both know life isn't fair. Art Hennighan. Big, bald, has a scar on one cheek. Tell me where I can find him."

Donat collapsed onto the ground, curling around his wounded stomach.

Simeon kneeled beside him and held his Hidden Blade at the man's throat. When it came to it, he didn't relish watching a man die this way.

"Here," Donat said, in a dry whisper.

"Hennighan's here? At the glass factory?"

Donat winced, shook his head.

"He's in Paris? Is that what you're saying?"

Donat, his face contorted with pain, managed to nod.

"That's not much to go on, is it? What was he doing with the Ankh?"

He had to get very close to hear the answer. "The Engine of History."

"The Engine of History? What do you mean?"

But Donat's face was slack and pale, and he said something else. It sounded like "Cold."

He couldn't take this anymore. Within seconds, Simeon's blade ended his life. With a shaking hand, Simeon brushed a calling card against the man's wound, and put it away into his pocket. A job like any other job, but he shivered. Perhaps it was a good thing to be reminded never to get used to this. He had decided years ago that he would never be a soldier: he would act according to his conscience. But sometimes his conscience failed him. More and more, lately.

He tossed the bloody newspaper on top of the body. It was open to the page about the upcoming war; there was an advertisement down in the corner for laundry soap.

The shadows were lengthening as Simeon walked through the streets, past brothels and workshops. As much to dispel the shiver as anything, he whistled.

> *Farewell and adieu to you, Spanish ladies,*
> *Farewell and adieu to you, ladies of Spain;*
> *For we've received orders for to sail for old England,*
> *But we hope in a short time to see you again.*

Simeon crossed the rail line that brought the animals to slaughter, and the line that brought the coal to be burned. The gasworks loomed ahead: a dozen cylindrical iron frames, each as tall as an apartment block, and each containing a massive tank. The tanks moved up and down within these cylinders according to the level of the gas, so each was at a different height.

There was something ghostly about this place, the source of the gas that lit the lamps of Paris. Maybe it was the hulking metal cylinders that seemed to dwarf everything around them, their shadows in late afternoon latticing the ground. Or maybe it was simply that the smell kept people away unless they had to be here. Simeon saw a few hunched figures wheeling carts of coal to the ovens.

The fourth gasholder from the left was half-full, as always. He stepped casually into the little booth beside it. It was no bigger than an outhouse and contained nothing but a telegraph machine. He tapped out a code and waited.

There was a distant sound of creaking, then a click as the secret door at the back of the booth unlatched. He pushed it forward and stepped into a cast-iron cage. In front of him was the inside of the "tank": an open circle, lined with brick, half of it underground. Simeon moved the lever, and the cage descended, bringing him down to the floor of the tank.

Michel Moulin sat in the middle of the tank, at a desk covered in papers. A young Assassin named Mary Fitzpatrick slouched in a chair across from him, and two other Assassins, young Sami Zidane and less young Jean-Baptiste Barbeau, were having a quietly heated discussion at the opposite wall.

As Simeon opened the door of the elevator, Michel gestured him over.

Mary rose from the other chair, and said to Simeon in her soft Irish accent, "I hope you've brought good news."

Although Michel was nearing forty, he still had a boyish way about him; something about his slightly awkward thin frame, or the smattering of freckles across his nose. But he had worry lines around his eyes now. He was the head of the Paris Bureau of Assassins, and it said a great deal about how beleaguered the bureau felt that his favorite place to meet was here, lit only by two electric lamps, where the faint stench of coal gas permeated everyone's clothes.

It was a good place to hide from Templars, who preferred to reap the benefits of their power. They kept spies in the poor neighborhoods, but they tended not to congregate there themselves. Michel looked at home here. He had a job to do and he would do it, although his own background was wealthy; his father was a government official. When he needed to, Michel could get information from socialites; when he needed to, he could get information from ragpickers.

Of all the Assassins Simeon had known in Paris ten years before, Michel was the only one still living in the city. Henri Escoffier, the first Assassin Simeon had ever met, was in Zurich now, on assignment. Michel had a talented group of Assassins around him, though. He was no longer the messy-haired young man who'd been the youngest of the Paris Assassins himself.

Michel looked at Simeon's expression. "So Donat is dead."

Simeon pulled out his calling card case and took out the topmost, still damp. He handed it to Michel.

"Well done. Any difficulty?"

"None at all. And I got something out of him. He said Art Hennighan is here in Paris."

Michel considered. "Information from a man in pain is always suspect. Still, it suggests it's worth focusing our efforts. If he's in Paris, we'll find him."

"There's one other thing. He said something about the 'Engine of History'. Some Templar phrase?"

Michel shook his head. "I've never heard it before."

Simeon could tell that Michel's mind wasn't on the elusive Art Hennighan. "What is it? What's happened?"

Michel smiled sadly at him. "Politics."

"Oh, is that all?"

"It's enough. You know the emperor is nervous about Prussia's growing power. A lot of diplomatic posturing and terse letters."

"Michel, I spent the last two hours reading every word of *Le Siècle*. I'm aware, believe me."

"Well, Prussia has its warmongers, just as France does. King Wilhelm's foreign minister, this Bismarck. He wants to unify the German states against a common enemy. To turn nationalist sentiment into support for a new empire – led by Wilhelm of Prussia."

"But foreign ministers don't rule their kings."

Michel smiled. "No, they work around them. We've just heard that Bismarck leaked a telegram that made it sound as if the French had given the Prussians an ultimatum, and the Prussians had responded with an insult. He sent it straight to the French press; it will be in the papers tomorrow. He has to make sure the French are the ones to declare war, you see. Prussia has to look like it's on the defensive, and then the German states rally to its aid."

Simeon thought for a moment. "Who was this telegram from?"

"From Wilhelm's staff, ostensibly, but the German Templars control half the telegraph lines in Europe, and they've suborned or trained many operators. There are Templars supporting Bismarck's plan, I'm sure of it. The bigger the empires, the easier the people are to control."

"Do you really think it will come to war?"

"If we can't stop it."

Simeon hated war as only a former soldier could. "What can I do?"

Michel tapped the table, a habit he had when he was thinking. It reminded Simeon of a telegraph operator, and maybe it gave Michel the same thought. "Prussia knows that its ability to win a war depends on how quickly it can mobilize. Communication. Transportation. That's its advantage, in large part thanks to your German countess."

"She's not my countess, believe me."

"Well, she's done a terrific job covering the German states with her fast trains and fast wires. If Prussia loses some of its communications network, it might be less willing to beat the battle drums. I'll get a message to our Brothers in Prussia, and if you'd take on some demolition work on the borders of France, Simeon, I'd be grateful. I know that's not why you came to Paris, but it's all hands on deck at the moment."

Simeon nodded. "Of course."

Michel looked relieved. "I'll send you two men to help. You can start in the morning. That means you'll have to wait to look for your man Hennighan, I know."

"I've been waiting eight months. We'll find him. Should I be worried about you, Michel? You have the look of a soldier about to go up over a ridge."

"Oh, don't worry about me. I'm going to talk to the politicians, that's all."

CHAPTER TWELVE

Michel sent two men to help Simeon with his sabotage operations. Jules and Fabrice Sabourin were brothers, eighteen and twenty years old, strong and smart. They wore their hair long like poets, under hats with short, round crowns and narrow brims. Neither of them was an Assassin. They worked for Michel. And they didn't ask questions when Simeon spread out the map and showed them where they would cut the telegraph lines.

They had no trouble crossing into the Rhine Province, part of the Kingdom of Prussia that bordered France. With dry weather and good roads, they'd made twelve cuts in four days. But Simeon felt slightly guilty about the fact that he always put Jules and Fabrice on the boring task of lookout while he climbed the poles and made the cuts himself. The young men were eager to try their hand at doing the real work.

So he let Jules go up. He immediately regretted it. It was easy to forget that most people, unlike Assassins, didn't train by climbing everything that could be climbed. Simeon lay on his stomach on the grass next to Fabrice and cringed as he watched Jules clinging to the pole, his feet scrambling for purchase.

He felt exposed here. The telegraph line ran along the railway, over to the left; to the right, the sun glinted off the Rhine River.

"He's going to make it to the top," Fabrice said, a clay pipe sticking out of his mouth as usual.

"Of course he is," Simeon agreed, though he didn't believe it. What would be best: to let Jules come down and ask for help, or take over now?

"You'd never know it, but he's afraid of heights."

"Now you tell me!"

"Don't worry. He's stubborn. Both of us are."

"You can call it stubbornness if you like, but I call it courage," Simeon replied sincerely. "You're both putting yourself at risk for the good of your country."

"For our own good as well," Fabrice said quietly. "Neither of us wants the emperor to declare war. Don't get me wrong. I'm happy to fight on my own terms, but it'll be on someone else's terms soon. Both Jules and I were called up in the Garde Mobile, and our fathers weren't rich enough to buy us out. At the time, we thought it didn't matter. They gave us fourteen days of training. We thought it was funny that we didn't even get guns or uniforms. I imagine they'll give us guns now."

Simeon had volunteered to be a soldier, and he'd spent years regretting that decision. The men who'd given him orders to kill and to die had been incompetent cowards. He'd decided that he'd only ever follow the dictates of his own conscience, and that conviction had driven him to seek the Brotherhood of Assassins.

He was searching for something comforting or inspiring to say when a shot came from nowhere. Jules slipped and was dangling from the line, one leg wrapped around the pole.

"Is he hurt?" Fabrice breathed.

Simeon was coiled, tense. "Get down, Jules! Get down now!"

Whether he couldn't hear him or was just ignoring the instruction, Jules scrambled up and got himself back in position, the massive shears in his right hand, ready to cut the cable.

Another shot.

Simeon leaped up, opened his pack, and pulled out a flashbang. It was designed by the Assassin Jean-Baptiste Barbeau, the best explosives man in Paris: a small tube with a pressure detonator filled with some mixture of magnesium powder. He ran toward the pole, and then lobbed the flashbang over to the left, past the telegraph line, hoping it would roll close enough to the railroad tracks to seem like an attempt at sabotage. Make Jules look like the diversion, instead of the other way around. At the least, he hoped it would startle the shooter enough to buy a few seconds.

The explosion was nearer than he intended, and whether or not it startled anyone else, it certainly startled Jules. He slipped again, and dangled from the shears, which were closed on the line. For a moment, he hung there, and then with an effort, he made the cut.

Simeon ran toward the crumpled figure on the ground.

"Good news," Jules croaked. "I landed on my arm, not my legs."

The arm was, indeed, dangling at a weird angle when Jules

got to his feet – but he did get to his feet. Simeon urged him on, and they ran back to the horse and cart concealed in a railway outbuilding. He got Jules and Fabrice in, leaped into the driver's seat, and the clever horse was moving before he even took the reins.

They were lucky this time, but Simeon was uneasy. The shots could have come from a guard who happened to see them – or they could have come from someone who had become aware of Simeon's activities. They could still be in danger.

It was a long night in their small hotel room in Metz. Simeon knew a doctor in the area, but it was nearly midnight when he showed up, and by then, Jules's face was white from pain. It only got whiter after the doctor splinted the arm, but soon he slept from the laudanum, and Simeon sat looking out the window, while Fabrice dozed.

The milky light of dawn was just creeping between the buildings when Fabrice woke and told Simeon he should get some sleep.

"I'm not tired."

"Nonsense. Besides, I'm already up. Going to the privy and when I get back – wait, what's this?"

Fabrice bent over and picked something up at the door to their room: a piece of paper, folded.

Simeon crossed the room before Fabrice turned it over, looking at the seal in red wax on the other side. A scythe and a flail, forming a cross. Circling it all, a Latin motto: TRITICA REGIT PALEAS.

"Some lookout I am," Simeon grumbled. "If you don't mind–"

Fabrice handed him the letter. "I'll run out and see if I can find whoever left it."

He was out the door, leaving Simeon holding the letter. He opened it gingerly, checking for powder. There was no date, no place, no greeting. Just a paragraph, written in English.

> *I have lost the taste for the primitive feud between our organizations, but I would appreciate it if you would stop destroying my property. If you have no respect for progress and science, if you truly want a world of darkness and chaos, know that I will not let that happen. This is a warning.*

He clutched it so hard that the paper crumpled in his hands.

Konstanze von Visler owned the telegraph lines he'd been cutting, and clearly she knew he was the one cutting them. What was her game? How had he been found out? Someone must have seen him doing the sabotage, or perhaps he'd been under watch for a while. He should have expected that.

Shouts outside: laughter, a distant song. Simeon went to the window, and Jules was up, raising himself in bed with his good arm.

Men walking – no, *marching* – down the street, with people cheering them on.

The door opened and Fabrice burst in. "They've declared war," he said, breathlessly. "The local members of the Garde Mobile are marching to the depot to report."

"Already?" Jules asked. "What good did it do, then? Yesterday? All our work?"

"We did what we could, and maybe it will slow things down,"

Simeon said. He wasn't sure he believed it. He'd been studying the maps of new telegraph lines and railroads that crisscrossed the German states, and it would take a lot more than three men working with a pair of shears to make a real difference. They should have started earlier. But war always seems like a distant threat, until a morning dawns with men in the street, holding rusty weapons.

Fabrice went to the bed and sat beside his brother. "You don't have to worry. You're injured. You're well out of it."

"But what about you?" Jules said. "And all the boys from our town? Will they say Dad's too old? Our cousins – they don't even know how to shoot a gun. They'll be called up."

"No, they won't," Fabrice said grimly. "We'll pull our teeth out. Can't recruit a soldier who can't bite the end off a musket cartridge. Don't worry. I'll keep them safe."

Simeon stuffed the letter from the countess into his pocket. "Nobody's going to be pulling out anyone's teeth. You won't ever be forced to kill, or to die, not if I have anything to say about it."

Chapter Thirteen

On a rainy afternoon in July, one cobalt blue umbrella stood out in a gray London street.

Pierrette's mood, though, was as low as the weather. Her morning had taken her by the new underground line out to Edgware Road to see a petty criminal named Tom Shallow. London was low on Templars these days, thanks to the efforts of the Frye twins, but most of the thugs who had worked for them were still in business. If the countess was in London, she might have used their services.

But Tom Shallow, like the rest of them, had nothing to tell her. She enjoyed putting a little fear into him, nonetheless. He was one of those bullies who set themselves up as saviors. He took people from the streets or workhouses, gave them a bed and a meal, and sent them out to thieve, dance or sing. Before long, he'd ask for more of their takings, extorting every penny with threats to send them back to the streets or to prison.

She had enjoyed bursting into his dingy office and holding a gun to his head.

Still, she had gotten nowhere in the search for the countess. She sighed, slowed down by a pair of women strolling in front of her.

Perhaps it was time to leave London entirely, strike out for somewhere else the countess might be. But where?

She tried to step to the left to go around the women. A man walked briskly up beside her, and she resigned herself to her fate. Wootton Street was busy today. Everyone was just trying to get home in the rain. Boring dark umbrellas everywhere.

Hunting the countess had kept her busy, so she hadn't spent as much time with her old circus friends in London as she might have liked. She sometimes visited with the Robinsons, and with Ariel Fine and Tillie Wallin, who were performing three nights a week at Astley's Amphitheatre – or Sanger's Amphitheatre, as it was now. They even called themselves the Aurora Troupe, although the other performers were not original members. It would have gladdened old Leo Wallin's heart to see the Aurora Troupe rise again.

Pierrette had seen the new troupe rehearse several times. A marvelous show, with three white horses, impeccably trained.

Tillie had been a little girl when her father had taken in Pierrette, and given her a home in the circus. Leo Wallin had trained his daughter to be a classical equestrienne, showing off the skills of the horse and emphasizing grace and precision.

But in recent years, Tillie had gone through a bad patch when she couldn't get work. She'd had a love affair, and a child. Pierrette had missed a lot, and she didn't like to pry, but she did want to help. Tillie was convinced that more daring tricks would bring the audiences in. And she seemed to be right. At Tillie's insistence, Pierrette had taught her a vault and toss she used to do years ago, in her knife-throwing days, and she'd even taught her an Assassin technique of landing from an impossibly high jump without getting hurt.

But when it came to actually sitting in the audience for two hours, it was hard to fit in the time. Pierrette always had an appointment with some unsavory character instead.

She turned into a side street, on her way to her lodging. The women in front of her seemed to be going in the same direction, and the man next to her matched his pace to her own. Now another man came up on her right, between Pierrette and the long rowhouse on that side of the street.

Footsteps behind her.

Pierrette realized she was surrounded. Her blue umbrella sailed in the middle of a small sea of gray ones. They were almost at the door of her own lodging, at the end of the rowhouse.

A gun at the hip of the man on the right.

Her silk umbrella collapsed, and she pushed the polished wooden handle to her right, knocking the gun out of the man's grip.

On the left, the steel point of the umbrella jabbed hard into an abdomen. She whirled, swinging the umbrella at the heads of the men behind her, one of whom she'd seen lurking outside Tom Shallow's door.

He'd sent them to intimidate her. Not to kill her, because she had a pretty good idea that he suspected she was an Assassin, and he seemed smart enough to know what attention killing an Assassin would bring. She was almost insulted. Intimidation was a waste of her time.

Following through on the swing, she landed a hard right

punch on the face of one of the women in front of her. The other woman, though, had time to land a punch of her own – with brass knuckles. Pierrette reeled as a cut opened on her brow.

Before she had a chance to think, she pushed the woman against the wall of the rowhouse, her umbrella in both hands held against the woman's neck, nearly choking her. The woman stared back fearlessly. Probably worth sending a recruiter to get her out of Edgware Road... she might be useful to the Assassins. But not today. Today Pierrette was not inclined to give her a chance.

"You tell Tom Shallow that his operations will close by tomorrow morning, or we'll close them for him," she growled. "And if you come after me again, it won't be my umbrella at your throat."

Pierrette let the umbrella drop, holding it in her right hand while grabbing the woman by the shoulder in her left. Two of the men were on the ground still, and one of them had a bloody head from where he'd landed on the cobbles. One was holding a wound in his side, which made Pierrette smile a little. She'd sharpened the point of her umbrella specially and wasn't sure she'd ever get a chance to use it.

She stared them down, as the standing ones pulled their comrades to their feet, and they all backed away.

Pierrette walked a few steps to the door of her lodging and saw the lace curtain in the front window twitch. Her landlady, Mrs Twill, let her in reluctantly. She was a middle-aged widow with a permanent worried expression, the sort of woman people tended to describe as "harmless". Given some of the other landlords and landladies in this city, Pierrette reckoned harmless was a compliment.

They stood in the hall and Pierrette shook the rain, and a little blood, off her umbrella.

Mrs Twill said, "I won't stand for any more bullets coming through the windows."

This little gang wasn't the first to try to scare Pierrette. There had indeed been a shot through the window, one night.

If the Templars were trying to kill her, she'd explained cheerfully to Evie, they'd be doing a much better job of the attempt. Besides, the countess had no reason to bother trying to kill her. If Pierrette was right, the countess already had the notebook, and she knew that Pierrette could tell her nothing useful about it. No, these were smaller and less competent bullies, just trying to stop her from asking questions that made them nervous.

Pierrette smiled at her landlady. "I paid for the plaster, didn't I?"

The long-suffering Mrs Twill pointed at the side table. "Two letters for you, in yesterday's evening post. I couldn't find you until now to tell you."

One letter was a long one from Safiya. The Templar cave had been a dilemma for the Cairo Assassins. What could they do but guard it? They could seal it, but the Templars were determined and resourceful enough to break concrete. They could blow up the damned place – and secretly, Pierrette would have liked to see it – but it would be a crime against ancient art. The Assassins were many things, but iconoclasts they were not.

Gamal's idea had been this: if they wanted to preserve the art, why not do what the British and French did, and loot it?

They even hired English antiquarians, who were thrilled to chisel out the paintings in vast panels and transport them to a warehouse they thought was owned by the British Museum. It was taking a long time to remove and transport everything, but the Templars had not managed to disrupt them. In the warehouse, the Assassins of Cairo kept the art, and the skeletons of the horses, under guard.

The second letter was from Tillie Wallin, inviting her to view a new trapeze act the following night, with a ticket enclosed. She was ready to show the tricks she had learned from Pierrette, and wanted her teacher and friend to be there.

The trapeze had become popular in London lately. The trick was this: Tillie stood on her hands, on the shoulders of another woman, who stood on the horse, traveling in a circle. A trapeze lowered from the rafters, and Tillie hooked it with her knees, rising to a dizzying height, swinging across the track to meet the horse and rider on the other side, grasping her colleague's hands and then vaulting herself to the ground using Pierrette's landing.

Pierrette looked at the ticket and smiled. It tugged at her heart, just a little, that her own circus days were over. Once, she had done the impossible too. But her version of impossible was a generation old. She was, mostly, content to sit in the stands and clap proudly. Tomorrow, she would do just that.

Tillie greeted her warmly backstage, kissing her cheek and then wiping off the makeup she'd left. "Oh dear, I'm sorry."

Pierrette laughed. "Trust me, this modern greasepaint is better than the stuff Mrs Robinson used to mix for us."

"Yes, well, when Harald gets into it, it's a real mess." Tillie scooped up her two year-old son and kissed him.

"This angel? I don't believe it." Pierrette smiled. The boy could indeed do a passable impression of a cherub with his wispy blond hair and big blue eyes, but he had a talent for getting himself into unlikely situations. He was fearless, climbing ladders and scaffolding and, once, nearly making it to the high-wire.

Tillie had named him Harald, but everyone else called him by his nickname: Spider.

Pierrette had a soft spot for him. Tillie had never said who his father was or why he was not involved in his son's life, and Pierrette didn't ask.

"That reminds me." Pierrette pulled a Fry's Chocolate Cream out of her bag. "Come on, Spider. Sit with me in the stands."

They waved to Ariel Fine, who was busy near the stage as the troupe's trainer, and took their seats.

It was a hot evening; the chocolate melted before Spider could get it from hand to face. She gave him something to wipe the worst of it off – one of her dwindling stock of unembroidered handkerchiefs. The show began with applause and three riders on white horses.

She could hardly hear Spider's words, partly because he still didn't speak clearly, partly because of the chocolate, and partly because of the music, which had risen to its frenetic jumble of honking trumpet and racing xylophone.

She leaned in close to him. "Say that again, please, Spider."

"I have a friend who is a leopard."

"Do you really? I might be a little afraid of him, if he were my friend."

"I'm not afraid. He's fast, like me."

"But you don't have teeth as sharp as he does."

Spider opened his jaws wide to show her an array of milk teeth. She shuddered with mock horror and looked out at the theater.

As always, Pierrette scanned the crowd for enemies, reading facial expressions and lumps in jacket pockets. She always looked closely at men wearing bowler hats, a fashion favored both by the men who had once tried to kidnap Ada Lovelace at a circus performance, and later by the Blighters, the street gang the Templars had used to keep their grip on London.

That grip had slackened, and she didn't fear the bullies left behind. All the same, she didn't want any thugs in the audience at her friends' performance. So she kept one eye on the crowd, always. From the beginning of the show to that final trapeze lift, as the music evened out to a rising duet in flute and violin.

That's why she missed the moment when Tillie fell.

It seemed impossibly fast. The first sound to break through the music and chatter was not Tillie's body landing on the sand, but the gasp of the crowd. Pierrette looked to the stage. Tillie was on the ground, twisted.

All at once, Tillie was again the little girl Pierrette had known. The girl who had once been so sick from fever, until a miracle happened, and she lived. The light in her father's eye who had picked up languages all over Europe. The girl Pierrette had taught, loved, and called friend. A girl raised by the circus, as Pierrette had been, and who inspired everyone else in the troupe. Not a girl anymore. A woman. An artist. A woman who always went to visit the Robinsons through each year of their advancing age. A mother to Spider.

Oh God, Spider.

The people sitting in front of Pierrette and Spider stood up to get a better look, which meant, luckily, that Spider couldn't see at all. Pierrette gathered him up and tucked his head into her shoulder while he squirmed and demanded to know what Mama was doing.

Pierrette carried him through the crowd and down the stairs, spotting a white-faced understudy standing at the side of the stage. The moment Spider was safely thrust into the understudy's arms with shouted instructions to get him backstage, Pierrette knelt on the ground, with Tillie.

Ariel was pushing people back; the theater's doctor knelt beside Tillie. But Pierrette could see from the doctor's face that it was too late.

Pierrette shouted in Ariel's ear. "What happened? Sabotage? Shall we lock the theater doors?"

"A simple accident," Ariel said, their voice strained. "I saw it. She made a mistake, put her hand wrong. I should never have made the call to go ahead. She said she was ready…"

CHAPTER FOURTEEN

The better-prepared of the troops that Simeon passed on his way back to Paris held maps of the German states, but they never got to use them. France declared war and was immediately invaded. The Prussian army was so fast, so well organized, that it seemed like magic. They were shooting while the French were still getting their boots on.

By September, they had the emperor's forces pinned at the Belgian border.

And Simeon had a visitor to his third-story rooms in Montmartre.

Monsieur Sabourin's skin hung loosely on his face, and there was a line of red below his eyes that reminded Simeon of Egyptian kohl. He said he had heard that the Englishman in Rue Simart had ways of keeping young men out of the fighting.

Those ways hardly required much effort, Simeon thought, given the tangle of contradictory orders and delays since the war began. In the first weeks of the war, it had almost been more difficult to find one's regiment than to avoid service. But now the bodies of the poorly armed men lay strewn over the broken and burned villages of northeastern France, torn apart by Prussian artillery. No one had ever seen anything like it. The Prussians had taken vast numbers prisoner, marched them east to places unknown. And from the ranks of the scattered French armies, came stories of hasty court-martials at which grumblers were summarily shot.

Simeon, who had survived a court-martial of his own, was determined not to let the Sabourin brothers be fed to the meat grinder. They bunked in his bedroom while he slept on the sofa in the sitting room.

So there was only a dozen feet between Monsieur Sabourin and the sons he was seeking, with Simeon in between.

Simeon had never been a comfortable liar. It was a skill every Assassin needed, but he went at it sideways, leaving parts of the truth in the shadows while he shone a light elsewhere. He was polite, welcoming, because why should he not be, if he had nothing to hide?

"I can't help you find your sons, sir."

The red-rimmed eyes looked right through him. "I believe you could, if you chose."

Simeon pulled out his pocket watch, and pitched his voice bored and casual, as if discussing some abstract principle, not the lives of two young men. "Why do you want them to fight?"

"France is suffering, Mr Price."

Simeon spoke too quickly, too honestly. "Perhaps if the emperor did not have so many troops in Algeria and Mexico, he would have some at home to defend his borders. Properly trained soldiers, instead of boys and old men."

"Bah, the emperor!" Monsieur Sabourin scoffed, taking

Simeon aback. "He's not long for this world. So sick, they say, that he chooses his battlefield positions based on whether they have a tree for him to lean against. Taking orders from his wife in Paris. I don't give a damn about the emperor."

Simeon didn't hide his surprise. "Then why, in God's name, do you want your sons to fight for him?"

"I didn't say I wanted them to fight for *him*. I want them to defend their homes. Prussian soldiers stroll through our towns, taking what they want, leaving us hungry or worse. I won't stand for it. I have an old rifle cleaned and ready. Why do my sons not stand with me?"

"I do not think your sons are cowards," Simeon said, his voice low, looking down at his hands.

Monsieur Sabourin swept his gaze over the room. What would Simeon do if this wheezing fifty year-old barged through the bedroom door and grabbed his sons by the collar? Would he hit the man, in front of his sons?

"Why are you here, anyway?" Monsieur Sabourin demanded. "You're an Englishman. You came to France for this? To separate young people from their families, take them to the city while their villages burn? What do you think will happen to Paris, if we can't stop the Prussians on the road?"

Simeon closed his eyes. This old man and his rusty rifle would not stop the best army in Europe, an army with railways that put its troops exactly where it needed them, an army that had made its own bridges and roads. Simeon couldn't stop the Prussian army. The only thing he could trust was his own heart and his own arm.

In that, he was no different from the man in front of him. And he also wanted to fight next to the Sabourin boys. He'd been teaching them some basic skills all Assassins learned – mainly to help keep them safe.

He had made them learn how to climb every train station in Paris – a phase he remembered from his own early days as an Assassin. Jules was always first to the top, and Fabrice was always gracious about it.

One day at the Gare du Nord, they had looked down through the rafters to see policemen arresting a blue-eyed urchin, no more than sixteen, who'd come in from Saint-Quentin without paying the fare. The Sabourin brothers had stood up to the police, called them bullies. It was no good. By the time Simeon offered to pay the boy's fare, the police were having none of it, and the three of them were lucky not to be carted off to jail themselves. No, the Sabourin brothers were not cowards. They only needed what so many young men needed: someone to keep them from utterly destroying themselves long enough for them to grow up into the men they could be.

He looked into Monsieur Sabourin's wet eyes and, at last, he lied to him. "Your sons are not here."

The door opened behind him.

Simeon stood and whirled around, and saw Jules, smiling slightly.

"You don't have to–" Simeon started.

Jules held up his hand. "We didn't want to fight on their terms. But we will take great joy in fighting on our own."

Fabrice elbowed his way past him. "You've trained us well, Simeon. It's time for us to go home. Father, is everyone well?"

Monsieur Sabourin stood, a little shakily from his age. "Your mother will be pleased to see you."

"Father, you should see how well Jules can shoot now. I saw

him hit a wine bottle sitting on a fence when I couldn't even read the label."

Two days later, Simeon sat in the driver's seat of a carriage on the Rue de Rivoli, in the shadow of the long galleries that connected the Louvre to the Tuileries Palace. The latter had PROPERTY OF THE PEOPLE written in chalk on its front steps, and a crowd firing guns into the air. Michel had anticipated trouble, so he'd told Simeon to go to a side door.

While Monsieur Sabourin had been collecting his sons, the French Empire had collapsed. When the news of the emperor's capture reached Paris, there were a few hours of strange nervous energy, as people walked out in the streets just to be out, seeing what was going on. People crowded around newspaper sellers and stopped each other in the street to ask what they had heard.

The empire fell, but Paris rose.

The Prussians would surely make peace now. Their enemy was not the people of France, but its deposed emperor. And if they didn't, well, let them come. Paris would resist them.

So many people climbed columns and pediments that day that one would have thought it was an entire city of Assassins. Everyone was singing. There would be a new republic, a republic of brotherhood.

Even Michel had looked hopeful. The Assassins had met, hastily, in their old rooms beneath the Gare de l'Est, because it was easy for everyone to get there.

"I think even the Templars have been taken by surprise by the French collapse," Michel began. "In trying to build one empire, they toppled another."

Sami Zidane, the youngest among them, cleared his throat. "But Michel, how long before we have a new Napoleon? Or a new king? Won't the empire just change hands?"

"That's why we must act quickly. The key thing will be getting good people into the leadership of a new republic. People who can make peace with Prussia, as a start." Michel scratched his chin. "Maybe this is a new beginning."

"Or maybe we will all soon be pledging allegiance to Kaiser Wilhelm," said Mary Fitzpatrick.

Simeon thought of the Sabourin brothers, of all the men and women ready to protect their families even when their government would not protect them – when there *was* no government to protect them. He thought of the scattered troops, the inadequate provisions, the regiments full of boys who had been farmers weeks ago. They stood now between the Prussians and Paris.

"We can't control what Kaiser Wilhelm does," Michel retorted, "but we can at least make sure that when he gets to Paris, he finds us strong and unified, and that he sees the wisdom of making peace."

And with that, the Assassins were given their assignments.

Simeon had been waiting an hour in the carriage. He'd tucked it into a small alley near one of the palace's side doors, and nobody seemed inclined to give him any trouble. Maybe he'd finally perfected the art of invisibility. Or maybe he'd reached the age at which he could glower powerfully enough to keep curiosity at bay.

The horse, though, was getting restless.

Finally, just as the sunlight was glancing off the windows of the palace, two veiled women came out of a door with a well-dressed man who helped them into the carriage, and told Simeon to go to an address in the Boulevard Haussmann. He chose the quietest streets, but he found them crowded, and didn't like the way people were peering into the carriage. So he made for the open space of the Place Vendôme. There was the statue of the first Napoleon, up on his column made from the melted cannons of his enemies. And there was someone celebrating the capture of his nephew: a figure clinging to the spirals on the side of the column.

As the carriage passed, the figure leaped down, and then up onto the carriage, right beside Simeon.

It was enough to startle him and the horse. He kept the carriage upright, barely, with his left hand, while he put his right hand to the person's throat. He could hear his passengers crying out. Damn it.

"I guess I can still surprise you too," said Pierrette, grinning. "Payback for Egypt."

Simeon's heart slowed enough for him to calm the horse and find a route that wasn't clogged with people. "Pierrette, how in God's name did you–"

"Michel told me your starting point and your likely destination. I calculated from there. You are predictable. Anne taught me about probability. But the bigger the group of people involved, the harder everything is to predict. For example, you and Michel think that if you get Empress Eugenie safely away, the killing won't start, and the revolution won't be a bloody one." She knocked on the carriage with a grin.

"You know who the passengers are, then."

"I know one. I assume the other is a lady's maid."

"Lady-in-waiting, actually."

Pierrette waved a dismissive hand. The carriage rounded a corner and Simeon caught a glimpse of the Opera House where he and Pierrette had saved the empress and her husband the first time, years ago.

"Third time pays for all," he muttered.

"What does that mean?"

Pierrette had spent as much time in England as he had, even though he was the one born and raised there. Sometimes he forgot that there were English things she might not know.

"It's just an expression. It means that sometimes it takes three tries to make sure something works."

"Well, I'm not sure I want it to work. This woman has been beating the drums of war, and we keep saving her life. We keep doing the same things over and over. We're always on the defensive. As long as we're fighting, they're winning."

"Why are you here, Pierrette?"

She said nothing for a moment, then: "Tillie is dead."

He felt her grief like a cold wind. Simeon had not known Tillie Wallin well, but he remembered his first meeting with her: a small blonde driving a circus carriage; and then later risking her life to help Pierrette. She was like a sister to Pierrette.

"How did it happen?"

"An accident. A dangerous trick. She fell." Pierrette brushed a hand across her face. "I should have helped her more or told her she wasn't ready."

"That's not your responsibility."

"No," Pierrette said bitterly. "I've been rather busy turning over every rock in London, for all the good it's done me. I know the countess has the notebook. I just know it. But I can't find any trace of her in London, so I've moved my search here."

Simeon brought the carriage to a halt at a tall house, hopped down, and rapped on the door. When a servant opened it, looking wary, Simeon gave the name he'd been told.

The woman shook her head. She didn't look as if opening the door was usually her job. "He's gone, sir."

"Gone?"

"Left Paris. With the others."

The others: wealthy people with connections to the emperor's regime. The servant peered behind him at the carriage, and Simeon thanked her and went to the carriage door, opened it.

The empress held out a gloved hand for him to take, to help her down, but he left it hanging in the air. "Madame, your friend has left Paris. Is there anywhere else we can go?"

A quavering voice came from behind the veil. "Left Paris?"

He didn't have time for this, and neither did she. The streets were full, and it wouldn't take long for someone to get curious about a carriage making social calls on this day of all days. He could feel Pierrette staring at him from the driver's seat. It seemed the passengers remained unaware of her presence.

The lady whispered to the empress, and the empress said, "All right. Let's go to my chamberlain's house."

"Not far from the Arc de Triomphe," the lady-in-waiting supplied. "The Avenue de Wagram."

Something told Simeon that the area around Arc de Triomphe was best avoided, so he went back to the smaller streets, but it was slow going.

Pierrette said nothing for a while, letting him steer the carriage through the crowds.

They were almost at their new destination when he said, reluctantly, "I had a letter from her."

"From *her*? From the countess? Good God, Simeon, why didn't you tell me? When? And what did she say?"

"She warned me to stop cutting her telegraph wires. Which was useless, I must say, as the war began that day and ended my sabotage campaign."

"What else did she say? Were there any clues about where she is now?"

Pierrette's voice was eager, almost desperate. He couldn't keep this information from her forever, but he regretted telling her. She was too focused on finding the countess and it was making her more reckless than usual. Even if she did have Ada's worm-eaten notebook, that was far from the biggest problem the Assassins faced. He had to wonder whether she only wanted revenge for the time the countess had held her hostage.

"That's everything," he told her firmly. "The whole letter. Just intimidation. Believe me, if there had been a postmark, I would have told you."

"And is there any news about Hennighan?"

"A dying Templar told me he was here, in Paris. Which is one reason I've stayed here so long. But I haven't found him. Michel says some Templars are leaving Paris. Not keen on popular uprisings, I suppose."

"Where will they go?"

"Some have country estates. A few went to Tours. Michel thinks they might be setting up a base of operations there."

They were in the Avenue de Wagram now, and the sun had sunk behind the buildings. Servants lit the lamps over the doors, but there was no light at the house of the empress's chamberlain. Simeon halted the horse a little before it, to keep his distance from a group of boys marching toward them, in uniforms that were too big for them, one banging a drum. They were waiting for the Prussians to come; they were going to show them what Parisians could do. They looked desperate, joyous. Paris might be free of its emperor, but these boys were ready to take orders from someone. Simeon could see a day, just over the horizon, when every person in Europe would be a soldier, and obedience to absolute masters the only virtue.

"Well," Pierrette said, "if you haven't managed to find Hennighan here in all these months, maybe I'll have better luck in Tours."

In all of this, what did it matter if the Templars had Ada's notebook? Simeon wondered. Her weapon, like half her ideas, had never been proven to work. It was all theory. What was happening on the streets of Paris today was real.

"You may have noticed there's a war happening around you," he said, regretting it almost instantly.

"I could say the same to you."

The chamberlain's house, at last. Annoyed and frustrated, Simeon was grateful for a chance to escape the conversation for a moment. Pierrette had always challenged him, but he'd lost patience with her grand gestures and heroic quests. Simeon hopped down to rap on the door, but no one answered it. Not even a servant this time.

An increasingly distraught empress told him to try the house of her dentist. When he climbed back up to the driver's seat, Pierrette was gone.

CHAPTER FIFTEEN

The dentist got the empress out of France, and there was no
bloody revolution; not yet. Instead, Simeon's nightmare of
a city of soldiers came to pass. Old women leaned on their
rifles as if they were walking sticks. Children ran in the streets
wearing military caps.

There was a new government in France, which called itself
the Government of National Defense. Some of its leaders were
in Paris, and some were in Tours, to make sure that this new
government could carry on if – when – the Prussians attacked
the capital. There was talk of moving the Tours delegation
to Bordeaux, just to put more distance between it and the
approaching Prussian army.

Despite the split between Paris and Tours, the new
government manufactured and distributed guns so quickly
that it made the old government's lumbering mobilization
efforts look even worse. Everything and everyone in Paris was
militarized. The Government of National Defense had sworn
to protect "religion, property and the family", but all were

in service to their power. Even the church bells were melted down to make weapons. The Prussians would not take the city without a fight.

The Assassins helped build fortifications and barricades. Simeon spent a few days helping to dig empty graves, so the city would be ready for a winter siege. Michel asked him to help keep the provisions flowing, while there were provisions to flow. That meant holding a judicious knife at the throat of any shopkeeper trying to gouge or ask for bribes. If the Prussians laid siege to the city, there would soon not be enough food. For everyone to live, that meant no one could have extra.

The Champ de Mars was full of men in motley uniforms, running drills. Most were Parisians who hadn't been called up before, but some were soldiers and Garde Mobile who made their way back to Paris. And some were people from the country who had picked up guns on their own and defended their homes.

It was there Simeon found Fabrice Sabourin, a bandage around his head, parading with a group of old and young. When the parade had petered out, Simeon called him over.

He could see from Fabrice's expression what the answer would be, but he had to ask, anyway. "Jules?"

Fabrice shook his head. "We were ambushed beside a church wall. My brother, my cousin and six other men died."

It was hell to think of Jules, his bright eyes, gone from the world. Simeon wondered what Monsieur Sabourin thought now, whether he could live with his regrets. Whether he would. He put his arm around Fabrice and pulled him close, tucked his bandaged head onto his shoulder, grateful for his own hood.

•••

When the Prussians came a few weeks later, the Government of National Defense did nothing. Michel said that the government did not trust the people of Paris, most of whom were not professional soldiers, to break the Prussian lines if they went out and fought on the field. Instead, the government was waiting for the Prussians to attack the city, where at least the fortifications would even the odds a bit.

But the Prussians did not attack. They encircled Paris, so completely that when runners were sent out, they either died or came back, exhausted, to report there was not even the slightest crack to slip through. There was no way out. The wealthy had left already; Paris was a city of workers, and the government was clearly nervous about it. It was also a city with more alcohol than food.

Simeon never considered leaving. He'd come to Paris to search for Hennighan and the Ankh, and the only evidence he'd found suggested Paris was still the right place to look. With all the disruption and panic, maybe Hennighan would at last slip up and give them some clue to his whereabouts.

Besides, it wasn't in Simeon's nature to walk away from a city that needed his help. The first lesson he had ever had in being an Assassin had come on a sinking ship, from Henri Escoffier, who helped the drowning when the men in uniforms would not. As far as Simeon was concerned, that was his personal creed, deeper even than the vows all Assassins made, and it meant that his place was always with the people whose leaders had abandoned them.

People kept waiting for news that the army was coming to help Paris, that the government would break the siege from without. Week after week, they waited. The telegraph lines were all cut. In the absence of newspapers from outside Paris, people hung on every rumor.

Then came the pigeons.

It was an innovation that Oscar Kane would have appreciated. Carrier pigeons were the only way Paris heard anything from the world outside, but there was only so much information a pigeon could carry. So the Tours government sent telegrams, letters, instructions, and whole pages of newspapers as microphotographs, rolled up inside the cartridges carried by these birds. In Paris, the government read everything by magic-lantern projection onto a wall.

As for how the pigeons got back out of Paris, well, that's what the balloons were for.

Three years before the siege, Paris had hosted a Great Exhibition, complete with a gas balloon tethered above the city. That balloon, and a few others belonging to scientists and hobbyists, were patched up with paste and paper, and filled with coal gas from the city supply, and to everyone's great surprise and relief – especially the first aeronauts who tested the idea – the Prussians could not shoot them down.

The Government of National Defense had also experimented with a heliograph: flashes of light, to send messages in Morse code. But they decided they couldn't trust government communications to it, because it might be seen by their enemies. Michel tried to convince them to keep using it, because after all, the messages were encoded, and there was no way for the Prussians to stop them from sending flashes of light, as all it required was a sun and a mirror. Pigeons, on the other hand, did not always make it back to the city. At one point, Simeon overheard Michel yell at an official: "At least a flash of light can't end up in a Prussian pie!" But it was no good; the government settled on pigeons.

Meanwhile, no food or medicine came into the city. There was no milk for the children; no meat for anyone. Simeon kept himself going with hard tack he'd made, just in case, when the emperor was captured; it reminded him uncomfortably of life on board ship, but it kept well and he had some salt pork that would stretch. The Assassins shared food among themselves and with the poor. People queued for hours for bread and counted themselves lucky if the flour didn't include plaster, or even ground up bones from the catacombs. Smallpox was spreading. The nights were getting colder, and the coal would run out. Before long, the city would devour itself, beginning with the zoo animals and ending with every stick of furniture.

What, people asked, was the point of all the guns, all the drilling? The people of Paris were ready to fight, but they would never get a chance. They would drop of hunger, and their bodies would freeze in the streets.

Michel convened a meeting in the Assassins' hideout beneath the Gare de l'Est. That long, open room with the tiled floor was where Simeon had met Michel, years ago, when he'd first arrived in Paris. There was still a map of Paris on one wall and a map of the world on the other. The room wasn't secret anymore; the Templars had found it a few years back, which was why Michel conducted business at the gasworks. But the train station was a convenient spot to meet with people who were organizing food, medicine and defense in the neighborhoods of Paris.

On the empty tracks above, dozens of people were sewing

and patching massive balloons. It was late October, and chilly, and Simeon was glad that there was still some coffee in the city, and that Michel had made some for their visitors: A dark-haired young doctor and writer named Georges Clemenceau, and a grim-faced, middle-aged bookbinder named Nathalie Lemel.

When everyone had their coffee, Michel smiled at the guests, and leaned against a marble table. He was wearing what Simeon thought of as his diplomat face.

"Thank you for coming, my friends. Tell me how things stand for you."

"We now have several restaurants where workers can buy food at cost," said Nathalie Lemel. "But this will mean nothing when we have nothing to sell. We need more supplies."

Michel nodded. "I've heard of a government storehouse on the Left Bank. Salt, sugar, flour, even bacon. I have two people ready to obtain and deliver it to your restaurant tomorrow, if you can tell us a time and place when we can do it secretly."

"And is there medicine in this storehouse?" Clemenceau asked. "All the stretchers are full at the Odéon Theatre. They can make bandages, but they need camphor, ipecac, laudanum. We need the government to listen to us and act, now, to break the siege. Or, failing that, we need a new government."

"We have a new government," Simeon said drily. "I see no reason to think that the next one would be any better."

Michel left the table he'd been leaning against and paced as if thinking. Simeon knew him well enough, though, to be certain that every word he said was planned. "I have been trying, and failing, to convince the Government of National Defense to attack the Prussians. Yesterday, as I was walking through Montmartre and I saw the women holding guns and the boys handing out food, I realized that the people are governing themselves. If the government will not lead the people, the people must lead the government."

"What does that mean?" Lemel asked abruptly.

Michel turned to her and held a fist high. "It means we break the siege. We shame the government. There's a village called Le Bourget, just outside the city. It's vulnerable to attack, and it will be even more so once my colleagues and I quietly remove a few sentries. There is a French division general willing to act without orders. Once he gains a foothold, the Government of National Defense will be out of excuses. The ring around Paris will be broken. But we must be ready to push through the gap. When the fighting starts, the government will need the people to rise and join the army."

His guests looked at each other. And Michel looked at Simeon. "Tell us the truth, Simeon. You used to be a soldier. Can we do it?"

Simeon scratched the back of his neck. Michel had put him on the spot, which was just as well, because Simeon was no actor. He thought about it, honestly. "The government says the common people are not disciplined enough. But I've seen what discipline does, and frankly, I would rather trust my life to a man with nothing to lose and no rich man to obey."

Michel gave him a grateful glance before turning back to his guests, who looked uncertain.

Before they could answer, Mary Fitzpatrick strode across the room, and whispered in Michel's ear. She stood just a little too close; Simeon had long suspected there was something between Mary and Michel, but whatever it was, it was their business.

A shadow passed over Michel's face, but he said, quietly, "Send her in."

Two minutes later, Victoire L'Estocq walked into the room.

Simeon tensed, on alert. Michel was not showing much outward concern about this surprise incursion from a Templar, but an enemy among them meant violence could be necessary at any moment.

The most powerful, best-connected Templars in Paris were a married couple, Robert and Victoire L'Estocq, who had somehow made both the Bonapartists and the Orleanists believe they were on their side. When Michel learned that Robert L'Estocq was among the Templars who had fled to Tours a few days before, he had made a snide comment that Templars always protected themselves in the end. "They know what happens to rats during a siege."

But Victoire L'Estocq had not gone with her husband to Tours. Like the government itself, the couple was split, so that Victoire could keep the ear of the leaders in Paris. Michel thought she had kept some lackeys with her, as a Templar was nothing without people to order around, but he didn't know who they were.

The highest-ranking Templar remaining in Paris was tall, with gray curls beneath a sloped hat heavy with feathers, and an expression that was one-third curiosity and two-thirds arrogance.

"It has been a long time since I was here last," she said. "And that time it was not by invitation."

She didn't offer her hand, and Michel did not reach for it.

"I'm sorry to say that I'm unaware of any invitation sent to you today, Madame L'Estocq. I assure you I would have prepared something more than coffee."

"Coffee will be fine, thank you. I assume that if I discover that a meeting is happening, that must mean you want me at that meeting. You are not clumsy enough to let word of your plans spread unwittingly."

Michel's jaw creaked. "It is a busy and difficult time. I have other things on my mind than what you know and what you don't."

L'Estocq touched the lace at her throat, her fingers brushing a golden brooch: a heavy gold bar with a large round bead of black jet in the middle, and two smaller beads on either side of it, and a thin line engraved horizontally along the middle of the bar. It reminded Simeon of a pillory.

She was nervous, Simeon realized suddenly: a lone Templar in the Assassins' den. Mary lurked a few paces behind L'Estocq. That made three Assassins to one Templar, and Mary had surely disarmed her at the door. The two non-Assassins in the room looked like they could handle themselves in a fight.

"I am here to ask for patience." L'Estocq's gaze took in Clemenceau and Lemel. "We are at one of those rare moments in history when the interests of our two orders are aligned."

Simeon shivered. It was cold in the station.

Michel's lip curled. "Pray, tell me how our interests could possibly be aligned."

L'Estocq strolled past them, ran her fingers over the map of Paris painted on the wall. It was out of date; when it was painted, the city had not yet absorbed some of the areas around it. "Michel, you and I have known each other for a long time.

I have come to you because I know you are a man of reason, a man who never severs a connection that might be useful, a man who tracks gossip the way shopkeepers track debts. You and I both know that this so-called government here in Paris cannot wipe its own arse."

It was jarring to hear this from a woman who looked like she ought to be pruning roses with silver shears, but no one in the room betrayed any surprise. She wanted them jarred.

Michel did not match her use of his first name. "What do you propose, Madame L'Estocq?"

She turned and smiled. "We are preparing to put a better government in place. I am here today because my message is not only for the Assassins but for all friends of the people. We are on your side. Once our preparations are in place, with your co-operation, I will leave the city and set our plan in motion."

"Leave the city!" Michel's surprise turned into a genuine chuckle, just quiet enough to be genteel. "Oh, now I see. How slow I am. You're trapped."

"I beg your pardon–"

"You may beg for more than that before the end." Michel's tone was as light as if they were discussing the weather. "The Templars may control the railway companies and the telegraph companies, but not the places where people actually work. We hold the rail stations, and the gasworks, which means we control the balloons. So if Paris burns, you burn with it. Yes, I do see your dilemma. How unfortunate."

She flushed. "If you think I have any intention of leaving Paris, you are a fool. I came here to say that the Order of Templars stands ready to serve the welfare of the people, as it always has. But yes, it would be useful in that work for me to have my own balloons. We both have things to offer. Do you want food, money, medicine? Newspapers from abroad? I can get you those things. We are all on the same side here. We all want order and peace. I know that you have worked to prevent bloodshed, Michel. I know that your lackey drove the empress to safety."

Her glance flickered over Simeon, who stopped himself from reaching for his knife. The two guests in the room exchanged glances at the mention of the empress, but Michel refused to be baited. "You left liberty off the list of things we supposedly all want, I notice, along with justice and compassion. Yes, we Assassins want to avoid pointless bloodshed, but pointless is the operative word, isn't it?" He shook his head, still smiling. "You have come to me because you want an escape hatch when things get worse. Well, you can't have it. The only thing I can't understand is why you want to prop up this government that is, as you so said, incompetent."

"I can." Simeon cleared his throat. He had learned a lot from Kane about the Templars, and Kane had taught him things he hadn't intended about people who tried to manipulate history. "They haven't been able to steer this government, so they want it to collapse. They're doing exactly what they did during the Terror, trying to ensure that the next government is under their control. They need Paris to suffer, to acquiesce, so that the city will accept whatever tyrant they choose to put on the throne. If I had to guess, I'd say they want another emperor. More power for them to wield that way."

L'Estocq turned to him with a face that now had no curiosity in it. She said coldly, "You are a fool, Simeon Price. An empire does not require an emperor. It does not even require that the windows and statues of Paris remain unbroken. There is nothing you can do to us here. We are not afraid of a mob of scrawny drunks with rusty guns."

"Whatever fate awaits the windows and statues of Paris, you will share it," Michel said. "And the only reason you will live that long is that you left your guns and knives at the door and came here to parley, and I am old-fashioned about that sort of thing. Next time you Templars orchestrate a war, perhaps you'll think ahead and plan your own escape. A fleet of submarines to take you out via the Seine, perhaps. You do like your toys."

L'Estocq gave him a defiant smile. "Michel Moulin, I look forward to the look on your smug face the day you realize that we Templars with our toys, as you put it, have a kind of power that humanity used to ascribe to gods. And my curiosity about just what your face will look like on that day is the only reason *you* will live that long."

Her exit was somewhat marred by the long walk, nearly the length of the train station above. At Michel's gesture, Mary stepped out of her way to let her go.

Then Michel turned to the two Parisians who had just witnessed this extraordinary conversation. His diplomacy fell away like a cloak falling off his shoulders, his expression fierce. "My friends, you see what they intend? They want to make themselves gods. They believe others are only fit to be their servants. In Paris we will have no gods. We will have no masters."

"We scrawny drunks stand ready," said Lemel, drily.

Clemenceau cleared his throat. "How will we share information when the fighting starts?"

Michel smiled and looked at Simeon. They'd anticipated this question.

Simeon said, "We'll use the heliograph – it's faster than pigeons, and we can teach everyone a simple code."

They spent the next hour with an up-to-date map of Paris, working out the plan. When Clemenceau and Lemel left, Michel sank into a chair with a cigarette, and Simeon poured them each a brandy. He tapped his glass and studied Michel.

"Have I got something on my face?" Michel asked.

"I'm just thinking that L'Estocq was right about one thing. You are much too careful to let news of a meeting with our allies reach the Templars by accident."

Michel shrugged and stubbed out his cigarette. "Everyone makes mistakes."

CHAPTER SIXTEEN

There was no moon on the night of October 27. It was the matter of moments for a half-dozen Assassins to slip their blades into twice as many Prussian sentries.

Simeon cleaned his knife and watched as a few hundred of the men and women of Paris walked silently down the dark road between the French and Prussian lines. They flowed into the narrow streets of the village. By morning, it was in French hands.

Fabrice Sabourin was among them, and to Simeon's great relief, he survived the attack, grim-faced with his long hair matted with someone else's blood.

At dawn, Simeon stood with his back to a stone wall, knowing that farther up the hill behind him was the Prussian artillery. The French could not hold Le Bourget for long, if they stopped there. They had taken the village because it was easy to take, out in the open surrounded by hills. But it would be just as easy for the Prussians to take it back. They had to press onward, quickly.

When the sun was high enough over the rooftops to strike the mirror on the tripod in front of him, Simeon took a piece of paper out of his pocket and read the encrypted message he'd written:

Village taken. Send reinforcements.

His Morse code was slightly rusty; he had to pause and think between words, carefully counting the seconds between flashes as he hit the mirror.

He sent it three times, trying to block out the noise of the victorious soldiers behind him, who seemed untroubled by their lack of sleep. At last, the message came back.

Received.

They're not coming.

Three days they'd held the village, and some reinforcements had arrived. On the second day, they'd even fended off a Prussian counterattack while the division general was inside Paris pleading with the government to send him troops. They'd held their position, the point of the spear, waiting for the government to see reason and press the advantage.

Three days of standing watch, in houses recently deserted by French families. Fabrice and Simeon played cards in a child's bedroom; there was a doll on the shelf.

On the third morning, the guns began. By the time the message came in – *They're not coming. Retreat* – Simeon could not respond, diving for cover at the base of the stone wall. Across the road, shells turned roofs and walls into powder. The noise was terrible, and in what might have been his final moments, Simeon thought of his old friend Sawyer Halford. Last he'd heard, Halford was living happily in some hamlet in

Essex with a wife and two children, deaf as a post from his years in the army. The noise. Simeon would do almost anything to stop that noise.

Then it stopped, and he was still alive. But a new sound began: the sound of many footsteps, all marching in time, approaching from all directions.

"Where I went wrong was believing the men who run this city were capable of feeling shame," Michel ranted a few days later, as they walked briskly down a street in Le Marais. "But the government has miscalculated too. The people will not sit quietly, not after this. We broke the siege, and the government squandered it. Squandered those lives."

It was cold, and Simeon was glad when they reached their destination: the home of a pigeon keeper. Michel wanted to know whether the balloon carrying the pigeon had landed safely.

Up three flights of stairs to the attic where Madame Charpentier was at the window, an open cage in one hand, cooing at her recently arrived bird.

The bare attic bore little resemblance to the laboratory in Vienna where Simeon's onetime teacher had kept his pigeons, but the smell brought it all back. His ears still rang from the guns at Le Bourget. Blood on a church floor. An overturned pulpit. Houses in ruins that had been standing that morning, men taken house by house, their gurgling cries. The dead, the wounded, the captured.

Fabrice Sabourin was among the missing.

Simeon tried not to show his impatience as Madame Charpentier gave Michel a lecture about the terrible cold, the hunters, the Prussians with their guns, and all the other horrors her bird had braved for this.

"Then let it not be in vain," Michel said, his diplomat face doing its utmost. "You're sure this is the bird that went with the last balloon? The pilots should have included a message in the canister if they are safe themselves. If you don't mind…?"

Madame Charpentier untied the canister from the pigeon and handed it to Michel, who pulled three sheets of photographic paper out and handed them to Simeon. The dispatches for the Paris branch of the government, from Tours. The government was supposed to have a man here ready to receive the pigeons, but this wasn't the first time the Assassins had got there first.

There was one more scrap of paper in the canister, and Michel said, "Thank God, they're both safe, but they landed near Lausanne. Well, we… Simeon, what is it?"

Simeon stared at the roll of photographic paper in his hands, at the tiny smudge on it that looked familiar. Just a bar with three dots inside it. The shape reminded him of a pillory.

"Michel, do you have your magnifying glass?"

Simeon could barely hold it steady. There was no doubt: the symbol was the same as the one on Victoire L'Estocq's brooch.

Beneath it was a letter in code, and at the bottom, a blurry cross.

"The Templars," Simeon said, pointing. "Don't they have their own bloody pigeons?"

"Not that they can get out by balloon," Michel said, his face waxen with fury. "Or perhaps they're out of the ones they had."

He pushed the roll of paper into a pocket.

All that talk about being on the same side, about peace and order and the welfare of the people. The Templars were using the city's one precious means of receiving word from outside, for their own ends. And where were they when the people were fighting for their lives?

Madame Charpentier protested, "But what shall I tell the government man when he comes?"

"Tell them the pigeon is in a Prussian pie," Michel said, and they left.

Mary Fitzpatrick was the best code breaker among the Paris Assassins, and she had a lot to work with, as Michel had been intercepting Templar communications for years. It took her an hour to decode the message, sitting at the desk in the gasworks, while Michel paced. Michel never smoked in that hideout, and that made him irritable.

"You can wait outside," Mary said mildly at one point.

Michel went and stood by Simeon against the wall.

Fifteen minutes later, Mary beckoned them over to read it.

I am disappointed that you have not yet got the artifact to safety, and I wish you had taken my advice to send it out of Paris with the others before the siege began. Time is running short, which I would think would be very evident to you.

The talks here in Brussels have gone as we hoped. We have a government ready for France, one that we can control, and one that will not stand in the way of a strong German Empire. All nations' interests are the same. Europe will rise out of the fire of this war strong and united, now that time and distance are not the enemies they once were.

We rely on you now to send us word when the people are ready to accept peace. Our people with the Tours government stand ready to assist you and they can get your messages to me any time. I urge you to find methods of communication that you can control.

In friendship.

"This is why they didn't want to use a heliograph," Michel said. "The government in Tours is passing messages directly between the Templars. Someone didn't want us to see what they were sending. That symbol at the top means Victoire L'Estocq. It's part of her family crest, I think. Good eye, Simeon."

"What about this cross at the bottom?" Mary asked. "It's not the usual Templar cross. It looks like…"

"A scythe and flail," Simeon said hoarsely. "From the crest of Konstanze von Visler. Now we know she's in Brussels."

Was she still in contact with Hennighan, who had once been her right-hand man? She was clearly keeping a close eye on Paris. Maybe Pierrette had always been right to focus on her. Pierrette's quest had been motivated by revenge, but that didn't make it wrong.

"It seems she is orchestrating a French capitulation. Damn." Michel banged his fist on the table. "No wonder the government here is doing nothing about the siege. They have their orders, it seems. If we're going affect what happens in Paris, we need to get word to the Brotherhood to send someone to Brussels."

He could get word to Pierrette. She would be in Brussels, a knife in her hand, before she rested. She was desperate to find that notebook, repair her mistake and fulfill her old promise to Ada Lovelace. If she confirmed her theory that the countess had it, she might have an excuse to get revenge on the countess for holding her captive. Simeon had failed to prevent that when he was her teacher. It was as much his task as hers. Besides, Konstanze had written to him before the war; maybe that was something he could use. He had no idea how to get a message to Pierrette, wherever she was.

"I'll go, if you can spare me," Simeon said. "I will take care of Konstanze von Visler."

CHAPTER SEVENTEEN

"You won't be the first Assassin to see Paris from the basket of a balloon," said Michel, hanging a scarf around Simeon's neck. "I suspect theirs was prettier, though."

The Émilie *du Châtelet* may not have been pretty, but it was certainly striking. The balloon had been stitched in the Gare du Nord out of emerald silk that had been sitting in a warehouse for twenty years. Old-fashioned green dyes had been unsellable since a case of arsenic poisoning in the 1860s. Simeon had once had to dissuade Pierrette, who loved to dress like a tropical bird, from buying a green cape she saw in a shop window. The seamstresses who made the balloon had worn masks and gloves; nothing could go to waste in a city under siege.

It was, at least, strangely suitable for an Assassin. Simeon wasn't sure how the balloon's other occupant felt about it, because the pilot, Monsieur Lebrun, was a taciturn railway engineer with a large black beard, who stood in the basket with his arms crossed.

The basket felt smaller than he expected, the wicker walls barely reaching his waist. On the outside of the basket, sandbags held ballast to help them rise, and a spiked iron anchor was tied up with the furled drag rope, for when they wanted to land. Inside, on the floor of the basket, was a box of letters. A cage of pigeons hung from the hoop above, between the basket and the balloon. The pigeons made a dreadful racket, but they had to get out of Paris somehow so they could return with messages.

The balloon was leaving from the La Villette gasworks, and it smelled even worse inside the balloon, since they'd filled the thing with coal gas that morning. Michel handed him a satchel and gave him the last few instructions. It was impossible to know where the balloon would end up, but the winds that morning gave them a good chance of traveling southwest. Simeon's task was to see what he could find out in Tours and set up a heliograph there for the Assassins to communicate with Paris, and then make his way to Brussels.

They cut the ropes and rose swiftly, silently. Paris soon became a map of itself, and beyond Simeon could see the broken bridges, the empty streets in no-man's-land. Before long, he saw the canals and palace of Versailles. Where Amira had taken him when he was inducted into the Brotherhood, for his dive of faith. It seemed a million years ago.

Now, he had another task to perform for the Paris Assassins. Michel's first instruction for his balloon journey: what he called diplomacy of the people. Simeon opened the satchel and pulled out a square of paper, with a few sentences on it in German: "We have done away with emperors and kings. If you do the same, we can stop killing each other."

He looked at Lebrun, who stared at him from the opposite side of the basket. Simeon kept his body only half-turned as he looked out; he didn't turn his back on strangers, out of long habit. He hardly ever even turned his back on friends.

"Does your satchel have pamphlets too?" Simeon asked.

Lebrun adjusted the strap of the bag he carried, and said, simply, "No."

Simeon shrugged and grabbed a handful of pamphlets. Below, he could see Prussian soldiers, tiny figures. The pamphlets left his hand and drifted over the sky like petals and he thought of Amira's newspaper. Cairo didn't seem so far, from up here. A fair wind and he could be sitting with Amira, asking her advice. And she, no doubt, would ask him about Pierrette.

Three loud bangs tore through the sky, and it took him a moment to realize what was happening.

"They're shooting at us," said Lebrun, surprised into saying four whole words.

"Come on," Simeon said. "We must get higher. Out of range."

He pulled his knife and slashed open one sandbag tied to the side of the basket, releasing a sparkling cloud into the sunshine. He could hear Lebrun on the far side, doing the same. Simeon stepped toward another sandbag when his peripheral vision registered Lebrun advancing across the basket, toward him.

With a knife in his hand.

Simeon's elbow flew back and cracked him square in the forehead. Lebrun staggered back to the far side as though the basket were a boxing ring. Simeon followed, put a knife to his throat. The basket only came up to Lebrun's waist, so Simeon bent him backward, leaning him out into nothingness. Another bang echoed. So far, the Prussians had not been able to shoot down any balloons, but it would only take one lucky shot to turn the Émilie *du Châtelet* into a fireball.

The balloon rose slowly, away from Versailles. In between shots, the world was totally silent, except for their panting breath. Lebrun held desperately on to the rim of the basket.

"Tell me your real name and your mission," Simeon growled, his knife pressing into Lebrun's Adam's apple.

The man spit in his face.

Simeon swore and debated letting his knife follow through. But most Templars would talk eventually, especially if they believed they were about to die. They were always so proud of themselves. Believed themselves martyrs, every time. And if Lebrun talked, Simeon might learn something about the siege, about the Ankh, about the countess.

So he settled for disarming him, running his right hand through pockets while his left kept the knife in place. The folding knife Lebrun had used on the sandbag Simeon tossed to the floor. An Adams revolver.

That left the bag over Lebrun's shoulder. Simeon grabbed the strap to pull it high enough to open, and was surprised by the bag's weight, as if there was a stone in it.

As if there was a stone in it.

The countess's letter to L'Estocq had urged her to get an artifact out of Paris.

Lebrun had the Ankh.

The Templar still hung onto the rim of the basket, his hands on the outside. His eyes widened and he breathed hard. Simeon was tempted to cut his throat now, and finally have the Ankh in his hands, but he resisted the impulse. The information Lebrun might give him was just as valuable. The man couldn't get away, after all.

"I've been searching for this damn thing for months."

Simeon patted the sandbag, his lips curling into a smile. "How good of you to bring it to me."

"You fool," Lebrun spat at him. "You don't know anything about it."

Sometimes, pretending to know information could get more out of a stubborn subject, and Lebrun struck him as stubborn.

"I know exactly what your friends were doing in Egypt," he said, deliberately calmly. "I was there."

Lebrun shifted, leaning backward and to the right slightly. Before Simeon could react, the drag rope from the outside of the basket was in Lebrun's hands, the spiked iron anchor flying through the air, connecting with the side of Simeon's head, a spike scraping the back of his neck. If he hadn't dodged the full force of the blow, he would have been dead. As it was, he staggered sideways, all the air whooshing out of him, and the basket seeming to reel and spin around him. On his hands and knees at the bottom of the basket, retching. Blood dripping from his neck.

He drew a breath.

The weight of Lebrun on top of him knocked him prone to the basket floor. Simeon wheezed. The man pulled off Simeon's cap, grabbed a handful of his hair and yanked his head up so that his chin cleared the ground. The wound on his neck screamed. His head rang – the artillery – the blood rushing in his ears – the water – he was going to drown.

Black water all around him. The screams of horses. The prayers of men. The shipwreck.

No, not that water. He could call up other water in his mind. The canals of Versailles. Amira in the boat above, telling him to reach out, to touch the bottom.

Lebrun was so heavy. Simeon pushed one elbow in and down, to get traction, but a rope was around his neck now. The drag rope, with the bloodied anchor resting now beyond reach near the edge of the basket. He tried to keep his eyes open, despite the sweat and blood. Tried to think.

The rope got tighter. He couldn't breathe and he wanted more than anything to get his hands to his throat, to pull even half an inch, even a second's worth of life. But his life depended on his knee, now. Think of his knee. Move his knee beneath him. Shift his weight – was the basket rocking? Onto the other elbow, and both knees under him as he pushed up with his hips – but Lebrun pressed him back down and his world was going black. He couldn't move without taking a breath. His body was going slack.

And then, just for a moment, the bloodied rope slackened too. Lebrun swore and adjusted his hands.

"You will die without understanding," Lebrun panted. "That is the choice you made."

Simeon put the last dregs of his will into one more push upward. A sharp jab, a grunt of pain. He could hardly believe it when he found himself kneeling with the bloody rope falling away from him. He tried to get air through his throat. He had broken Lebrun's hold.

Meanwhile, he had his back to his enemy.

Simeon lurched to standing and turned to see that Lebrun had grabbed onto the ring above them, and that he was swinging through the air, his feet aimed squarely at Simeon's chest.

The pigeons in their cage cooed all at once.

Simeon ignored the instinct to dodge Lebrun and instead, he grabbed the Templar's legs, wrapped his arms around his knees and pulled. Lebrun half-fell into his arms and then they were wrestling on their feet, fingers grasping for anything soft. Simeon's knife was gone, knocked out of his hand when the anchor had smacked into him. The folding knife and gun he'd taken off Lebrun were somewhere on the floor of the basket. Not that it mattered; Simeon couldn't get a hand free for long enough to reach for a weapon, and Lebrun was expertly keeping the Hidden Blade out of range. Somehow, he had to get the bag off Lebrun's back and claim the Ankh. He couldn't wrench it off Lebrun… he'd need to cut it free.

The man's big hand jammed into Simeon's throat now, and this time, the blood didn't slow him down at all. Coughs and gasps tried to escape Simeon and choked him instead. He couldn't keep this up much longer. He pushed forward, like swimming downwards. Everything was dark. He pushed forward until they hit the edge, and with every bit of strength he had, he pushed the man over.

He saw the dark figure of Lebrun falling as though it was an image in a daguerreotype, with blackness at the edges. And then, feeling that he was dangerously close to toppling over the edge himself, he stepped backward, and sat in the middle of the basket, wet with sweat and blood and making some sort of hideous noise that might have been a gasp or a sob.

The pigeons kept up with him, cooing with alarm.

As the world set itself back in order, the realization sunk in that the Ankh had just fallen out of his grasp, somewhere between Paris and… somewhere.

He stared down at the floor, trying to memorize the shape of the skinny river, the patchwork of forests and farmland, so that he could tell the Brotherhood where to look. Damn Lebrun!

His only consolation was that it might take the Templars time to find it. After all, their only witness to its location was lying dead beside it. Maybe they would never find it. Maybe the damn thing would break.

The pattern on the basket floor shifted, his view growing wider and wider. The balloon, suddenly freed from a two-hundred-pound piece of ballast, was rising quickly.

He lurched to the side of the basket, pulled out his compass, and tried to get his bearings. The balloon was traveling southwest; that was good. He could see a gray patch amid the green below, but from this height, it could have been Chartres, Orléans, Le Mans or Tours. At least he couldn't see the ocean yet; that was something.

The air fogged, and he could see nothing, and his cheeks were damp with something other than blood. A cloud. He was inside a cloud. It seemed impossible, as if he'd knocked on the door of the realm of the gods. His laughter seemed to echo, and he was suddenly cold despite his wool coat. He sank back down onto the floor of the balloon and picked up his wool cap, but it was half soaked with his own blood.

Simeon put his hand to his cheek, his forehead, the back of his neck. He didn't think his wounds were still bleeding, but he felt sick. And the balloon was still rising.

Simeon caught a brief glimpse of the sun warming a landscape on the wrong side of the clouds before he yanked on the valve rope and let a bit of the gas escape. He was back in the clouds; he'd descended, or maybe a rise in the white landscape had met him where he was. *Was* he descending? He had nothing to measure against; the first balloons to leave Paris had carried several navigation instruments, but there seemed little point in wasting them on an escape mission for two men who were not scientists.

After what seemed a long time, he pulled again on the rope, and again. The clouds dissipated, and the world below rose to meet him. Rising too quickly, he thought. He grabbed the folding knife Lebrun had tried to kill him with, and he sliced open another ballast bag. He was running out of time. Below him, a patchwork quilt of fields stretched out, but ahead of him was a forest. He did not relish running into a tree, or getting tangled in one.

But if he let out more gas and tried to bring the balloon down quickly before they reached the forest, it would slam into the ground.

He had just enough time to open the cage and free the pigeons. No time for a message or to feed the birds beforehand, but they'd find food in the fields below.

"Farewell, my friends," he said, lifting the birds one by one into the air. "Paris, I think you'll find, is that way."

The ground was close enough now that he could see the chimneys of houses.

The difference between a leap, and a leap of faith, was that there was always a good chance death was waiting at the bottom of the second kind. This was especially true when the Assassin doing the leaping was trying to land in a millpond from a moving balloon. As he stood on the edge of the basket, holding the rigging with both hands, he wondered if he would ever again feel the moment of weightless peace that came as he spread his arms and stepped out into the sky.

Chapter Eighteen

Pierrette sat on a rooftop in Tours and stared at the café window opposite. It took her a few minutes to convince herself it was Simeon behind the thick glass. A slightly distorted view of the man she'd known for sixteen years. On the table was a high glass vessel with taps on either side: ice water to be poured over sugar, into glasses of absinthe. Pierrette was sure it was him. That mark on his temple might be a fresh wound, and he pulled idly at his collar.

How had he got out of Paris? There was only one way out, as far as she knew: the balloons.

She didn't recognize the man sitting across the table. Perhaps a functionary in the faltering Government of National Defense. There were no Assassins in Tours, other than her.

It had taken her nearly two months to find Hennighan here. She'd taken a room and started asking questions. A newspaper boy in the old town said he had sold a paper to a man with a scar on his cheek, so she had taken to watching the corner where the boy worked. It was not comfortable, sitting on this sloping roof, wedged between a chimney stack and a gable, but it was decently concealed from the street. Templars were trained to always look up.

So were Assassins. She thought Simeon would look up and see her – and she would wave, or do a backflip down to the balcony below to make him laugh. When her instincts proved wrong, and he didn't turn after all, she found herself oddly relieved. The fact was, she wasn't sure what to say to him, for the first time. There had been no letters between them during the siege, with communication so difficult and precious. He might not even realize she was still in Tours. Perhaps he planned to look for her, once he'd concluded whatever this business was.

It started to rain.

She pulled herself up to a crouch, suppressing a groan at her stiff back and shoulders. Sitting for a long time on a chilly afternoon seemed to resurrect every bruise and sprain from her circus days, and every punch a Templar had landed on her since. Her body held its grudges. The rain was hardly more than a mist, but it was enough to chill her.

She was nearly standing, one hand on a chimney stack, when she saw the sniper.

He lay on the roof of the neighboring building, a man in dark clothing, blending into the blue-slate roof. He was staring across the street, at the café. His rifle was pointed at Simeon.

It would be a matter of twenty seconds to run from her roof to his, take him unaware, give him no chance to escape or shoot at her. But he could kill Simeon in less time.

"Hey!" she screamed, drawing her revolver as she leaped

over the small space between the two buildings, from her roof to his.

The sniper readjusted to his knees and aimed a handgun at her, his rifle still resting on the rooftop. How had she missed him up here? She'd come so close to witnessing Simeon's death. Her mouth tasted like metal, and her shoes slipped on the wet slate as she recognized the sniper's face.

It was Hennighan, smirking at her.

Startled, she slipped further, fell flat and slid down the roof on the far side of the building, out of sight of the café. She dropped to her fingertips and glanced down long enough to see her gun fall to the pavement below. Her feet found a windowsill. The window was open, and a woman stared up at her, a hairbrush in her hand.

"Bit damp out here," Pierrette said breathlessly to the astonished woman. "Mind if I come in?"

The woman stepped out of the way just in time to avoid Pierrette's heeled boots, and the rest of Pierrette followed. She ran through a messy bedroom, through a sitting room in which two children played. Damn it. She'd best keep the fight as far from here as she could.

What had possessed Simeon to sit in a café in full view of the street? The old man was losing his edge.

At least she'd managed to distract Hennighan and get him to chase after her.

Back out through the front window. Hennighan would have run to the roof edge by now, would have had time to ask himself whether Pierrette had dropped to the ground, climbed around to the side of the building, or gone through a window. If he guessed wrong, she would have a second or two to catch him by surprise. It would be slow going for him, walking on that steep, wet roof.

She climbed up, putting the chimney stack he'd been using for cover between them. The Templar, still looking for her, stood with his back to her a few feet up the roof, looking down into the space between the buildings. As he turned toward her, she picked up his now-abandoned rifle by the barrel, climbed toward him and swung the rifle butt at his head.

He would have stumbled backward on level ground, but as it was, his head went back and his feet went down. She was on him then, sitting on his chest with her knees on his arms, and it didn't matter that he was twice her size, because she had a knife to his throat. The roof worked to her advantage, every time he tried to get purchase to push her off, he failed.

"It won't do you any good," she said, breathlessly.

He growled, "I told her we should have killed you."

"You were right. All of that for a notebook. And now she has it again. Doesn't she?"

He snorted. There was a fresh cut on his temple, where the rifle butt had made contact.

She had wanted to find him, but not like this. Torture, she knew, was basically useless as a means of getting information. She had planned to follow Hennighan, to search his things. To find out where the Ankh was, and what the Templars were doing with it. To find out why they'd gone to such horrible lengths to get Ada's notebook, after all these years. To find out where the countess was, and what her plans were.

And *then* to kill him.

He'd robbed her of that, and he even robbed her of the choice of what to do with his final moments. The toe of her boot slipped briefly on the slate, and she came unbalanced for a moment. He used that moment to push her off and to the side, trying to roll on top of her.

Her Hidden Blade was in his ribs before he got the chance. His eyes went wide as he realized he was dying, and a soft gurgle came from his mouth. Pierrette wiped her eyes, wet from fury, frustration, exhaustion. Or maybe the rain. Her eyes stung and her throat hurt. She remembered a cold room in Mayfair, she remembered the chains, she remembered his fists. How Hennighan had done everything the countess asked.

"Where is she?" she shouted. "Where is the countess?"

She leaned forward to hear Hennighan croak two words: "Ask *him*."

His body went slack, his eyes staring at something no one in this world could see.

Suddenly aware of another presence, she turned and saw Simeon, standing higher up the slope of the roof, looking down at her.

The rain subsided and the gas lamps were lit as Pierrette and Simeon walked quickly out of the old town and through the gates of the botanical gardens. Open land, with no rooftops or dark alleys, where they could talk. She tucked a rain-soaked, bloody handkerchief into her pocket; it bore the initials A.H. She'd embroidered it years ago, and she'd been carrying it ever since. Simeon watched her with some concern, so she made her voice light.

"What in God's name were you doing sitting in an open window in a narrow street?"

"My companion insisted," he said drily. "A low-level official with the government of Tours. He said it was for his own safety, to make sure we were in public view. Tried to make it appear that he just had a low opinion of Assassins. But it seems he was in league with the Templars."

"So a low opinion of Assassins indeed. A terrible risk, Simeon."

"One I thought worth taking. The Templars are manipulating the French government, this so-called Government of National Defense. They want the Parisian half to prove itself incompetent, so the starving people will welcome a terrible armistice and whatever government they get."

"That doesn't sound like something the people of Paris would do."

"Indeed. There was an uprising in Paris right after I left; the news just came. The Government of National Defense used the army to put it down, but it won't be the last. Still, I had to make some connection with the government here. There are no Assassins currently in Tours, from what I can tell. Present company excepted. I didn't think you'd still be here."

"Yes, it took me a long time to find Hennighan."

"Well, I'm glad you're here, and not only because you saved my life. Made it worth coming to this place. I don't think there's any headway to be made with the Government of National Defense. There are two Assassins in Le Mans at the moment, and I happened to land near there last week, so I helped them set up a heliograph line to Paris from there."

"Landed," she said, delighted. "So you did leave by balloon!"

"No other way out." He sounded amused.

"Tell me everything. What does the world look like from the air?"

"Like maps."

"But then what does the sky look like? Is it blue when you're in it? Did you see clouds from close up?"

He smiled at her. "I saw them from the top. You'll never believe. They're purple on that side."

"Purple? Really? Is it an effect of the sun, or–"

"Not only that, but there are entire cities. Towers. They look like spun sugar. And little people in flying–"

She smacked his arm. Despite their brush with death – or maybe because of it – it felt like the old days between them. It was a relief to close the door on that terrible room in Egypt, and all their frustrations with each other since.

But Simeon looked pained.

"Are you hurt? That wound, on your head."

"It was a hard landing, and a hard fight inside the balloon. A Templar tried to kill me. Hennighan was the second in a week. I suppose once I left Paris, I was fair game, and they aren't fond of me for the sabotage I did before the war." He paused. "Pierrette, before I left Paris, we intercepted a message. It seemed to be from Konstanze von Visler, and it said she was in Brussels. So that's where I'm going next, now that it's clear there's nothing I can do here to influence the Government of National Defense to try to break the siege."

"Brussels! Finally! We've got her. All right, we leave tonight."

He hesitated. "I don't think it will be easy to find her or kill her. She wrote that warning to me. If she knew where to find me in that hotel in Metz, she could have sent me something deadlier than a letter. I don't know why, but she tried to connect with me. Said something about being tired of the feud. Maybe we can use that. If I go alone, maybe I can flush her out, take her off guard."

Pierrette bit back her first response, and her second. When they were old and gray and comparing sore knees – if they lived that long – he would still treat her like his student. But she didn't say that, because it had been a bad year for both of them, and she wanted to hold on to the feeling of being friends again.

Instead, she said, "I have been searching for her all this time."

"I promise you, I want her dead as much as you do. She kidnapped and tortured you. She is puppeteering the lives of Parisians. That's why Michel gave me the assignment. I must play it the way that makes sense to me. You killed Hennighan. Let me kill her. Listen. I promise I will burn Ada's notebook and send you a page from it as a Christmas present. And I promise I will stain a card with the countess's blood. If I fail, you can come and do what you like."

She turned away, frustrated, and looked at the shadows between the trees. "All right. I'll go to Le Mans and see to this heliograph line of yours. I'll keep in touch with Michel as best I can that way. You'll keep him informed, won't you? If a week goes by without a telegram, or if you need help…"

"I know. You'll show up and jump into my carriage, or fight a sniper across from my café, or ride a horse onto a rooftop, or spell my name in letters of fire. I look forward to it."

CHAPTER NINETEEN

It was a long journey from Tours to Brussels, with the rail lines cut, avoiding Paris. Simeon took three stagecoach trips, giving a false name to Prussian soldiers at crossroads. He kept his cap low over his brow and said nothing to anyone.

He found Belgium in much the same mood. It was neutral, but it lay between two empires at war. He could feel the anxiety in the way people stared at each other in the street, and then looked away.

Simeon was exhausted by the time he arrived, and knew he wasn't up to a fight. He took a room near the cathedral at the heart of the city: a simple, clean room, with a bed, a wash table and a chamber pot. Everything a man needed. He even had a book to read; the last stagecoach had kept a basket of them for travelers to leave and take, and Simeon had helped himself to a battered copy of Hugo's *Notre-Dame de Paris*.

Perhaps that's why the cathedral of Saint Michael and Saint Gudula reminded him of Notre Dame, with its two towers. It stood in a wide square high above everything, a vast stone staircase leading to it. The best way to get to know a city was to climb its highest buildings, or so he'd been taught. It was cold like the day he'd climbed his first cathedral, in Vienna.

Simeon walked around the cathedral, looking for the best place to climb it and be hidden from public view. He paused to gaze at a giant window made of brilliant stained glass, showing a scene of people gathered around a table.

"That's new," someone said, and he turned to see an old man in a battered hat, holding a basket full of maps. "Put in just this year for the celebrations."

"Celebrations?" Simeon asked.

The old man cocked his head, no doubt catching the English accent in Simeon's French. "Ah, a visitor, are you, sir? You'd be interested in a map."

Simeon stepped forward politely and took a cheap folded map out of the basket, and handed him a coin. "What celebrations did you mean, sir?"

"Five hundred years since the miracle of the sacrament. Some Jews stole some consecrated host, and when they stabbed it, blood came out."

"Why on earth would they do such a thing?"

He shrugged. "Who can say? They were burned at the stake for it, the story goes."

Of course they were. An excuse to murder Jews five hundred years ago, celebrated with beautiful light and color today. Somehow, despite all the work of good people, history and the future felt like a circular trap. Simeon felt ill. He put the old man's map in his pocket and left without another word and found a spot where the architecture would screen him as he climbed.

It felt good to get his hands on the cold stone, to make his acquaintance with a building he'd never climbed before. From the roof, he looked out over the city and wondered where his enemy was, and whether she was still in Brussels at all.

Back to the room he'd rented, climbing up the uneven staircase with the musty carpet. Someone called his name – the false one he'd given. He turned to see the landlady, an exhausted and thin woman, holding out a small card.

"You had a visitor," she said.

He frowned, his heart racing suddenly, and took the card from her.

I shall expect you at the Château Aarden, to the south of the city, after five o'clock.

The card was plain, the ink black. On the other side was the countess's seal, in red ink this time. He held the edges with the finger and thumb of both hands and stared at it as though it might tell him more.

"My cousin has a cab, sir," suggested the landlady.

But Simeon didn't want to wait here until late afternoon and then get into a cab where the driver might be anyone. The city's new horse tram ran southwards. He pulled out his watch. Two o'clock. Plenty of daylight.

A trap is not a trap when you know you're walking into it, he reasoned. All the same, he stopped at the telegraph office – the one Michel had told him to use, which was dingy and out of the way and didn't even have a sign on the door – and sent a message to Pierrette and one to Michel, letting them know that he'd found her, that he was going after her, that if they didn't hear from him tomorrow, to send someone else.

Simeon was one of four passengers in the little wagon, all of them glad to be out of the chill. The horse pulled them at a lugubrious pace down the track, with the first pinprick snow of the year nearly invisible except where it fell on the black horse's broad back.

The wagon took Simeon to a large park. He walked until he noticed spaces between the houses, then long stretches of no houses at all. He followed a narrowing road until he found himself deep in the forest, like a child in a fairy tale. He rounded a corner and there it was: a small lake, and on the island in the middle, a castle barely big enough for the name. More a tower, really. Nearly a perfect square of stone, with a single turret capped in black.

He walked around one side of the lake, keeping inside the wooded area. The chateau seemed deserted, though there must be guards. What was her game? She had someone watching the cathedral, it seemed. Perhaps the old man with the maps. She could have tried to kill him there, or had someone follow him to his rooms. But she wanted him here.

Whatever her motives, he would not walk in the front door. He checked his watch: half past four. No need to wait to be polite.

He considered his options. The narrow causeway that connected to the castle was, no doubt, watched closely. But it was a damned cold day to be swimming, and if it came down to it, he'd rather not be firing a wet revolver from a wet hand. There was no guardhouse, at least. He decided to risk it, and ran across the causeway, his hood up and his cloak flying behind him.

A dark wooden porch opened out from the front door, but Simeon darted around to the side. He assumed he'd been seen, but as Amira used to say, if you couldn't stay out of sight, you could always *get* out of sight. Keeping low, he walked around the base of the tower, so close to the walls, he didn't think he'd be seen from any window.

It was a strain to reach for the cracks in the massive stone blocks as he climbed. By the time he reached the top, he was exhausted. He pulled himself through the opening in a crenellation, glanced around for danger, and then collapsed to catch his breath. The tower rising in one corner had a small, medieval-looking door opening onto the roof, and a row of chapel windows near the top. That tower was the obvious place for a sniper; there were even loopholes in the stone, halfway up. Damn it. He'd been lucky so far, but…

One of the narrow, leaded-glass windows at the top of the tower swung open.

He drew his gun, pointed it at the window. He couldn't see anyone but heard her voice.

"You can shoot if you like, but this glass is older than sin and I'd really rather you didn't. Besides, you'll want to hear what I have to say. I can serve you better alive than dead."

He hesitated, playing for time. "Say it, then."

"This is a terrible way to have a conversation, Simeon. I don't intend to let down my hair, so perhaps you'd do me the courtesy of coming up the stairs? You'll find that small door unlocked. If I wanted to kill you, I could have by now. I wanted to get you somewhere where I could show my willingness not to shoot at you, and I needed you not to be shooting at me for long enough to make that demonstration. A puzzle! I'm rarely trying to work out how *not* to kill people. But I do like novelty. Are you coming in?"

He kept his gun in one hand and pushed open the little door. The tower was bigger than it looked inside. There was a staircase, and each floor had a room opening off it. The level with the windows was three up. He dashed up and pushed the door open.

It had been eight years since he last saw Countess Konstanze von Visler. She was just as striking as she'd been years ago in Vienna, and even more imposing. She had a single streak of gray in her brown hair, now, done up with a tortoiseshell comb on one side. She stood at the window but turned toward the door. A fire roared at one end of the room, alongside three settees and two chairs, in different colors of upholstery, and a thin red and gold carpet on the floor. Over the fireplace were two crossed sabers.

The countess did not move. "You'll notice a small table there, just beside the door. You can help yourself to the whisky, and pour me a glass, if you like, so you'll see it's not poisoned. And you can also take that odious book. Are you wearing gloves? It's been fumigated, but even so, I hate to touch it."

Simeon stepped sideways, keeping his eye on her. There was a half-full decanter on the table, with two glasses. And a notebook. He recognized it with a sudden surge of grief. It had been Ada's, then was torn apart by Pierrette, then rebound by the countess. It was misshapen now, as though it had been soaked, and the long edge looked like it had been chewed.

"What's the game?"

"No game. I am tired of games." She walked toward him, her brown silk dress swishing. "I want to tell you that we were wrong. Oh, not morally – don't misunderstand me. We hoped it contained information that would be of use to us, and once again, we were disappointed."

He opened the cover, gingerly, and saw Ada's familiar handwriting. He choked back his sorrow. Ada had been a dear friend.

"Information that would be of use to you," he said. "Are you building something? A weapon?"

"Of a sort. It was an idea. A project."

Simeon, going on a hunch and a scrap of memory from Virgile Donat's last words in his glass factory yard, asked, "Was it the Engine of History?"

She seemed genuinely startled. "Where did you hear about that?"

He said nothing. Donat had been on the edge of death, and sometimes people in that moment spoke as if in a dream. His only answer to Simeon's questions about the Ankh was to utter the words "the Engine of History", whatever that was. A metaphor, or an actual machine? It implied that Hennighan had been working for Konstanze after all, in Egypt, or at least with her knowledge.

After it became clear Simeon would not answer her question, Konstanze sighed, and said, "I suppose it doesn't matter now. Yes. I found correspondence that shed light on the contents of Ada's notebook, which I had foolishly let get away from me. I assumed you and your acrobat protégée had destroyed it. Imagine how my hopes soared when I learned from John Elliotson that there was a second, secret book in the coffin of that poor woman. Very grisly. So, I did what I felt I must. But it was all for nothing. Much like the terrible weapon that your friend Oscar Kane tried to build, the Engine of History is a phantasm. The trouble with Ada Lovelace is that she was *nearly* a genius. She could be very convincing. I'm sure she convinced herself."

He ran his finger over the cover. It was, nonetheless, Ada's. The product of her remarkable brain. The only thing he had that was hers. "And you're giving it to me? You've made a copy, haven't you?"

"I'm telling you, it's worthless. My colleagues tried to tell me that my pet project was a waste of time, and now I see they were right. Burn it if you like. Or leave it on the table. It makes no difference to me. It is only there to show you I mean to make this visit worth your while. I have things to offer."

He ignored that, for the moment, but he holstered his revolver and picked up the book. He'd promised Pierrette he would burn it. Remembering his promise to send her a page, he opened the book at random and tore one out and stuffed it into an inner pocket of his cloak.

All those years, trying to protect this book and keep it out of dangerous hands. His own hands shook slightly as he walked to the fireplace and placed it on top.

It took a while to catch. Finally, he saw it framed in orange, like the impossible dream of a medieval illuminator, and then it was as black and dense as any log.

He could smell nothing but the burning book. His eyes stung. At last, the book and its mysteries were gone forever, safe from Templar machinations. And a part of his old friend Ada was gone too.

"What do you want from me?" he asked hoarsely.

"For the book? Nothing. It, like me not killing you, is a gesture. I want to win your confidence for the real negotiation."

"Start negotiating, then."

"You don't want whisky first? I might have something."

"This is not a social call."

"Oh, but it is! I left you a card, and you came to my house. I would have had the valet take your coat at the door if you'd been so conventional. Now we do what men do: we drink whisky, and we can smoke cigars, if you like. And we will make some political arrangements."

"The only political arrangement I want is for you to stop manipulating the government of France."

"You have it."

He wasn't sure he'd heard her right. "You're wasting my time."

"I'm quite serious. I will withdraw all my pieces on the chessboard when it comes to the Government of National Defense and whatever follows it. If your friends in Montmartre want to replace the government with a mob, so be it. I can't promise it will work out well, but I can promise that once I give the word, no Templar will do a damned thing about French politics."

He shook his head in disbelief. "For how long?"

"For as long as our arrangement holds."

"And what is my side of this arrangement?"

She said nothing for a moment, then turned and closed the window. Simeon felt trapped, for the first time, despite the gun at his hip. He felt trapped by bad options and regrets, by all the ghosts who would not rest. Two murderers in a room, and both of them thought they were right. An ordinary person might make no distinction between them.

Except, of course, that he was filthy, dressed in a cloak in the colors of the butt-end of November, and she had pearls around her neck.

He was tired of this. He walked to her and grabbed the pearls with callused hands. "Tell me what you want from me."

She didn't move, didn't flinch or squirm. "I want you to tell me all about your Brotherhood."

A smile broke on his face. So it was very simple after all. "You've chosen the wrong man if you want a spy."

She swallowed. "I don't mean like that. Teach me what you believe, and why you believe it. Teach me the history of your order. I want to understand why you cut the telegraph and rail lines that are building the modern world. Why you destroy everything good. Why you hate progress. I have learned everything my Order can teach me about the Assassins, but I still don't understand. I believe the Templars will be stronger if we understand our enemies. That's all."

He let go of the pearls. "I'll give you one lesson for free. Your first and last. I will never compromise the Brotherhood. A strength for the Templars is a weakness for the Assassins."

"What a simplistic way of looking at things you have, Simeon."

It was exhausting, these fishhook barbs, back and forth. It reminded him of the drawing rooms he had glimpsed as a child in Ada's home, when her mother had tried to improve him. The army had seemed simpler, if not nobler. He'd rather fight openly.

Wearily, he asked, "Why me, then? There are other Assassins who might be more to your taste."

"Yes, but you're the only Assassin I've ever danced with."

"And then you had someone try to kill me. Two someones, in fact. I assume both Lebrun and Hennighan were acting on your orders."

"If they had succeeded, it would have shown I was wrong about you. Instead, you showed me that Lebrun and

Hennighan were weak. Vulnerabilities. I never hold a grudge when someone kills a comrade in a fair fight."

"Don't you have any human feelings at all?"

She looked out the window, while he looked at her. They were an arm's length apart. Killing distance.

"I decided long ago that I would put the universal above the particular. I reserve my affection for humanity as a whole; individuals can only get in the way of that. Ties lead to corruption and compromise. The only thing that matters is building a better future. But then we come to the paradox."

"More than one, I should say."

She looked back at him with glittering eyes. "The goal of the Templar Order, and my own singular goal, is to bring order to the world. Order is light, safety, harmony, progress. Like an engine cleaned and oiled, all its parts working perfectly together. We build walls around our cities to keep the wolves out. I am trying to keep the wolves out, Simeon."

"And I'm a wolf, I suppose."

"The Brotherhood of Assassins spreads chaos. You seek the darkness."

"Lesson number two. We work in the darkness to serve the light."

"An easy bromide," she snapped. "Try stepping into the light sometime and seeing the world for how it really is."

"Then what is the paradox you meant?"

She rubbed her temple. "We are order; you are chaos. But war is also chaos, isn't it? Anything can happen in war. I admit we were surprised by the way the French Empire crumbled this summer. War can cleanse, like fire, when it's controlled. But unending war between the Assassins and Templars does not serve the cause of progress. As long as we are fighting, chaos wins. As long as we are fighting, therefore, *you* win. Order demands peace. Now, there are two ways wars can end. The annihilation of one side would do nicely. But we can never eradicate you because you are an idea. We need to channel that idea instead, make it serve us. So, we come to the other way to make peace. Negotiation. Compromise. There. There's your paradox. To serve my singular goal, I must compromise after all."

He was astonished. He wanted to laugh and he wondered what Pierrette would say. The truth was that she wouldn't have let the conversation get this far.

"You're wondering what your acrobat friend would say," the countess said.

Simeon looked at her sharply.

She waved a hand. "I'm not a mind reader. Of course, you would find it difficult to talk about peace with me, of all people. Let me show you something." She pulled the brown hair at her temple back. "Can you see it?"

He leaned closer and saw a small patch of red on her skin, a finger's breadth from the end of her perfect eyebrow.

"The scar I bear from the day your friend blew fire in my face. Peace is always made by people who have hurt each other. That's the whole idea."

Simeon shook his head. "I can't speak for the Brotherhood."

She put up her hands, placating. "Of course not. We are not yet at the peace talks. We are at the beginning, when each of us tries to open up the possibility of peace within our own orders. All I ask is for a truce between you and me. I ensure no further Templar action in Paris. All you have to do is satisfy my curiosity, and whenever I ask a question you think would compromise your Brotherhood, don't answer it. Do you want peace, Simeon?"

Did he? Pierrette wanted victory. Simeon focused on doing what was right, protecting the innocent and standing with his friends. But what the countess offered could help the innocent of Paris, and his friends there too. And he might learn something that would help Pierrette get that victory, although she might not see it the same way.

He said, "I promise I won't kill you... today."

She laughed. "That's a start."

My dear friend,

Thank you for your letter of 16 November, and for sharing your concerns and progress with me. You asked for my thoughts.

I gave you a target given what we knew at the time, but no command in our Brotherhood is absolute or unchanging. The purpose of an assassination is not vengeance or blood lust. The purpose of an assassination is to eliminate a threat to humanity. It seems there may be a way to remove the threat of Konstanze von Visler, at least for a time, without eliminating the countess herself – and there could be benefits to us, as you may be able to learn about her methods, contacts, and plans.

The wisdom at the heart of the Brotherhood has never been ours to hoard or keep secret. I know you will take care not to compromise your brothers in the field, and I see no reason why we should not teach a Templar about our beliefs. There have been Templars, in the past, who converted to our cause. I know that may be a faint hope in this case, but faint hopes have always been our stock in trade.

You're right that Pierrette may see this differently. Give her time to make peace with the idea. None of us knows for sure which course of action is best; that's one thing we mean when we say we work in the darkness. Death is not the only thing that happens in darkness; diplomacy often happens there too, as I know very well myself.

Be careful but trust your judgment. I do.

In brotherhood,

Michel Moulin

Simeon,

I knew I should have been the one to go to Brussels.

For the sake of our friendship, I'll give you what you ask for: time and patience and trust. And for the sake of our friendship, I'll be there with my blade sharp the moment all three run out.

Thank you, at least, for burning the book.

Pierrette

Chapter Twenty

The countess was true to her word. The French state barreled down the tracks she had laid down, straight into a fiery wreck, with no interference from her.

Simeon read newspaper reports and Michel's dispatches with increasing guilt and alarm, as 1870 turned to 1871. The people were starving, cold and sick. In January, the Prussians surrounded the city with artillery and bombarded it. When the people rose up to demand a change of government and civil control of the army, the government used that army – the parts it still controlled – to clear the demonstrators with violence.

The Government of National Defense signed an armistice, promising to pay a shocking amount of money for the privilege of not starving to death.

By then, there were no Templars left in Paris. Victoire L'Estocq had left to meet her husband at her country estate, a fact the countess had relayed to prove to Simeon that there would be no more Templar manipulation in Paris. She had given him an account of the movements of all the Templars within a hundred miles of the capital, in fact, including the man who had found the body of Lebrun.

This conversation occurred in a sleigh, while Konstanze held the reins, and the runners whooshed over the snow. There was so much empty forest around the chateau, and the countess said it was the best place to talk.

"So if you have the body of Lebrun, you have the Ankh," Simeon said.

"Alas, no sign of it. My people have combed the area. The one bright spot is that we have found no pieces of it, which suggests it is lost, not damaged. Lebrun was found on the bank of a river, which makes the search for the Ankh difficult."

"So I suppose you can't resurrect whoever you were going to resurrect."

She looked sharply at him. She did that a lot. "What do you mean?"

"Once you completed the test on the horse. The next step would have been – who? A Templar from the past? Is that what it means, the Engine of History?"

Konstanze didn't answer, suddenly occupied with steering the horse through a copse of oak trees. "You're so clever, Simeon. Sometimes I forget how clever you are."

"Then you won't tell me."

"I've clearly told you too much already. You're supposed to be the one telling *me* things, remember? If our arrangement stops being valuable, I might as well send my colleagues back to Paris. In the state it's in, the city would be ours to do as we like with."

Simeon hid his frustration, like the ember in a cold fire.

"Tell me about the paradoxes again," Konstanze

demanded. "Tell me how you have any order and discipline in an organization devoted to holding opposite beliefs simultaneously."

He told her what he could, echoing the things his teacher had told him. When they got back to the chateau, the butler, Lambert, was waiting for them. He took their snowy coats, put a silver service with hot chocolate on a side table, and built up the fire. Then he left them alone. Lambert was one of the chateau's half dozen staff and the only one Simeon ever saw up close. He was the perfect butler, an almost invisible presence, who always anticipated what the countess wanted next.

In addition to the hot chocolate, he'd laid out a copy of the *Journal de Bruxelles*.

"Tell me the news." Konstanze warmed her hands by the fire.

Simeon read, and then he told her bitterly that one part of her plan had come to pass. Kaiser Wilhelm had gone to Versailles and declared the beginning of a vast and powerful new German Empire.

"So half of Europe is united," the countess declared, taking the paper from Simeon and holding her gold-rimmed reading glasses up. "No more squabbling. Peace, prosperity, and progress. I look forward to my next coffee with King Leopold. He'll be so pleased that Belgium won't be caught in the middle anymore."

Simeon did not point out that this empire was to include some of the territory that had once belonged to France.

France, in turn, declared its Third Republic – though the majority in the new parliament were staunch monarchists, and the only issue to be decided was what man to put on the throne. In the meantime, the government tried to take away the cannons that the people of Paris had paid for by public subscription.

And this time, the people of Paris would not be put in their place.

As winter turned to spring, Simeon read with astonished delight about the departure of the regular army and all government departments from Paris. Even better, Fabrice Sabourin had been found on a stretcher at the makeshift hospital, and when he recovered from his injuries, he joined in the defense of a free and independent Paris.

He read with cautious acceptance about the Central Committee of the National Guard declaring Clemenceau and the other mayors invalid, and holding a quick election to choose the men who would sit as the council for the new Commune. This council seemed all to the good, though. It abolished the death penalty, child labor and conscription. It passed laws to ease the debts and burdens of working people. The council even established programs to give children clothing and free education.

It was, all things considered, a good start. But a messy one. As the weeks passed, the letters from Michel were delayed and increasingly terse. The Paris Commune, knowing an attack was coming from the French army that surrounded the city, had banned pro-regime newspapers. They held executions, suspicious of dissent. Freedom, yes, but let us win first.

It was when they decided to create a Committee of Public Safety, like the one that oversaw the Terror, that Konstanze laughed as she was reading the *Times* of London. She liked to read the newspapers from several countries.

"You have to admit it's funny," she said. "We Templars were

the ones behind that original Commune, in the 1790s, you know. Now your friends and allies emulate it, right down to the name. How long until *this* Committee of Public Safety starts cutting off heads? What will the Paris Assassins do now, I wonder? Whose side are they on?"

That was in her morning room, soon after he'd arrived for their twice-weekly meeting. She had offered, more than once, that he could stay in a guest room at the chateau, but he insisted on staying in the city. A détente was one thing; a friendship was another. Plus, it was difficult to see the value in teaching a Templar about Assassin philosophy when his colleagues were fighting for their lives.

In May, the army entered Paris. Pierrette had moved into the city after the Prussian siege ended, and she wrote to say she'd defended a barricade with thirty other women, with rifles. She must have thought of her parents, who had died doing the same.

At least Simeon could be of some use, collecting information about the countess. There were limits, though. She had proposed what she called a "gentlemen's agreement" not to use their arrangement to spy on each other's order. Simeon had responded that neither of them was a gentleman, but that he agreed anyway. He kept his word. It amused her to think of him as fatally moral, so he did nothing to disabuse her of that. He picked no locks and listened at no doors.

He did buy himself a camera apparatus and taught himself to use it and kept it in his room so he could send photographs of her letters and telegrams, even of her calling card, to Michel and Pierrette. He kept lists of the visitors who came to the chateau, and how long they stayed. The countess did not invite him to the chateau while Templars stayed there, which was a secret relief to him; it suggested that her motivations were personal, and maybe even genuine, and that she wasn't showing him off: her Assassin on a leash.

The information he shared might not have been secret, but it was useful. Michel said that understanding her patterns in writing letters helped Mary break codes. Even Pierrette grudgingly wrote that the whole business might be of some value after all, when he told her he had seen her workshop.

Her letter continued:

> I have to admit that the heliographs you set up last year have also been helpful, not for communication with Le Mans or Tours, but from neighborhood to neighborhood. There are so many rumors flying as the regime tries to turn us against each other. Every day, there is someone yelling that an attack is imminent, or we have been betrayed. But we can tell each other the truth in a flash of light, faster than telegraphs even. We use a favorite phrase of Michel's to keep up morale, sending it out at the end of all our communications: 'no gods, no masters'. I have faith in the strength of the people, but it is being sorely tested. We need time to build this Commune, and time is what we don't have.
>
> I don't suppose you could convince the monster you have befriended to tell the regime to back off? You should have asked for more than non-interference. Might be time to kill her. Just a thought!
>
> Write soon,
> Pierrette

By the time the letter came from Michel Moulin telling him about the fall of the Commune, he'd already read about it in the newspapers. Michel was able to add only the terrible news that Sami Zidane, one of the youngest Assassins in Paris and a bright and cheerful young man, had been captured, lined up and executed by a firing squad. Fabrice Sabourin was alive but seemed to be suffering from some sort of head wound, or perhaps just from a surfeit of grief. Everyone else he knew in Paris had come through alive and unscathed. The Communards had burned down the Tuileries palace and had fought to the last, among the tombstones in Père Lachaise cemetery. When it was all over, and the streets were full of bodies, the Third Republic took its place at the head of the French Empire.

That day, Simeon had little stomach for Konstanze's gloating. He sent her a telegram with his regrets, saying that he would see her the following week.

The next morning, he woke up to see her sitting in his ratty armchair by the glowing embers of last night's fire.

He sat straight up and pointed his gun at her, more as a kind of physical swear word than a real threat. She didn't flinch.

There had been a change in the fashion since they'd met, years ago, in Vienna. The skirts were narrow now, a long line up to the bodice. He liked the new styles; they made it look as though someone had gift-wrapped the woman. The bustles made them sit on the edges of their chairs, so that there were two modes of sitting: Very upright, as if ready to spring, or, if leaning back, leaning so far back that it looked halfway like lying down.

That was how Konstanze sat now, her bustle tucked beside her, leaning backward, her arms spread over the comfortable wing chair. Deliberately relaxed. Her dress was a golden yellow, tightly tailored.

He was wearing nothing but his shirt.

"I've come to give you my sympathies," she said, as if this were an ordinary social call. How the hell did she get in without him hearing?

"I didn't ask for your sympathies," he grumbled, putting the gun down on the mattress. "Or your company."

"No, but I know how hard you worked to help your friends in Paris. I understand a little now why. You truly believe that individuals will act for the collective benefit. Despite all evidence to the contrary."

"The evidence is that you and your allies attempt to stop humanity from ever getting the chance to try. The Commune might have been a moment of real change, if it hadn't been for the threat of the army."

"There will always be threats. There will always be armies."

"Then you truly don't believe people can ever genuinely care about others, and act in the collective interest? Not without being coerced or manipulated?"

Konstanze shrugged. "Hives need queens."

He pushed the hair out of his eyes. "Your kind regards have been delivered. Surely you can wait until next week for another of our conversations. Frankly, I'm not sure there's much left to say. If you don't understand our creed now, it's not because nobody's explained it to you. It's because there's a kind of understanding that doesn't happen in the brain."

She looked at her hands. "You could say that I grew up in the Templar Order. It raised me. My father was a Templar, a man of science, and a dreamer. He spent our family's money searching after artifacts, and eventually bankrolled an expedition to an island that, to his dismay, turned out not to exist. He'd been swindled by a Portuguese adventurer. We had to leave our house, sell everything. My parents sent me to live with my aunt in Munich. My aunt was a Templar as well; most of my family was. She was cruel, but she taught me many things. And she kept my father away from me, for my own good. I learned much later that he spent his final years making himself an embarrassment and a nuisance, demanding that the Order pay him all the money he'd lost. The Order offered him a suitable house and a small income, but it wasn't enough. He believed that every penny he'd lost had been in service of the great cause, you see. We had been a very wealthy family."

Simeon swallowed. "So he turned on the Order?"

"He became a liability." The room was freezing. "My aunt told me about it. He had been making threats, exposing our work and putting his colleagues in danger. We share at least one part of your creed, Simeon. We never compromise the Order. So someone – I never found out who, and it doesn't matter – had the unpleasant duty of killing him. My mother had always been fragile. She accepted the offer that my father had refused, of a house and small income. I am told it was a pleasant house, in a village in the mountains. She had enough for a housekeeper."

"You never saw the house?"

She shook her head. "My aunt wanted to protect me. If I had gone to live in that village, I would have learned nothing but how to milk goats and spit curses. Instead, I learned mathematics from the best professors in Germany, and how to fight, and how to sneak into a man's room without waking him up." At last, she made eye contact, weary and wary. "You think I'm cold-hearted. But I have fulfilled my father's dreams in ways he never could. I've found treasures he only hoped were real. I've honored his memory and rebuilt the family's fortunes."

All of this could be invented. But it fit with what Oscar Kane had told him about Konstanze, years ago, when Simeon had danced with her in Vienna. The night of his first kill.

"The best way I know to love someone is to carry on their work," Konstanze said. "That's what I'm trying to say. I think your friends would feel the same. I believe any member of either of our orders would. Isn't it funny how we believe the same things in opposite ways, or opposite things in the same ways?"

"You have a strange sense of humor."

"That's true." She stood, smoothed down her already perfect skirt. She had curled a few strands of hair on her forehead, and one of them bounced as she pinned a small hat onto her head. "I'll go now so that you can get out of bed without damage to your modesty. I expect to see you at the chateau on Tuesday, as usual."

In Brussels, Simeon met some people he'd known in Paris, such as Hippolyte Fontaine, who had organized the production of the now infamous cannons there during the war. Fontaine introduced Simeon to scholars and factory workers. Many of the factories were closing, because the Vienna stock market had crashed and there was no one to buy the things that anyone made. So Simeon would buy his friends a beer and they'd agree that the world was a terrible place and then they'd talk about everything and nothing, all of which was helpful for keeping his head straight in between his philosophical tutoring sessions with Konstanze.

He wondered, sometimes, what Oscar Kane would have said, if he'd known that one day, Simeon would teach a Templar about Assassin philosophy. Occasionally, Simeon even found himself using the same phrases Kane had. He wanted to get away from the games and strategies, even the old ideas. He wanted new books and new conversations. One of the booksellers in Belgium introduced him to Jules Verne in French. He liked the new one, *Around the World in Eighty Days*, but was disappointed by *Five Weeks in a Balloon*. He read Zola, Hugo and Flaubert, and George Sand, who was Amira's favorite writer. He read Turgenev's *Fathers and Sons* in an English translation. He wished he could read Dostoyevsky and Tolstoy, but it was hard to find their work in translation, and though he'd picked up conversational Russian during his time there, he wasn't able to read it very well.

When Gamal Sabry came to Brussels in the summer of 1873, Simeon was in a good position to tell him exactly where to find books and publishers. Gamal was on his way to Russia for some book-related task, and stopped in Belgium because, "all the most courageous publishers are there now." He believed firmly that the Brotherhood had a responsibility to preserve human knowledge, and he was fond of saying that the history of the Assassins was the history of books and libraries. Simeon enjoyed the conversations, as he took Gamal to the cafes he liked. It was grounding to hear him talk; it reminded him of Pierrette.

Gamal, for his part, listened to Simeon explain his arrangement with Konstanze.

"So," Gamal said at last, tearing into a piece of bread one evening in the back booth of a dim cafe, "her side of the bargain was not to interfere with the Commune. But now the Commune's dead. So what is she doing for us now?"

Simeon shook his head. "It's a good question. I hoped for a long time that the people might rise up again, or force the government to change, and I didn't want the Templars to interfere with that. Then I told myself that I didn't want them to make the whole situation worse. But the fact is, Paris is no longer under siege, and we can fight the Templars the way we always have. Besides, I'm running out of things to tell her."

Gamal grinned. "What *do* you tell her? It doesn't take long to say the basics of what we believe."

"Mostly we argue about philosophy."

"Ah, that I do understand." Gamal paused, looked at him seriously. "So you don't really have a reason to stay?"

"You'll call me naïve."

"Try me."

"She is not happy in the Templar Order. She chafes at the Order's strict control. Of course she says she just wants to understand her enemies, but I think she might be seeking a way to come over to our side."

Gamal whistled softly. "Has she told you this?"

She hadn't, and Simeon hadn't dared to put it in words himself. It was not the sort of thing he would have put in a letter to Pierrette. And it wasn't a solid enough analysis to pass to Michel. It was just a feeling. Maybe wishful thinking.

He said, "I'm not sure she's even admitted it to herself. But she's always trying to persuade me that there's no real difference between her order and mine. Maybe she thinks I'll come over to the Templar side, but if she thought that, wouldn't she be trying to tempt me? Showing me the wonderful weapons they have, the artifacts, the powerful connections? She doesn't. She keeps me away from the Templars, barely lets me see her workshop."

"Maybe she's trying to tempt you in other ways."

Simeon snorted. "It's nothing like that, believe me."

"All right then." Gamal shrugged. "If you believe there's even a small chance that one of the most powerful Templars in Europe might defect, then obviously that's something you must see to the end. Of course, even if she did want to join us, there'd be a long way for her to go to earn our trust and a place in the Brotherhood. Can you imagine what Pierrette would say?"

"I can," Simeon said grimly. "But maybe it's a castle in the air, anyway. Maybe she is precisely what she appears to be. And in that case, my usefulness to her is running out."

CHAPTER TWENTY-ONE

A few days later, Simeon left Gamal to putter happily around bookstores while he went to the chateau for his regular visit.

Lambert the butler took his coat. He was a little taller than Simeon, with a bald spot that gave the impression of a tonsure, and a perpetually pleasant half-smile that made him look like he knew a secret. He probably knew many secrets. What sort of interview process did Templars have for their butlers? Maybe they bred them.

Instead of showing him into her study or morning room, as he usually did, Lambert asked him to wait in the drawing room. The countess regretted that an earlier appointment detained her.

It was the room least like Konstanze, of all the rooms he'd seen in the chateau so far. There were yellowing lace antimacassars on the furniture. Over the fireplace hung a large painting of a train on a bridge, dreamlike and hazy. It looked like a Turner; not Konstanze's usual modern taste in art. For the first time, Simeon wondered how she'd come to own this strange block of stone in the woods. The place was ancient. He'd assumed that she'd bought it with her own fortune, built up from the bottom, like the house in Vienna where he'd first learned she was a Templar. But perhaps it had been in the family; maybe an inheritance from the infamous aunt, or some other relative.

The drawing-room window looked out on the gardens at the side of the house, and a moving shadow pulled his gaze there. Out beyond a boxwood hedge, Konstanze stood in a pale ivory dress and hat, talking to a man in a dark suit. He looked familiar – yes, he was certainly one of the scholars Hippolyte Fontaine had introduced him to. A mathematician, Simeon thought. He couldn't remember his name.

The mathematician – if that's what he was – waved his arms wildly, as if alarmed, but Konstanze just nodded in response. No, he wasn't alarmed. He was excited. Explaining something. One of her projects or inventions, no doubt.

Their agreement had said nothing about conversations spoken in the open air. And it would feel good to send Michel some concrete information about her inventions and ideas. To prove to himself there was some use to his time here, even if the countess never defected. Voicing that hope to Gamal had made him realize how unlikely it was. He had known others who claimed the only difference between the Assassins and Templars was which of them was winning. He'd been taught by one. And he'd killed him, when the time came, because Simeon had chosen his path long before, on a ship going down, when he'd decided to protect the lives of drowning men nobody else would. To protect the powerless, you must be ready to kill the powerful, no matter how charming, intelligent and beautiful they might be.

Yes, he admired the countess. How could he not? She was brilliant, fascinating, and occupied his thoughts constantly.

But she cared about people only in the abstract, representing everything he stood against, making him stand where he always did, in the shadows, holding a knife.

He stepped carefully, quietly, to the wall, out of view of the window. From behind the yellow curtain, he reached forward and put his finger on the latch.

The garrote cut off his air and sliced into his neck before he named it in his mind, but his body responded. His head slammed back against the attacker, weakening his hold. Body rotating into the space. A punch to the man's gut, a palm to the ear – it was Lambert, the fucking butler – and a knee to the chest, but that didn't connect. His throat was free and Lambert's hand had dropped, the wire dangling free from one hand. The other hand punched Simeon in the face.

He'd taken a few good punches in his life, but this one sent him into his own world of dizzy agony. He lashed out with his fists, knowing he couldn't spare the time to come back to his senses. His knuckles connected with flesh and bone, and his left hand was wet. He knew where Lambert was now, even if he couldn't quite see him through the blood in his eyes. His Hidden Blade shot out from his right wrist and pierced Lambert's neck.

Simeon wiped his eyes with his left forearm and braced Lambert as he fell. The blood trickled around the man's neck in a mirror of the stinging line on Simeon's own. He was dead before Simeon could say a word to him, before Simeon could catch his breath.

Then he looked up and saw Konstanze standing in the doorway in her ivory garden dress.

He had never seen that look on her face before. Shock, surprise, dismay? Was she surprised that he was alive, or surprised Lambert had attacked him? Whatever the reason, it was as though a mask had dropped. It was terrifying, because he had no idea what she would do next.

He stood, pulled his revolver, and pointed it at her. She did not move.

"It seems our agreement is at an end," he croaked.

Her eyes focused on him, and she nodded briefly. "I've been forced into a choice."

It hurt to swallow. "Will you let me walk out of here?"

She said nothing for a moment. Then, quietly, "I don't think so."

Every heartbeat seemed to last a day. He wasn't sure how she was armed, but she always was. His gun was pointed at her heart, and his hand wasn't shaking, because he was an Assassin. The trigger was warm against his finger.

"Lambert didn't work for me, not really." Konstanze gazed at the body on the floor, speaking almost dreamily, as if having a gun pointed at her had the opposite effect than it would have on other people. "He was here to keep me in line. To make sure you never became dangerous."

Simeon, dripping blood on the carpet, said, "It seems I became dangerous."

"You gave him reason to think so. Or you gave him an opportunity to carry out the decision of someone else. My colleagues must have decided to do me the favor of removing you from my life. For my own good, I expect."

He tasted blood. "You're trying to talk your way out of this."

She shook her head. "I can't make your choices for you, Simeon. I can only make mine. I can try to kill you first, like a good Templar would."

"Or?"

She leaned back against the doorframe, as if it was holding her up. "Or," she said weakly.

Michel had sent him to Brussels to kill Konstanze; their agreement had delayed that, and now their agreement was over. But whether it was Konstanze who had broken that agreement was not something he could sort out now, not with his head ringing and that strange look on her face. Lambert had tried to kill him; he had killed Lambert. The balance was even.

He kept the gun on her as he walked to the doorway and passed through.

She reached for his lapel, grabbed it, pulled him to her, and kissed him.

It was a kiss full of blood and two years' worth of conversations. He pushed her against the doorframe, pulled himself back. As much as he wanted this – and he finally admitted to himself that he very much did – it was dangerous. Kissing Konstanze was like leaping off a cliff. He couldn't foresee the consequences, but the pull of it was almost too strong to resist.

"What the hell are you doing?" he asked, talking to himself as much as to her.

She said, "Let's find out."

The Templars would kill Konstanze if they learned what she was doing. And what was she doing? She couldn't say, but she knew she wanted freedom, to act according to her own conscience and not out of obedience. Not out of fear.

"Then you're an Assassin, whether you join the Brotherhood or not," Simeon said.

"I think joining the Brotherhood is rather crucial to the

question of whether one is an Assassin or whether one might be killed by one."

"Then what do you want?"

"I want to go on learning what I want."

They had this conversation in her bed the following morning, with eastern sunlight coming through the window onto a painting of a woman by Édouard Manet. There was blood on the ivory dress she'd been wearing yesterday, which was flung onto the chair. There was blood on his clothing, on the floor. Blood on the bed.

"In the meantime, three Templars are coming this morning," she said brusquely. "If you leave now, and you're careful, you won't meet them on the road."

She remained a puzzle to him. If the day ever came when he solved that puzzle, would the fascination end? Fascination, no matter how sublime, could not be enough to compensate for her cruelty, her treatment of Pierrette, her manipulation of empires without regard for the people in them.

There had to be something deeper – or else all of this was a horrible, selfish mistake.

He could walk out of here, consider it a conquest, a move in the game, and put an end to it. But that felt like cowardice, turning his back on the possibility that people really could change for the better, and build connections with each other, against all odds. It was something he had to see through. That was, in fact, the only thing he felt sure of: He was going to see through the consequences of his decisions, and not sneak around like a lovesick teenager.

"I'm not afraid of Templars," he said.

"You should be."

In response, he pulled her down to him, smoothed her hair off her face, and kissed her. "Whatever comes, we'll face it together. I'm not leaving you here alone, not after Lambert acted without your consent."

She groaned. "Fine. But at least stay out of the room. I have to handle this my way."

Konstanze had told her maid not to disturb her. They dressed and went down the stairs, hand in hand, and she told him her plan. There were few Templars in Belgium; it was an overlooked country in the Order, because of it being neutral ground politically. That was why she had settled here; she liked some space to work on her own projects, and most of her colleagues saw her as an arrogant eccentric and were happy to leave her alone. But occasionally, groups came to meet with her, check on her, tell her what they needed from her – because eccentric or not, it was her ideas that had made the trains of Europe faster than anyone had thought possible. The next thing was steamships, and she had ideas about that too.

But they all knew about her pet Assassin, as they called him, and they might well have known that Lambert had been ordered to kill him. They probably thought that the Order had been doing Konstanze a favor, removing a weakness she wouldn't admit she had.

She was going to tell her visiting colleagues that Lambert had attacked Simeon, and that Simeon had killed him and escaped.

As they reached the door, they heard horses and carriage wheels outside, and Konstanze pushed him into her study. "They're here already. Go on, get out of the way."

Her study had several curiosities on shelves: models of

steam velocipedes, hunks of rock, carvings. The art here was all family portraits: a man with long muttonchops, a woman with a thin, pinched face and dark hair pulled back with punishing severity.

It was next door to the drawing room, and he could hear wisps of their conversation. Just a phrase here and there: "the Order" and "long gone". Simeon walked cautiously closer to the adjoining door. There was no gentlemen's agreement now. No reason not to eavesdrop. No butler waiting to garrote him – he hoped.

He had said something to Konstanze once about a kind of understanding that didn't happen in the brain. Maybe that explained why he trusted her now, despite all the reasons not to. It could be mere lust, or infatuation, but he really believed there was a connection between them. They sought each other last night like two people who have been wandering alone for a long time. They did understand each other, in ways neither of them seemed able to put into words.

So he listened at the door not because he thought Konstanze would betray him, but because he was worried about what the Templars might do if they decided that she, like her father, was a liability.

The door swung open, and he sprang back. It was Konstanze, and when the door had closed, she pushed him against the wall, her mouth on his, her hands on his shoulders.

"I was thinking of you in here and it was driving me mad," she said, her mouth twisting into a reckless smile. "I told them I needed to fetch a document."

That afternoon, Simeon arrived late at the dingy office of a

publisher in central Brussels. Gamal was already there because
he wanted the publisher to send him books in Egypt regularly,
and he had asked Simeon to help arrange it.

Luckily, Simeon's tardiness didn't affect the meeting,
because the publisher was detained at the back of the long,
untidy room, deep in an animated conversation with a young
man with wild hair. The room was stuffy at the end of a mid-
July day and it smelled of paper, ink, metal, tobacco and sweat.

Gamal greeted him warmly. "I had a telegram from Pierrette,
just before I came. She's arrived safely in London."

"Oh, good," Simeon responded. Had he known Pierrette
was going to London? Gamal hadn't mentioned it, perhaps
he thought Pierrette would have told him. But he hadn't had a
letter from her in weeks.

The young man finished his conversation with the publisher
and strode past them with an amiable grin. Then he turned and
pointed at Simeon with a lit cigarette. "I know you."

He did look familiar. "I'm sorry," Simeon said. "I can't recall…"

"It was in the train station. In Paris. Yes! In 1870. I was such
a child then. You and some friends, you tried to prevent me
from being arrested for not having a ticket. It was you, I'm sure
of it." He put the cigarette into his mouth and expertly talked
around it as he stuck out his hand to shake. "Arthur Rimbaud.
I never forget when someone does me a service. Happens so
seldom." He said this loudly, good-naturedly glancing back
toward the frowning publisher.

Gamal stepped closer. "Rimbaud? Rimbaud, the poet?"

"Believe me," said Rimbaud to the publisher, "I didn't set
this up."

"I read your poem – 'Gifts for Orphans'. Very stirring, the

way you paint with words. I was recently in Paris and everyone there is talking about you. Your talent, I mean."

Rimbaud snorted. "You mean they're gossiping about the fact that Paul Verlaine and I ran off together. It's all true. He left his wife for me."

Gamal acknowledged this with a nod, and said, "I'd heard you were in London."

"We were, but Verlaine tried to escape me by running here, and then he summoned me." He turned to Simeon, as if to an old friend. "Love. It's terrible, don't you agree? It's an addiction of the senses like any other. It's a fire that you use to burn yourself up, to disappear, which is the only honest thing a man can do. Oh, don't listen to me – I can see you're a man in love, there's no use talking to you. What is your name, anyway?"

Simeon gave it, not looking at Gamal. When Rimbaud had left, promising to send Gamal some of his work, Gamal looked at Simeon and said only, "Well, that was interesting."

"He's a poet, and they all talk nonsense," Simeon grumbled. "Go talk to your publisher friend and then let's go somewhere safe. The Templars are likely to be out looking for me by nightfall. They've decided to eliminate me."

Gamal's expression cycled through half a dozen different questions, but he settled on, "What are you going to do?"

Simeon hesitated. He felt like a man waking up from a dream – or from a hangover. Suddenly sick to his stomach. Why hadn't he been able to tell Gamal the truth about Konstanze? Because he was ashamed. Rimbaud was right. Love – or whatever you could call the "addiction of the senses" currently afflicting him – was a fire that could only destroy. And fires could spread. His duty was to the Brotherhood. Perhaps

Konstanze had really changed; perhaps she hadn't. But the fact remained that he couldn't look Gamal in the eye and tell him what had happened, and that told Simeon what he had to do.

"I'm leaving Brussels by the first train I can."

Simeon considered sending a telegram to Michel through the Assassins' trusted line, but he couldn't think of what to say. It was not only that he was leaving, without having killed his target, and with no intention of monitoring her henceforward. It was also that he didn't think the Brotherhood should send anyone else to kill her either, because he genuinely believed that she was willing, if not ready, to betray her order, and come to the Assassins' side.

But he was also aware that he might not be thinking clearly on this subject.

In the end, he decided to go straight to Paris. Then he could explain in person and help Michel make a plan for what to do next. In the meantime, Gamal would be in Brussels for a few more days, and had promised to keep an eye on Konstanze.

The only seat he could get on the train was in the last car. It was full, which brought him a strange sense of comfort; he'd been trained to disappear in a crowd. Easier to do in one of these modern cars, with the aisle down the middle dividing the bench seats. He wore a battered, wide-brimmed working man's hat, and a gray coat. Smoke swirled outside the window. Metal squealed, men shouted final boarding calls, and the train rumbled out of the station.

They sped through green fields and villages. He had just started to relax when the metal squealed again and the train slowed to a stop. Simeon's hand was on the window latch. He had it open by the time a man in a railway uniform burst into the car and announced in three languages that everyone would have to evacuate.

Simeon craned his head out of the window. The train was on a bridge, over a small river. Good of the Templars to evacuate the train before they attacked him, at least. It meant he could get away without worrying about helping the passengers. He'd rather face whatever they had for him in the open, on top of the train or on the bridge, than here where they could corner him.

He had grabbed the top of the window frame, ready to pull himself out, when he heard the man in the uniform say to one of the young men, in a whisper too excited to be as quiet as he intended, "It said there was a bomb."

So the evacuation might matter after all. This wasn't the Templar style. Someone else, then? Something political? Or perhaps a mere hoax. A bad prank.

In any case, he had to help get everyone out first. He moved away from his window and ushered a young woman to it, trying to clear the aisle of anyone who didn't need to be there. It was slow getting everyone off, because most people did not relish walking out onto the narrow slice of bridge between the train and oblivion.

Soon, he was the last one in the train car. All the same, when he went to the door and looked back, just in case, Konstanze suddenly stood in the aisle, wearing a flared green traveling jacket and smart hat. There were no weapons in her hands.

"Tell me you haven't endangered all these people to get to me," he said, thickly.

Her voice shook. "They aren't in danger. They're all going to get away. The bridge is perfectly sound, and it's not slippery."

"Then it's just me who has to worry."

"I'm not here to kill you. Not exactly."

"I am tired of games."

"This is no game. I'm only here because you left before I could answer two questions you put to me. Once you asked me whether I'd let you walk away. My answer has changed. Now I answer yes, fully and wholeheartedly. I give you your freedom. If you walk away from me today, I won't follow. If any Templar stops your train or chases your horse, it won't be me. Not ever again."

"I'm not sure that message needed to be delivered in person," Simeon said drily.

She took a step closer to him. "But you see, I didn't want you to walk away until you'd heard the answer to the second question. You also asked me once whether I had any real feelings for anyone. I've changed my mind about the answer to that too. I think you've taught me. You are teaching me. Things I didn't intend to learn." She laughed shortly.

He wanted to go to her, and he wanted to run. It was, he knew, the most dangerous moment of his life. But he didn't know which way safety lay.

"It's no good, Konstanze," he said quietly. "It doesn't matter what you and I feel. We can't be together in secret. That may be how Templars work, but I can't be an Assassin and lie to my brothers and sisters."

She nodded. "You may tell your comrades whatever you think is best. I trust you, which means I have to trust them. I have to trust someone. It feels awful. But there it is."

"If you leave the Order to be with me, you'll be killed. And your friends are already hunting for me."

She spread her arms. "That's why there's a bomb on this train. A bomb you set, or so it will appear to my Templar friends. I have informed them that I was coming here to stick a dagger into you, to clean up my mess. They have also just intercepted a telegram from you, telling your friends that you know of my plan, that you intend to trap me here and blow up the train with both of us on it, that you are willing to die to carry out this assassination."

He scowled. "I sent nothing of the kind. And no one would believe I did. I'd never use a train bomb to assassinate you or anyone. Assassins do not shed the blood of innocents."

"I believe that, but my comrades do not. They think you Assassins are dangerous anarchists who will stop at nothing, no matter what philosophy you spout." She stepped forward. "Simeon, this is the only way we can be free. After this, I won't be a Templar. I'll be dead to them. And I can rise again as an Assassin. I will take whatever pledge you ask of me."

Simeon looked in her eyes. He had spent the last hour believing he'd never see her again, and he'd taken no relief from that, only dull misery. For so long, he had hardly dared to hope this moment would be possible. That something good could come of all the cruel decisions and mistakes that had pushed the two of them together. That what he felt for her was real, and more than just an addiction to the feeling of vertigo she induced in him. He could never predict what she would do from one moment to the next.

"Is there really a bomb on the train?"

"Yes. We have..." she consulted a watch chained to her jacket, "two minutes and forty seconds. I think it's about time we both took a leap of faith into cold water. The only question is whether we take it together."

CHAPTER TWENTY-TWO

Pierrette was disgusted. Paris was rebuilding, but she was in the mood to burn things down. Another battle in the streets, behind the barricades, just like the one that had claimed the lives of her parents in that bloody revolution in 1848 that had changed so little. And in the end, the Paris Commune had also been for nothing. The Communards had toppled the column with the statue of Napoleon on it, the one that she'd perched on the day she surprised Simeon. And now, the government was re-erecting it, as though nothing had happened. At least they couldn't do much about the burned wreckage of the Tuileries Palace.

She asked Michel what she had once asked George Westhouse: "When do we *win*?"

And Michel had answered, "We win every day that we keep fighting," but he had looked exhausted when he said it.

Amira had come to her rescue, as she had done more than once before, by giving Pierrette a job to do in Egypt.

Now she stood in a dim and dingy office on the outskirts of a village near the Suez Canal at five o'clock in the morning, staring at a wall of wooden filing drawers. Everything about the place screamed ordinariness. The room smelled of stale tobacco and sandwich crumbs. The window shutters were closed, letting only a few shards of light through to illuminate the dust.

But it was a deception. The window had bars concealed between the rows of shutters. She knew this because she had been forced to pick the lock of the door, a lock that turned out to be complex, which had meant she had to kill the guard whose patrol took him past it every few minutes.

There was no doubt about it: these were Templar files.

The English antiquarians hired to move the cave art had, unwittingly, tipped off the Cairo Assassins to a ring in Egypt that was sending artifacts to Manchester. That was near the end of the long process of moving the art. And even then, the Assassins weren't sure how to act on it right away. All they had, at first, was the tip.

Following threads for months had led them here, to this unassuming place. So unassuming that Pierrette had volunteered to scout it alone.

On the table, beside the overflowing ashtray, was a brass ball-shaped typing machine, and other metal devices. Such up-to-date machines for such a cramped and ugly office.

The drawers had small, neat handwritten labels, in English. One of the four cabinets was labelled with the names of countries. Another with kinds of transportation: coaches, steam omnibuses, velocipedes, rail lines, steamships, horses, underground railways. And the third with materials: rubber, diamonds, artifacts, cotton, tobacco, paper, tea, silver, bricks, tin, silk, coffee.

The fourth seemed to be labelled with a kind of code:

J&J:M, HINC, etc. She couldn't make head or tails of it. But those labels were older, yellowed.

The drawer that most interested Pierrette was the one marked "artifacts".

The Assassins still had many questions about what the Templars had been attempting with the Ankh, what their ultimate plan for it might be. Now the artifact was missing again, or so Simeon reported… although Pierrette didn't trust the information learned from the countess. Be that as it may, the Templars were busily digging all over Egypt. What other artifacts might they have, and what might they do? Simeon had mentioned an "Engine of History", which he seemed to think was connected to the Ankh somehow.

Pierrette did what she usually did these days when she was trying to clear her thoughts: she put her hand to the locket where she kept the page from Ada's notebook, the page Simeon had sent her. It was folded into a tiny square inside a silver oval, and for some reason, touching it seemed to help her think.

The answers might be in front of her, but she had to keep her wits sharp. These were Templar filing cabinets, and that meant traps.

She kept a long, thin hook in her lockpick kit. Standing to one side, she used the hook to gingerly pull open the drawer.

The dart that had been meant for her throat struck the wall opposite. Probably poisoned. Damn Templars.

Carefully, she approached the drawer, and stood on her tiptoes to look inside. When she was fairly sure there were no other traps, she pulled out a stack of papers.

Dig reports, drawings, long essays. She flipped through the pages, looking for mentions of the gods, of powers, of the Ankh. Nothing. They all seemed to be ordinary pieces of pots, tiny statues of cats, bits of papyrus or tile bearing official pronouncements or merchants' tallies.

A ruse? She held the papers to the light, checking for signs of invisible ink. Nothing.

She turned back to the desk in the middle of the room, the one with the strange machines on it. There was a blotter in the middle of it, and ink had seeped through from a recent document. A letter, it seemed.

Dear Sirs,

I am happy to elaborate on the benefits of the partnership I beg you to consider. What good is your string of London warehouses in today's world? The consumers of Europe no longer need you to keep goods on hand from places that used to take months to reach, where supply might be interrupted by bad weather, pirates or war. Now, the Suez Canal has cut the length of many journeys, so that a textile merchant in Prague or a rice merchant in Milan will simply buy from the nearest port, and have no need for your warehouses.

You would be well advised to transfer your shipping business to a partnership with us. Our organization recognizes the possibility of civilizing Africa, of bringing light to every dark spot on the map, and recovering the riches there for–

Her reading was interrupted by a small sound. When the door opened, just a crack, slowly and quietly, she waited for the tip of a shoe to appear at the bottom.

When it did, she shot it.

The door flung open and a man crumpled against the doorframe, trying to aim his wavering gun at her.

"Drop it, or die," she said calmly.

She spoke in English, the language of the letter and the labels. He was a pale man, thin, young, wearing a shirt that was too big in the chest. The sort of man who had ambitions.

"You'll kill me either—"

She shot again, just wide of him, so the bullet went into the doorframe. It was enough to startle the gun out of his hand.

"I don't play games," she said. "Come in and sit. For God's sake, your foot is bleeding."

He obeyed, warily sitting in the room's only chair. She tied his arms to it.

"There's nothing of value here," he protested, in a crisp English accent that spoke of boarding schools and cruel older brothers.

"I disagree," Pierrette said. "Tell me about the artifacts."

"The artifacts?" He glanced at the open cabinet drawer. "Which ones? You have the papers already. Nothing terribly secret. This is just a business office."

"People don't put poisoned darts in drawers that contain nothing very secret."

At that, the young man nearly smiled. He was paler now, probably from the pain. "We don't like some of the people who come poking around in our affairs, that's all."

She made a small curtsey. "Present company included, I'm sure. But there's something special about those drawers, in the first three cabinets. New labels, aren't they? Fresh looking. Your innovation, I'd wager."

He snorted. "Hardly." After a moment, he seemed to decide he had nothing to lose by explaining. "The design for that system just came in from Europe, and we do as we're told out here in the back of beyond," he said with a faint trace of bitterness. "Cross-referencing, tables, records. All has to be very precise. I told you, this is just a business office."

"But you have ambitions for it," she guessed, thinking of the letter she'd just read. She took a chance. "The fourth cabinet. That's your own special project. Related to the letters you send to England, isn't it?"

Her arrow hit the mark. His face went blotchy red. "I won't give you a single name," he sneered.

Names? She looked again at the labels, the abbreviations.

And in that moment, he lunged forward, scrambling to get his tied hands just underneath the desk to press something.

Pierrette exhaled hard with annoyance, strode over to the drawers and pulled the labels out, one by one, as fast as she could.

"How long until your friends get here?"

"I'm not going to tell you that!"

"You are a most irritating young man. You'll go far in the Templar Order."

She considered putting a bullet in the back of his head, but she didn't have the stomach for it, and she'd already killed one man today. Besides, she had a feeling this one would be just as irritating to his colleagues as he was to her, and the Cairo Assassins might well come to appreciate having a slightly bitter and ambitious young Templar to pressure.

Pierrette left and rode her camel back to downtown Cairo in the morning heat, thinking hard. The labels were names. Names of people and companies in England. People and companies that expatriate Templars were trying to do business with.

Evie and Jacob might have flushed most of the Templars out of London, but the remnants of the British Order simply spread out to the rest of the British Empire, like tentacles. Exploiting and exporting. The young office clerk had mentioned a system coming from Europe, a system to organize the first three cabinets: countries and materials and modes of transportation. Maybe it really was just business.

How dull it must be, to live in this age of balloons and locomotives and canals, and see only money and power in it. Pierrette had traveled with the circus from an early age, but she'd never been to the East, or to the Americas. Maybe one day, she'd take a long journey, not to perform or carry out an order, but simply for the joy of it.

She went straight to see Amira, and between the two of them, they made a list of people and companies in England who might match the abbreviations on the labels. Diplomats, politicians, and enterprises that the British Assassins might not realize were or might become Templar fronts, or connected to Templar fronts.

"It's going to be a big job, to investigate all of these," Amira said. "I'm not sure any of this is connected to the Ankh, but they hastily built a railroad to the cave where they used the artifact, and they must have needed to transport something out of there. Something other than a horse, surely! But as you say, the artifacts they're exporting seem to be ordinary baubles for rich gentlemen to put into their drawing rooms. We are missing a piece of the puzzle. The more we learn about the Templars' plans, the better our position."

Pierrette could see where this was leading. She said that if Amira needed someone to go to England, Pierrette was always ready to serve. She never did like to stay in one place too long, anyway.

Besides, this would give her a chance to see her old friends in the Aurora Troupe, for the first time since Tillie's death.

Spider Wallin didn't remember Pierrette.

He was five years old in the summer of 1873, living with the circus, which had taken to touring in the summers. They were in Brighton when Pierrette landed at Dover, so she went there first. Pierrette, exhausted from a rough crossing, hadn't remembered to buy a Fry's Chocolate Cream. Spider greeted her politely, by firelight, beside the old wagon with TWICE PATRONIZED BY HER MAJESTY THE QUEEN written in red paint. She could barely see the baby she remembered in his little boy's face. So many moments of his life that she had already missed. Had it really been that long?

Ariel Fine gave Jim, the horse trainer, a small smile of thanks as Jim left with the boy by the hand, taking him to get ready for bed.

"What's going on with you and Jim?" Pierrette asked, smiling.

"Is it that obvious?" Ariel groaned. "Let me put the kettle on. We've shared a tent for the last year. In Cardiff, Penzance, now here. He's kind and good with Spider. We've all done our part in raising him. I keep waiting for someone from the government to take the boy from us, but nobody seems bothered, thank goodness. Better with us than an orphanage. Nevertheless, sometimes I think he should have a proper family, with a steady home."

"A circus is as good a family as any."

"I hope you're right. Nell teaches him reading and writing when we're in London. He's clever and good at art. And he can already stand bareback and loves horses more than people. Not to mention, you should see him ride a penny-farthing on a tightrope. Don't worry, it's barely a foot high when he does it. Utterly fearless with heights, that boy."

Pierrette smiled. "Perhaps he gets that from you."

Ariel raised an eyebrow and poured the tea. The thing Pierrette liked best about being around performers was seeing them when they weren't performing: how the private side of themselves stretched out quietly and cautiously when the lights went down. Pierrette had once been the female Mazeppa, in a skin-tight pink costume, so that she could be anything she wanted afterward. Ariel had found a way to be themselves in public in a manner they hadn't yet in private, by announcing the performer known as Ariel Fine on posters as "Neither Man Nor Woman But Spirit of the Air" and then that was all anyone needed to know from then on; Ariel was a *they*, and being a *they* in the circus was not so difficult, and one could then be *they* while having a nice cup of tea with an old friend too. The circus made room for people, and it would make room for Spider, too.

In the morning, when she'd had a bath in a tub behind a screen in the big wagon, Pierrette went into the stables to see the horses. She found Spider there, cleaning horse tack.

She stood over him, offered to help. He looked up at her suspiciously. "Jim told me to do it."

"Yes, but he won't mind. Hold on, I'll get another bucket."

She settled in next to him on a plain bench, with a bucket of soapy water and some old leather. And she got a look at him in the daylight. He was not very big, but he was strong for a five year-old. Floppy blond hair and a determined mouth.

Once, when she snuck a glance at him, he was sneaking a glance at her.

She laughed. "You look like you have a question for me."

"I want to know whether you knew my mum."

Ah. The knife to the heart. She wanted to say, *Don't you remember? I was there when she died.*

Instead, she said, "Yes, I knew her well. She was a little younger than you are now, when I came to live with her father's circus because my parents had died in a revolution."

His brows furrowed. "A revolution is what a bicycle wheel makes. Ariel and I talk about that when we plan out where my feet will be at each part of the tightrope."

"Yes, it is a turning. But sometimes it means a changing over. Sometimes, what's turning is the world."

"The world is always turning," he said, pedantically.

She chuckled. "Ariel warned me you were clever."

He looked as if he wasn't sure what to make of this. They worked in silence for a minute. Then he asked, "What tricks did you do in the circus?"

"I was an equestrienne."

"Like my mum!"

"Yes, but she was more talented than I was when it came to horses. I did a lot of tricks, though. I used to spell out words with fire."

His eyes grew. "I have to use chalk. Because I'm still learning to spell. I can spell six words now."

"Yes, well, it starts with chalk." She tried not to laugh.

"But everyone is still learning something. And everyone has something to teach. Your mum taught me many things. Ariel taught me some of the same lessons they're teaching you. Oh, and you know Hugh Robinson, in London, who runs the costume shop? Would you believe he taught me to throw knives and shoot guns and even blow fireballs?"

He dropped the tack into the bucket and turned to her. "Will you show me?"

Belatedly, Pierrette realized she hadn't thought this conversation through – or the consequences for the adults who would be there for Spider after she had moved on again, hunting Templars.

"Maybe someday," she said softly. "Tell me. What have you been learning?"

"Nell teaches me to spell words and count out the tickets and programs. Hugh is teaching me how to run fast. Harriet is teaching me the names of places in the world. Jim is teaching me about animals and stories. What I like best is riding. But Ariel is also teaching me rope dancing and tightrope walking, because I am not afraid of heights, and because 'a valuable performer can always do more than their own act.'"

Pierrette grinned at the impression of Ariel's tone when giving advice. "Well, that's true. I studied an act called Mazeppa, and when a chance came to perform it, I was ready. And it brought me many opportunities."

He looked morose. "I wish I could ride the horses more and stop the other lessons. But I don't tell Ariel that, because I don't want to hurt their feelings."

Pierrette thought for a moment, drying her hands. "It's always best to be honest with Ariel about what you like and dislike. Your grandfather used to say that if your heart isn't in it, you'll fall to your feet. I think it made more sense in Swedish. Or maybe it just made more sense to him." She winked at him. "If one of us has a secret doubt, that can endanger everyone in the troupe, we have to be honest with each other. Always."

He nodded. "But it isn't *we*, is it? You're not in the circus anymore."

"No. Not for a long time."

"What do you do now?"

Her throat closed. "I try to help people. I protect people."

"Do you still throw knives?"

"Every chance I get."

Pierrette spent three days with the troupe, treasuring every moment. Home had never been a place, to her. Home was the Aurora Troupe. It had kept her fed and safe during her childhood. She owed the same protection to Spider.

And truth be told, the boy had her heart. Pierrette had never wanted children of her own, but she found spending time with Spider to be a joy. He taught her how to ride a penny-farthing bicycle, and laughed when she fell off, so she fell off again.

But she couldn't stay. She had to do what she'd promised Amira, and track the Templar connections, to get a better sense of how they were moving material around the world – and what they were moving. And she needed to let the British Assassins know her plans. Evie was in India, with her husband and her brother, and there were no other Assassins she knew well and trusted in England. That left George Westhouse.

George met her in a pub in Crawley, on a hot night in July. There was a private room near the back with a door that closed, and windows that looked out on the rest of the establishment; not that it mattered, as the rest of the establishment was empty. The floor stuck to her shoes, and the table wobbled when she put her list down on it.

George smoothed it out and took a stubby pencil from his waistcoat pocket. He was looking weathered; he was well over fifty by now, Pierrette realized. It was the first time they'd really talked, just the two of them, since that day when he'd suggested she go to Egypt. Five years ago. A lot had changed, and nothing had.

He ran his finger down the list of names in Pierrette's messy handwriting.

"These are British trading companies? And all connected to known Templars in Egypt?"

She nodded. "Doing business with them, at least. With some financial and insurance companies mixed in. But most of them are tea, rubber, ivory, rice, that sort of thing. Also artifacts, which drew our attention in Egypt. It could be that the Templars are interested in shipping and railroads purely because they love to be rich. But we want to see whether there's any connections between all these plans they're making in Egypt, and the strange business with the Ankh a few years ago. Amira wanted you to be aware of these names, anyway. Keep an eye on this end of the connection."

He looked at her. "She could have put it in a letter, then."

She blushed. He always did have a way of making her feel superfluous. "She also wanted to find out more about them and assumed you would be busy with other things and happy to have my help."

He didn't respond to that, just tapped the first name on the list. "A.C. Vise and Company. They've closed. And The United Atlantic Company. Closed. Southgate and Rowntree. Never heard of them; I'll look into it. Oh no, wait, that's Nelson Rowntree, who's just gone bankrupt. Universal Mercantile Assurance Society. If they survive the week, I'll be shocked. Algiers Trading Company. No, they're gone too."

She leaned back and stared at him, shocked. "What on earth happened? Don't tell me the Frye twins had another unsanctioned adventure?"

He grumbled, "Nothing of the sort. It's nothing to do with us, in fact. The economy is on the brink everywhere. Didn't you hear about the Vienna stock market crash?"

"Well, yes, but–"

"It was partly because of all the money flowing into the German Empire from war reparations, and all the spending on railroad speculation. One could say the Templars have been the authors of their own misfortune. Of course, it's not only Templars suffering – businesses of all kinds are closing everywhere."

"My task is easier than I thought, then."

"Indeed." He glanced at the empty glass in front of him. "A glass of bitter? I'm buying."

"Yes, please."

She went through the list, using George's pencil to cross off the companies he'd mentioned. There were a few more at the bottom.

"What about Drake Trading?" she asked as he put her beer in front of her and slid back onto the bench opposite.

"No, never heard of... well. Hmm."

"Hmm?"

"There's the Drake Line, of course. Steamships. A year or two old, like so many of these shipping lines."

"Do you think it's the same company? I've got some names written here, of the staff we know about in Egypt. Any names look familiar?"

He took the paper back, read, and shook his head. "No, I don't think so. I'm not sure who the people are behind that line. But I will monitor it."

"It makes sense," she said, and took a sip of her beer. She'd missed British beer, though there were a few places in Cairo she'd come to appreciate. Some Frenchwoman she was now.

"What makes sense?"

She counted on her fingers. "Starrick and his telegraph company. Pearl Attaway and her streetcars. Konstanze von Visler and her railroads and her telegraph lines. The Templars crowding around the Suez Canal. They like to have their fingers in transportation and communication, don't they? Why wouldn't they have steamships of their own?"

He shrugged. "It's a leap, but you may be right." He tapped his finger against his glass, thinking, and then switched subjects. "Pierrette, Michel tells me you showed great skill and courage in Paris, and Amira says the same about Cairo. It seems you're well on your way to becoming a Master Assassin. I'm proud of how far you've come. I hope you know that the British Assassins are always happy to have you here."

She did not know that, she realized, though she hadn't thought about it in those terms. Her home had never been a country; her home had been the people she tried to protect.

Pierrette received a telegram the following evening, written in the Assassin's code. She worked it out with a pencil in her bedroom and then sat staring at it, her fingers playing with the silver locket around her neck.

My oldest and dearest friend you will by now have heard terrible news concerning me I want you to know it is all right.

It was an echo of a letter she had read for the first time more than twenty years before. The letter Simeon had sent Ada, to say that the reports of his death were wrong, that he had not gone down with the ship.

It puzzled her all night long. From Simeon, certainly, but what did it mean?

The next morning, when George Westhouse came grim-faced to her hotel room to tell her that Simeon was dead, she smiled and said, "No, he isn't."

CHAPTER TWENTY-THREE

Brussels wasn't safe for Simeon and Konstanze. She was too well known in Germany, he was too well known in France, and they were both too well known in England. So they made their way south, to the Swiss Alps, and Konstanze sold some diamonds she had sewn into her pockets. They rented a cabin in the mountains.

"Just like the one my mother must have had," Konstanze said, squeezing his hand.

They were almost giddy, setting up their little cabin, lying in bed as long as they wanted, getting to know each other without pretext or sparring. After they had been there a month, a grizzled St Bernard started coming around and sitting on the back porch. They were reluctant to feed it – after all, they might leave any time, and the life of an Assassin was not kind to pets – but the dog was patient and persistent, and took to barking any time a stranger approached the cabin. They named him Javert.

Konstanze turned forty a few months after they moved into the cabin, and she joked that middle-aged domesticity really was indistinguishable from death. Simeon, who had been in his forties for a while, told her it just felt that way on damp mornings.

But the truth was, their new life was an adjustment for her. Their bedroom had only a few luxuries: a silver hairbrush, her pearls, a glass bottle of Guerlain's *Eau de Cologne Impériale* that she rationed. She had access to some money, because she had always made sure that nobody knew all her names and connections, not even her Templar colleagues. They found a way to be together without arguing, and sometimes that felt like a precipice. Simeon would watch her, sometimes, silhouetted as she walked their small garden at sunset, and feel that she was still a cipher to him, and he ached to decode her.

Their life was quiet, but it was not seclusion; it was nothing like the time he had spent with Laura on Lake Como, years before. That had felt like retreat; this felt like a war room. They strategized and schemed, and they trained together, which made up for the lack of arguing.

One reason Simeon had chosen to flee to Switzerland was that he knew Henri Escoffier was there, in a small bureau of Assassins in Zurich. The first Assassin Simeon had ever met was now in his sixties, and had found new ways to serve the Brotherhood that didn't require ice packs, as he put it. He'd gone to the congress of the League of Peace and Freedom in 1867 in Geneva, and had stayed on in Switzerland afterward, to guide and watch the anarchist Mikhail Bakunin and his underground group of revolutionaries.

Soon after Simeon and Konstanze arrived in Switzerland, he sent Henri a note, heavily coded, to let him know he was still alive, and that he had an unlikely ally to introduce to him.

Simeon knew from Henri's letters that the Assassins of Zurich met in the musty drawing room of an imposing, somewhat dilapidated old house on the edge of the city, owned by a respectable, dotty old widow – or so she appeared to the outside world. Not many Assassins made it to advanced age, but Irene Egli had, and was happy to continue to serve the Brotherhood in her way. That mainly meant being cover, and allowing the use of her drawing room, while she sat in the corner and nodded along, or nodded off, as the mood struck her.

Simeon and Konstanze stood on the front step of Irene Egli's house in Zurich, just after midnight, in traveling cloaks.

Henri opened the door.

Simeon's old friend had always been a bit gruff. A practical man, but one with a deep mind for politics and intrigue. He ushered them into a narrow hallway with fading yellow wallpaper.

"So this is the unlikely ally," he said, looking at Konstanze. "I win the pool. I hope you won't take offense at leaving your weapons at the door."

She looked a little uncomfortable. "Of course not."

Two guns and three knives clattered onto a silver salver. Simeon put his own down next to hers, as a gesture of solidarity.

"I can offer information about the Templar Order, in exchange for your protection," Konstanze said.

Henri put up one hand. It shook slightly; he was getting on in years. "We don't work that way. We operate on trust, and mutual aid, not transactions. Of course we want to know what you know, but you need not use it as leverage. We'll protect you as we would any ally or friend, and if you choose to join the Brotherhood, we'll protect you as we would family."

She bowed her head and seemed genuinely moved and taken aback.

Henri continued: "But if you break that trust, we will not hesitate to protect ourselves. Now, let's go in. The night is not getting any younger and neither are the occupants of this house."

The drawing room was exactly as Henri had described it in his letters, including the tiny old woman in the corner, watching everything with bright eyes. The other Assassins were two young people Simeon didn't know, a man and a woman. Henri introduced them, and they set about discussing the most urgent business: how to keep Simeon and Konstanze supplied and hidden.

After some time, the youngest Assassins went into the kitchen to get tea, and Konstanze, eager to be useful, went to help. Simeon took Henri aside.

"Tell me honestly, old friend. You know I would never knowingly compromise the Brotherhood. But I worry about doing it unknowingly." He remembered the long years in which he had thought of the selfish, treasonous Oscar Kane as his mentor. "Henri, do you think I'm being a fool?"

Henri shrugged. "I believe that any human being can choose to be nobler and wiser, at any point in their life, no matter their choices before that. You proved me right, didn't you, when you took off your silly uniform and stopped following the orders of terrible men?"

Simeon made a face. "That's different."

"Put it this way, then. If I believed it was impossible for Countess von Visler to become an upstanding Assassin and an asset to the Brotherhood, I would have stuck a knife between her ribs at the door. I don't know what's in her heart. But not knowing is the point, isn't it?"

It was the first of many monthly meetings. The group would talk about what the Templars had been doing, and Konstanze would answer the Assassin's questions. Then she and Simeon returned to their mountain haven, with freshly bought books, instruments and tools for Konstanze's "tinkering" as Simeon called it, and paper and ink. Konstanze wrote and wrote. Sometimes she wrote notes about her inventions, all her terrible machines. Sometimes she wrote long histories of the Templar Order, especially the family trees and connections established in recent generations. She drew plans of their safe houses and jotted down lists of their informants and connections.

Her inventions she kept to herself, but her notes about the Templars, she brought to Zurich, every month, in a little bundle.

It was an extraordinary windfall for the Brotherhood, as even Pierrette grudgingly admitted in her letters.

Konstanze was used to shouting to be heard in an organization that valued hierarchy and centralized control. She was used to jostling for power. Simeon could see that irked her, sometimes, that the Assassins of Europe would take what she said, politely note it down, and then apparently do nothing about it. Everything the Assassins did was less efficient – less effective, Konstanze was prone to grumble some days.

But she was also charmed by the decentralized nature of the Brotherhood, and the independence it afforded. She couldn't seem to believe there was no inner sanctum directing things; this was something Simeon had not spoken about, during their philosophical talks. But now that she had forsworn the

Templars and was working in alliance with the Assassins, things were different. He let the Zurich bureau take the lead.

She would need to gain more trust before being inducted, but Simeon had permission to train her in the areas she hadn't learned. Templars were taught to execute, not to assassinate. They were taught to guard secrets, not to hide in the shadows. They were taught to control, not to protect. Sometimes, the differences were subtle, but sometimes Simeon got a headache from trying to make the woman he loved see the world the way he did.

Konstanze did nothing halfway. Once she had betrayed her Order's sacred vow not to divulge its secrets, she was eager to divulge all of them. This was particularly true once she tried to obtain some of her most valued items by sending an Assassin to a hidden chest in Brussels; the Assassin reported the chest was empty. Konstanze was livid; she was sure that her erstwhile comrades had emptied it, and taken things she had kept to herself, including an Apple of Eden she had obtained years ago in a trade with Oscar Kane and hadn't told the Order about. Including, as well, several of her inventions.

"What about this rumored Engine of History?" Henri had asked

She had glanced at Simeon, then looked back at Henri. "Believe me, that would not have been the sort of thing one could fit inside a chest. Anyway, my colleagues already know that I could not make it work."

One of the young Zurich Assassins, whose name was Beatrice, asked, "What would this machine have done, if it had worked?"

She hesitated. "It would have destroyed the Brotherhood

of Assassins. Wiped them out. It would have allowed us to finally win. Changed history, you see? Or changed the future, which is the same thing from another perspective." And then she smiled sadly, repeating, "But alas, I wasn't able to make it work."

"Alas?" Henri asked with a little movement of his eyebrow.

She shrugged. "A weapon is a weapon, and just as useful to the Brotherhood as it would have been to the Templars."

"And no one else is working on this project now?" Simeon asked.

"It was mine, from the conception. I had many people working on components around the world, but the central idea fell apart."

She had always treated her Order like a family, but like the kind of family in which the strict father does not need to know his daughters are climbing out the windows. Family, to Konstanze, meant rules and protection, and a complex web of secrets.

Just as she had not told her Order everything (or handed over all her treasures to it), there were many Templar secrets she didn't know, as she was not a member of the inner sanctum. She was able to tell the Assassins that there was an enormous map on which the last known location of each Piece of Eden was marked; a new copy was made every year, and the previous year's copy burned. But she did not know where it was kept. She'd seen it once, recently, in a meeting about the search for the Ankh. As someone who had hunted her whole life for Pieces of Eden, she'd been fascinated.

"What struck me most was how blank much of Africa was on that map," she explained at one of their Zurich meetings.

"Surely those who bequeathed us the Pieces of Eden must have left as much behind there as anywhere else. But the Templar Order has neglected that part of the world. Modern science is laying rails into the desert. There's a chance – a brief chance – to beat the Templars at the chase. We can find these treasures before our enemies do."

Rails in the desert. Simeon, with a shiver, remembered the terrible cave, the effects it had on him and his friends when the Ankh was present. The strange moment when the horse came to life – an experiment, Konstanze had called it. How little the Templars seemed to know about the forces they were playing with.

To Konstanze's frustration, the Zurich Assassins were not as excited by the idea of hunting for Pieces of Eden in central Africa as she was. But she did not press the matter.

Simeon had been dead to the world once before, and this time he found it surprisingly easy. Both the Brotherhood and Konstanze knew he was alive, and that was enough. Sometimes he felt a twinge about Sawyer Halford, his one friend from his days in the British Army, and the man who had stood by him and helped him win his freedom. The man who had fought at his side, not because of a command from the Army, and not even out of loyalty to a creed with which he was barely familiar. No, Halford had fought out of personal loyalty and friendship.

But Halford was safer believing Simeon was dead. Probably happier, too.

When it came down to it, selfless friendship was the best thing Simeon could offer anyone now, as his fiftieth birthday approached. Like Henri, he thought of ways to serve that didn't ask as much from his body, as he aged. He would have liked to help young men as restless and friendless as he had once been. But his efforts to find such men and steer them away from killing innocents had failed, time and again. His two great successes in his life to date had been matters of judging character: He had brought Pierrette into the Brotherhood and taken Oscar Kane out of it. He'd been too slow in both cases, but he liked to think he had learned.

So he did not begrudge this time spent taking Konstanze out of the Templar Order, and taking her in to the Brotherhood, in their secret cabin, where the world could not intrude. It was as if they'd stepped out of reality. They dispensed with the idea of getting married one night over red wine, because, as Konstanze said, dead people could not obtain a marriage certificate.

He grew used to sharing their cabin not only with the aging Javert – who disliked expending the energy to chase strangers anymore but who barked all the louder because of it – but with her collection of metal arms and leather bellows and rubber tubing, none of which he was allowed to touch.

Three years after Simeon and Konstanze had officially died, she asked for her first assassination, and the Zurich bureau said yes.

King Leopold had scheduled an international conference in Brussels for September 1876. It was to gather experts in geography to discuss global exploration. Henri had become the Assassins' usual eyes and ears at international conferences – a task most Assassins considered so tedious, they were happy to let him have it. But Konstanze pointed out that one of the scientists traveling to Brussels was Maynard Poole, a cartographer and a known Templar. She felt sure he was the main keeper of the map of the Pieces of Eden, and she might be able to get information about it out of him. At the least, his death would slow the Templars down in their hunt.

Konstanze had arranged things to make it look as though she'd gone to the train to kill Simeon, and that as they fought, they were killed by a bomb he'd set. As far as the Templars knew, she had never abandoned or betrayed them. So it would be easy for her to gain access to Poole, and possibly other Templars as well. She'd have an explanation for her apparent death if need be, but she planned to shoot them all before the conversation became too detailed.

Simeon was wary, when she proposed this idea to him. "If any Templar survives their encounter with you, the whole Order will know you're alive."

She nodded. "I can't stay in this cabin forever, Simeon. You know that. Should I be like Daedalus, walled up in my prison, making my toys? I can't ever be inducted into the Brotherhood unless I prove myself – not only my skills, but my willingness to take real action against the Templars. I don't want to hide forever. We will keep each other safe, Simeon. You and I, and all our Brothers. Don't ask me to stay here and be something I can't."

He kissed her, which was not any kind of answer except goodbye.

Chapter Twenty-Four

For two months, Simeon waited. He walked in the mountains with Javert and winterized the cabin. Wood needed chopping, the stove had a temperamental flue damper, and bats had found a way into the bedroom on the top floor. He tried not to wonder whether Konstanze would return to him.

When he saw Henri Escoffier trudging up the path to the cabin, he felt as though he'd swallowed a stone. He stood in the doorway, his hand on Javert's head. The dog knew Henri, but anyone other than Simeon and Konstanze got a growl on principle.

Henri had never been one to waste time on pleasantries. "She's fine," he said, still puffing from the walk. "And she got her man. Maynard Poole is dead. The map was not on him, but she got information from him that might lead us to it. While she was at it, she managed to destroy select Templar records, including those about the Ankh. No Templar is left alive to tell that Konstanze von Visler was in Brussels instead of the grave. An immaculate operation, no unnecessary bloodshed."

Simeon felt relieved, not only because she was alive and well, but also, he realized with a sick feeling, because he had not been proven wrong about her. She had not betrayed the Brotherhood.

"Where is she now?"

"She'll be here tomorrow. I made an excuse to take an earlier train because I wanted to tell you something. I said no Templar is left alive who saw her, and that's true, but while she was in Brussels, she had an audience with King Leopold."

An audience with the king! That had not been in the plan. "How do you know?"

"I watched her in ways that she knew about, but I also watched her in ways she didn't. I don't know whether this conversation is anything the Brotherhood needs to know about. But I thought you might want to."

Konstanze knew the names and locations of Assassins, and some of their plans and missions. He couldn't believe that she would betray that trust. But then, what was she up to? It might be innocent. She might have an explanation.

Simeon nodded. "Yes, all right. I'll find out what happened and make sure we're safe. Henri, come in, for God's sake, I haven't even offered you anything. Come in, and we'll drink beer. I have fresh bread, even. We'll worry about tomorrow tomorrow."

Konstanze returned like a conqueror, peeling off her gloves and eyeing Simeon like a predator. And she had a guest in tow, without warning.

Henry Morton Stanley was in his mid-thirties, and had one of those careful, unplaceable accents that suggested he was in the habit of making it very clear to people that he traveled a lot. His droopy mustache accentuated his habitual downturn of the mouth. Simeon knew the name; he had been in all the newspapers shortly after Simeon moved to Brussels, when Stanley had "found" the explorer David Livingstone in a village near Lake Tanganyika – even though Livingstone wasn't actually lost. He knew exactly where he was, and was happy living there, but had just stopped contacting Europeans, which counted as being "lost" to the newspapers. Nonetheless, this supposed rescue made Stanley famous.

Stanley had attended the conference in Brussels, and was now on his way back to Africa. Konstanze said she had traveled with him as far as Zurich, and then asked him to come and stay a few nights with her and Simeon.

Simeon put Javert out to growl at the moon, handed Stanley a glass of whisky, and then followed Konstanze into the tiny kitchen. He was irritated with her for bringing this stranger here, when they'd been apart for the first time in years, and had so much to talk about. Private things, including the urgent question of what her conversation with the Belgian king had been about. He hadn't felt this distant from her in a while. Attempting to understand her used to excite him, but tonight it was giving him an angry headache.

She was opening cupboards, taking things out. "Have we got the wherewithal for sandwiches? I'm still not in the habit of having no servants – I didn't think."

"And you didn't warn me you were bringing him."

"No time. We only decided in Zurich." She turned to him, holding a butter knife, and then put an arm around his waist, pulled him close. "You don't mind, do you? We had so much to talk about. He's an interesting man. King Leopold has asked him to do some work for him in Africa."

"And what did the king ask you to do?"

She froze. Her arm dropped from his waist. "Ah. Spies. Henri, was it? He's very good at not being seen when he chooses, isn't he?"

"He's the best."

"There's nothing scurrilous about it. I wanted to find out what the king was really doing, with this conference of his. And I know he won't tell the Templars I'm alive. If anyone can be trusted with a secret, it is Leopold of Belgium, believe me. I knew the Brotherhood would dither if I asked about it beforehand. I learned very young that nobody great asks permission."

"And you want to be great."

"I want to be good," she said. "I do. But some habits are hard to break. Do you want to hear what the king has planned? He is going to build himself a country. Imagine the foothold–"

"I'm not in the mood. We can argue about it in the morning."

"Oh, you're out of sorts. What will I tell Stanley? He was so looking forward to meeting you. Don't worry, I didn't give him your real name. Just said you were an adventurer, like him."

"I suspect I am absolutely nothing like him."

Her face froze. "All right, then. We'll try not to disturb you. Go on – I'll make the sandwiches. I can manage that, I'm sure. Do you want me to bring you one up?"

He shook his head and left her holding the butter knife, staring after him.

The only stairs to the bedroom on the top level required him to go through the main room, where Stanley was poking around the countess's shelves of models and prototypes.

"I say," Stanley said as Simeon came in, "you wouldn't

happen to know the trick of that stove? I dare say it's as cold in here as it is outside."

Simeon nodded curtly and went to build up the fire. The damper was still broken; the one task on his list he hadn't got to.

"You work together," Stanley said. "And live together."

It was almost a question, but Simeon ignored it, yanking open the stove door more vigorously than necessary.

Stanley picked up Konstanze's latest design from the table: a tiny flying machine. "She's a regular da Vinci, isn't she? Do you think she'll truly shape the future?"

Simeon was elbows deep in the stove, wrestling with the flue. "If anyone can, it's her."

"Yes, but I wonder whether her ambitions are realistic. All those plans in her battered notebook, her great project. She'll never get it done if she wastes her time here."

The tone was casual, but Simeon paused to parse it.

And in that pause, he became aware of two things.

The first was the motion in his peripheral vision of a gun being drawn.

The second was a flash of memory, so familiar it was wordless and instant, of the argument he used to have with Pierrette about defensive positions. She loved nothing more than to throw a knife from afar; it made her feel safe. Simeon, though, preferred to be within hitting distance. If Stanley had been standing a few feet closer, Simeon would have picked up the fire iron and swung it at his head.

Instead, he had to make do with Pierrette's methods.

"I suspected you were the countess's weakness," Stanley said. "She'll–"

Simeon stood, the fire iron in his hand, and threw it in the general direction of Stanley.

At the same moment, a stinging burn in his upper arm registered at the same moment the gunshot did. He was moving by then, flinging himself toward the man. The fire iron had hit its mark. Stanley was staggering, blood gushing from his temple. His gun dropped to the floor.

Typical bully, Simeon thought. No good in a fair fight.

Konstanze appeared in the kitchen doorway, holding her revolver.

It was pointed at Simeon.

Simeon didn't slow. He grabbed for Stanley's wrist, but then he heard Konstanze say, "Simeon, stand down."

Cold, sickening certainty settled in his gut. He forced himself to do what he was trained to do, to think of the woman pointing a gun at him as a point in space. Stanley was recovering, however he was still dangerous.

He pulled Stanley into a choke, Simeon's arm around his neck, Stanley between him and Konstanze. A shield while he made his escape.

And now they were looking at each other, he and Konstanze, with this odious stranger between them.

"It was all lies, then," Simeon said. "These last few years. Your change of heart."

"That was real," she protested, but the gun in her hand didn't waver. "But there are bigger things at stake. If you let me explain–"

But he knew that there was no explanation now he would believe. About eight backward steps, he reckoned, to get out of the cabin. He could dispatch Stanley there, and then – but then he saw Konstanze's eyes, and he knew she was about to shoot. To shoot him right through Stanley, if that was necessary.

Simeon pushed Stanley forward with all his strength right into Konstanze, to unbalance both of them for the few seconds he needed to burst out of the front door of the cabin. He ran into the darkness, the cold air stinging his wounded arm. Through the beating of his own blood and breath, he heard a gunshot, but he was safe. He stayed in the woods but kept the road on his left, winding his way down the rocky, root-strewn hillside. It would be a long way to the nearest town, but he could not afford to slow down.

Then he stopped outright and swore as only a former soldier could.

The dog. The bloody *dog*. Javert would be all right, surely. Konstanze – no. He couldn't assume anything about her. Javert would be better cared for with his friends in Zurich.

He climbed back up, taking a long way around the ridge surrounding the cabin, and snuck silently in the darkness toward the fence door. Unlatched it; cursing the tiny squeal as it swung open. Yet another thing he'd never get a chance to fix.

Javert padded over, and he grabbed the lead off the fence pole. If Konstanze knew him at all, she'd know he'd come back for the dog. She'd be waiting for this.

But he got away into the night, with Javert trotting along beside him, every jingle of the dog's collar a reminder that she hadn't caught him. She'd let him get away, or she did not know he'd come back for the dog. He wasn't sure which possibility hurt more.

CHAPTER TWENTY-FIVE

Pierrette had seen some bad fogs, but none as thick and relentless as the pall that settled over London in the winter of 1879. When she walked near Sanger's Amphitheatre in the evening, she could see the new electric lights on the Victoria Embankment, like a firmament that illuminated nothing. On the good days, it was as if the whole city was stuck inside a spirit photograph, with tendrils of sepulchral mist reaching around the lampposts and groping into the alleys. On bad days, the city was drowning in it; you could only find other people by their coughing.

This particular Monday was a bad day. The fog had settled in and everyone was in an irritated mood at rehearsal. The Aurora Troupe was spending the winter in the city, to rehearse a new act before another summer on the road.

Spider had a role to play, introducing the act by juggling on horseback. Nell Robinson was to measure him today for a special purple suit. This sort of thing went over all right with the audience; he was still short enough that he was obviously a child, which added novelty, but he had no sense of showmanship. For him, the tricks and stunts of the circus were as natural as breathing, and he never conveyed to the audience that they should be impressed.

Perhaps the reason was that he wasn't impressed himself. On this morning, when he should have come for his fitting and rehearsal, Spider was nowhere to be found.

However, Pierrette had a good idea where to look.

The troupe had taken a set of rooms near the busy thoroughfare known as the Cut, because it was affordable and close to Sanger's Amphitheatre. They had two floors of a rooming house, and Spider was in with the new strongman, who was nearly seven feet tall but was a gentle spirit who would believe anything Spider told him, and who seemed genuinely shocked to discover that Spider had not been right behind him in the fog as he arrived at the amphitheater that morning.

The circus, no matter how bright and busy, could not compete for Spider's attention with the streets of London. In the troupe, he was the only child, but in the streets, there were newsboys and newsgirls, bootblacks, and children whose parents found the board schools too expensive or too cruel or who were too tired to care. The children ruled the ground and the sky, with the fearless sweeps' apprentices climbing the rooftops.

All day and night, there was a constant sound of children chanting as they played their games, banging tin cans, throwing pennies against walls. Strings of indecipherable insults shouted at passersby and peals of laughter afterward.

It was a world in which an eleven year-old boy who had grown

up in the circus could be a king. Pierrette knew well enough
the exhilaration that came with claiming a city's rooftops and
alleys. So Pierrette had advised Ariel not to forbid Spider from
playing outside. It would have been impossible to stop him,
anyway. But they had insisted that he keep up with his studies,
and training for the summer shows. As Jim reminded him
from time to time, the newsboys and bootblacks and sweeps'
apprentices had their trades, and he had his – and his was a
safer and better paying one, if he did it well.

But at rehearsal this morning, no Spider.

Pierrette had dropped by, on her way to visit a banker. She
had been busy all over England, tracing the connections of a
steamship line, finding out precisely who their owners were,
and then paying them visits. But companies were complicated
things to assassinate. It was not work she enjoyed, but it was
important. And George said she couldn't very well blow up a
steamship, so she had to settle for destroying the companies
that owned them.

She was not absolutely *sure* that one couldn't blow up a
steamship, but she was getting more prudent in her old age.

And she felt badly that she hadn't spent much time with
Spider lately. So when a tired Nell told her he wasn't where he
should be, she offered to go looking for him. She put up her
cloak against the cold and damp and started the walk toward
the troupe's rooms in Southwark.

In the fog, she followed the sound of the noisiest children.
No tin cans or chanting rhymes today, instead there were
shouts of victory and recrimination. When she heard an
outright scream, she picked up her pace. A child streaked past
her, running with her skirts in her hands, barely visible from

one moment to the next. Another darted in front of her, nearly knocking her down. She heard something crash, and a rock smashed a window next to her head.

Two boys became visible now in the middle of the street, one with his jacket yanked up halfway over his head, protesting and shouting as the other pummeled him. Pierrette resented the interruption in her day, but she hated bullies and was not about to let this pass. She paused, then, with a heavy sigh, walked over and pulled the aggressor off. He was as tall as her, with a wicked expression on his freckled face, and as slippery as an eel. It was harder than she liked to admit to get him off the other boy, who picked up a bit of broken bottle and hurled it at the one Pierrette was holding back.

"Get off!" she shouted at the bottle-thrower. "Go home. You too." She pushed the larger boy, and he loomed for a moment in the fog before moving away, no doubt to go find another victim to pummel.

She followed him, tracking him as he loped down the street.

The wrongness of the lamppost's shape struck her just as the bully was nearly underneath it, and it took a moment for her to believe her eyes. Surely that great lump on the top of the light couldn't be a person, perching–

–but it was, and the person leaped, crushing the bully into the cobblestones, before Pierrette was close enough to see that the leaper was Spider.

She pulled him off the bully, who yelled something indecent and ran off.

"What the hell were you thinking, Spider?" she sputtered. "Do you want to end up in jail or worse? What were you fighting about, anyway?"

"It wasn't a fight. It was a game of Bedlam. We take prisoners, they take prisoners, and then everything is settled."

"Sounds like war."

"You have no idea what you've done," Spider said bitterly. "The Larrikins are after our rooftop back on Roupell Street. If we don't stand up for Batty Fang territory–"

"Then someone else will run games on that rooftop. It doesn't matter, Spider."

"You don't know what real life is like," he protested, and stopped dead. He wasn't tall enough to look her straight in the eye yet, but it wouldn't be long.

"Oh, I don't, don't I? Come on. You made a commitment. Let's not keep Nell waiting any longer."

"I didn't make a commitment. You all made it for me. I don't want to wear a purple suit and juggle pins."

"If you want to juggle knives and fire, you start by juggling pins. What do you expect?"

"I can juggle knives already. I do it all the time. It's not fair. I can't do *anything*–"

She laughed. "Spider Wallin, you have more freedom than you know. I know it's hard living without parents but you have to admit that it comes with–"

"I have a dozen parents and every one of them is always trying to protect me, every way I turn. I wish you would all forget about me."

And with that, he dashed into the fog.

The new act went into the show without Spider. Over time, the troupe knew where he was, for the most part, and they kept him fed and housed. However, he stopped coming to lessons or rehearsals. He didn't stop spending his free time with the Batty Fangs – a loose territorial association of children of several blocks of Southwark. But it was the best his many guardians could do.

Pierrette understood when to give a horse its head, and when to rein it in. A boy of twelve – Spider celebrated his birthday that spring – was another matter.

She was relieved when the time came for the troupe to pack up the wagons and begin the summer touring season. It would get Spider out of London and rekindle his interest in the circus. The first stop was to be Brighton, so she told the troupe she'd meet them there, and made her own way down by train, stopping in Crawley overnight. She was overdue for a visit with George Westhouse, and they had a polite conversation over coffee.

But she was looking forward more to seeing Anne Blunt, who'd just returned from two years traveling in Arabia, and stayed at her estate near Crawley. It was a grand house, big enough, Anne said drily, to allow her and her husband to spend the entire day without seeing each other. But what Anne was most eager to show her was in the stable yard.

They changed into walking boots and Anne pointed the way.

"Did you travel through Cairo?" Pierrette asked, eager for news.

"No, we went through Syria. But the talk is all about Egyptian politics in that part of the world these days."

Pierrette had followed Egyptian politics too. The khedive whose life she had saved had sunk deeper into debt, eventually selling his shares in the Suez Canal to England. His projects had meant to free Egypt from the domination of empires, but his debts gave England and France an excuse to seize more control. When a revolt rose against European domination, Khedive Ismail did not crush it. So Britain and France pressured the Ottoman Empire to depose Ismail and install his son in his place.

"The new khedive is in a terrible position," Anne said. "The Egyptians are suspicious of him, the Ottomans are contemptuous, and England and France treat him like a servant. I hear he was happily farming somewhere and had no desire to take the job. Mind your shoes here."

They entered the stable yard, with its familiar smells of horse and hay. Pierrette's eyes were drawn to the distinctive heads poking out of a few stalls. She had seen Arabian horses around Cairo, but never in England.

Anne called the groom, who brought out a dark bay mare, her tail held high, with a fine head and strong shoulders.

"This is the Queen of Sheba," Anne said proudly, patting her. "Our best horse. Worth a king's ransom, if kings were still worth ransoming."

"You brought her from Arabia?"

Anne nodded. "We intend to breed horses here, you see. It's something worth doing, something I can put my mind to."

There was a sadness in her face, a dullness in her eyes that Pierrette hadn't noticed at first. Pierrette said lightly, "I should love to ride her. Is she as fast as she looks?"

"Faster," said Anne, handing the rein to the groom. When he had left earshot, she whispered, "But she's not as fast as Tulpar. Come and see."

They walked a narrow path through the woods to a secluded paddock, where a stallion was running. He was a chestnut with white stockings that stretched up onto his belly, and a long white blaze down his face.

"He's beautiful," Pierrette whispered.

"And he can carry a rider on his back at fifty miles an hour."

"Fifty! That's impossible, surely."

Anne shook her head. "We have three of these horses now, and we're keeping them very quiet, because I don't want people coming to have a look. I call the breed Pegasi. Sometimes it really does seem as if they have wings. I've heard rumors about a new bloodline appearing, some miraculous horse that had escaped from a breeder near Yenbo and sired a family like no one had ever seen. All three of ours come from that same sire."

"Miraculous?" Pierrette went cold, despite the warm spring sun. She remembered the last time someone had mentioned the port of Yenbo: the first sighting of Art Hennighan after the strange events in the cave so long ago. He'd gone to a horse dealer. What if that poor creature had lived long enough to sire a horse that might well be the sire or dam of the one in Anne Blunt's paddock?

It seemed beyond believing, but Pierrette had seen an impossible thing with her own eyes. That resurrected horse hadn't been a trial run at all. The horse had been the *point*. A faster horse, to go with the faster trains and the faster steamships and the web of telegraph lines.

She remembered Simeon saying once that it was funny that the only transportation that the Templars had not bothered to gain control over was the gas balloon.

Gas balloons were slow.

"Anne, would you mind terribly if I wrote some letters before dinner?"

Pierrette didn't want to leave the horses, but she had to get word of this to Amira and Michel – and Simeon, wherever he was. He'd taken Konstanze's betrayal so badly that Pierrette couldn't bear to say she had warned him all along.

Michel would know where he was. Maybe Simeon, who now knew the Templars better than anyone, could shed some light on all of this. She couldn't quite see the whole picture, but it was clear that the Templars were interested in speed.

CHAPTER TWENTY-SIX

After Simeon arrived at Irene Egli's home and told his tale, the Zurich Assassins burned the house down, and found a new safehouse. Simeon paced in the empty rooms, making plans to return to the cabin and deal with Konstanze.

"Are you ready to kill her? Tell me honestly," Henri asked, with dark circles under his eyes. It had been a long night.

"I'll do what I have to do."

"She's not in the cabin anyway," Beatrice said. "The place is empty."

"Then I'll find her."

Henri put a kind hand on his shoulder. "Let us worry about the countess. The Brotherhood would never give you this mission, and you know that."

There were a lot of things the Brotherhood wouldn't trust him with, Simeon soon discovered. At a loss, too angry and restless to go to Paris or London to his old friends, he went back to Russia, to finish the work that had been interrupted by the Ankh years before. There were still small reparations he could make there, families he could help. But it didn't take away his anger.

Henri wrote to him regularly, keeping him apprised of the search for Konstanze. So far, the only news they had was that she seemed to have re-joined the Templar Order. Simeon wondered whether she'd ever fully left it, in her heart.

One spring day, a young man came to see him in the village where he was staying, asking for help. His cousin in Saint Petersburg was involved in radical activities, and he had been talking like a man who expected to die soon. The cousin's name was Nikolai Rysakov.

It was a day's train ride to Saint Petersburg. Simeon went straight to the Assassin headquarters, a small flat in a working-class neighborhood. A young woman with thick brown hair opened the door.

He gave one of the Assassin passwords, and she looked relieved, and brought him in. He couldn't see the rest of the flat but could hear arguing from around the corner.

"We know precisely when they'll reach the road mine," a middle-aged man insisted. "They'll have it clear of innocents. It's easy there. That's why we chose Malaya Sadovaya Street, after all."

"And if something goes wrong?" a woman retorted.

"Then there's the backup plan."

"I didn't know we were getting any more help," said the young woman who'd let Simeon in, distracting him from overhearing the conversation. "Let me take your coat. We need everyone we can get today. What is your name, sir?"

Simeon gave it.

The girl's face went pale. She disappeared around the corner for a moment, and the voices sank to a low murmur he couldn't make out.

Finally, she returned, wringing her hands. "There's been a mistake," she said.

"A mistake?"

"I thought you were a friend of a friend. We are putting on a play, you see. It's rather silly."

"The password..."

"Oh, is that what that was? I thought you were making a joke."

She looked desperate, and Simeon took pity on her. A young Assassin, or an ally, and clearly she'd been told that Simeon Price was a Brother and not an enemy – but not someone to be trusted, either. Whatever the Brotherhood was up to in Saint Petersburg, they didn't want him involved.

He grabbed his coat from her and left without another word. His rage about boiled over.

He'd caught the name of Malaya Sadovaya Street, and he asked directions to it. It was still cold, for March, with a few inches of snow on the ground and a stiff wind. He put up his collar and walked through the city, feeling more like a stranger than he ever had anywhere. The Brotherhood did not trust him with information anymore, or at least, parts of the Brotherhood didn't. Fine – he didn't ask to be involved. He was here only because a young man had asked him for help.

But he was curious, and, he had to admit, angry and hurt.

Malaya Sadovaya Street was hardly a street at all. A single city block, narrow, and oddly quiet. No pedestrians. Strange, for the middle of the day.

He felt even colder, standing on the corner. Then he caught

sight of a man through the window of what seemed to be a cheese shop, sitting at a table. Simeon walked closer, then stopped suddenly when he saw what was on that table. Some sort of device with a wire sticking out of it, and in the man's shaking hand, a second wire.

The mine.

Simeon wasn't sure when that mine would go off, but he wasn't about to stand around to find out. He kept walking, up the small street, where he paused again. Several men in military uniforms stood at the next intersection, looking expectant. Pedestrians lined Italyanskaya Street, as if waiting for a parade. Perhaps this was the reason there was no one in the adjoining street; they'd come up here to see a spectacle.

In a moment, it was clear what that spectacle was. A black carriage pulled by a pair of horses, moving remarkably quickly so that the sleighs following kept losing ground by comparison, and the Cossacks on horseback all around had to trot to keep up.

The tsar.

Heading for a road mine. Dynamite under the street, no doubt, connected to that man in the cheese shop, holding a wire.

It wasn't Simeon's place to stop this assassination, especially given the tsar's well known Templar connections. But he would keep watch for his friend's cousin, make sure he got to safety. So far, he'd seen no sign of him, or of any conspirators other than the man in the cheese shop, who was too old to be the one he sought. He crossed to the far side of Italyanskaya Street.

The carriage slowed, started to turn to the left, into Malaya Sadovaya Street.

Simeon ducked into an alley and climbed a rickety iron back staircase up to the rooftop, to be out of the way and to get a view.

He spotted a figure on another rooftop, over the cheese shop, waving a flag.

The carriage was almost at the mine when it stopped, so quickly that the carriage careened behind the horses.

And the horses did something impossible.

They turned in that narrow street and burst into a full gallop before the carriage even straightened out. A gasp went through the crowd, and the military men pushed everyone back, out of the way of the carriage, which had doubled back the way it came. It turned left, and continued along Italyanskaya Street, as if it had never changed course. Simeon had never seen such speed before.

The man who'd waved the flag was gone, off the rooftops.

Simeon needed answers. He raced across the slats, staying off the ground as much as possible until he reached the cheese shop, where he burst in the door.

The man with the wires stood, a good three feet between him and the device on the table.

Simeon quickly said the same Assassin password he'd used in the flat, but this time, he gave a false name.

"What happened?" he demanded, pretending to know all about it. "What went wrong?"

"I don't know!" The man was clearly shaken. He had probably expected to die today. "The carriage was supposed to come this way, but it's taking the other route. We always knew that might happen, but we did everything we could to make sure its path was irreversible."

"What's the other route? Is Nikolai Rysakov there? I have a message for him."

"Yes, he's at the canal. We still have time. The carriage will stop on the way, and our goal will still be achieved. Nikolai will be all right. But this would have been better, cleaner…" His voice trailed off as he looked out into the street, on which a few people now walked, going about their business, unaware of the dynamite beneath their feet.

Simeon turned to go, when the man said, desperately, "I don't understand why the carriage turned."

It gave Simeon a chill. He didn't say anything about the man he'd seen, waving a flag. He wanted to get more information before he spread any around. "Could someone have signaled them to change course?"

The man shook his head. "Only if they knew about us. But none of us would have talked. There are no traitors among us."

Everyone thinks that, Simeon thought bitterly. And everyone is wrong.

"Is it possible someone could have predicted it?" the man asked. "Studied us, and known what we would do?"

The man seemed desperate, in denial that someone had betrayed him and his friends. But something about his theory made Simeon uneasy. He hadn't known anything about this plot to kill the tsar, which meant Konstanze hadn't known anything about it either. Yet she had made a study of the Brotherhood's methods, connections, and ideas.

The man began babbling. "And those horses – where did they get such fast horses?"

Simeon wanted answers to those questions too, but in the meantime, he had a young man to watch out for. A young man who was about to do something reckless, and who believed he would die as a result. Simeon couldn't stop the first part, even if he'd wanted to, but maybe he could prevent the second.

He ran back into the bitter cold, in the strange normalcy of a city resuming its business in the wake of the emperor. Maybe this city would rise in revolution if the assassins succeeded. And maybe it wouldn't.

After asking someone to point him toward the canal, he walked as fast as he could without attracting unwanted police attention that might slow him down.

He reached the street that ran along the canal and elbowed his way through a crowd of people when he heard an explosion, followed by screaming. Someone ran toward him, and to his shock, he recognized the description of Nikolai Rysakov: a heavy brow, wide nose, long auburn hair, a characteristic silk scarf.

Behind Rysakov was a group of police officers, running at a great clip.

Simeon stumbled into their path, pretending to be drunk. He rambled random phrases in Russian. One officer swiped a club across his shoulder and the other knocked him across his head. He fell at their feet. The confused chaos of the crowd kept the officers from going around him, so they stepped over him. Maybe those few seconds would be enough.

Simeon got to his feet, and turned, just in time to see a man throw something right in front of the fleeing Rysakov. The young man fell flat on his face. The police closed around him. Simeon's heart broke.

Then erupted the second explosion, and more screaming. Someone ran past, yelling, "The tsar! They've killed the tsar!"

Chapter Twenty-Seven

Spider was no happier with the circus outside London than inside it. Pierrette suggested to Ariel that Spider could stay with her at the Crabbet horse stud for a while. Ariel was relieved as they had romantic ideas about the miraculous properties of country air. Although Pierrette was reluctant to ascribe anything mystical to the ever-present whiff of manure, Spider did settle into a rhythm there. He lived with Pierrette in a three-room cottage on the estate, close to the secret paddock. Anne was grateful to have helpers with the Pegasi, as she and Pierrette had agreed that it was crucial to keep the special horses secret – from the competition, in Anne's view, and from the Templars, in Pierrette's.

She asked her friends to send reports of Templar movements that seemed too fast to be possible, even writing to the Fryes in India in case they saw any evidence there. It seemed clear that the escaped horse that had apparently sired Anne's Pegasi was not the only one of its kind the Templars possessed.

She told Anne about the resurrected horse. It seemed right

she should know, and a fair compensation for the years Anne had spent wondering what some mysterious cabal was doing with her mother's resurrected notebook. As far as the notebook went, Pierrette had reported to Anne what Simeon told her: that he had burned it, and that the countess had said she found it unworkable for her plans to build a device called an Engine of History. Anne said she'd never heard her mother use that phrase. Every answer seemed to lead to more questions.

Spider did not know the origins of the horses, but he knew they were a secret. He was reliable that way, and a good worker. Anne had looked him over much like she might look over any urchin from the city but took Pierrette's judgment and hired him on. While Anne worked on her breeding plans, Spider and Pierrette rode and groomed the Pegasi. He asked her questions about what she had done after she left the circus, and she told him pieces of truth, including that once she'd helped to rescue an emperor and empress, by riding a horse up onto a Paris rooftop.

Spider was impressed, but she never mentioned the complex subject of the Brotherhood. She wasn't sure he could understand that Templars and Assassins were not mere gangs, like the young terrors of London streets. At least, she had convinced herself that they weren't.

On the day that George Westhouse visited, Pierrette rode Tulpar, and Spider rode a gray mare of the same lineage named Delilah. Usually, when an ordinary horse approached a jump, Pierrette felt a bubble of nervous excitement in her chest, feeling the muscles beneath her prepare for that moment of possibility. On Tulpar, the moment of possibility arrived and passed before she even noticed any change in the horse, so that the bubble of excitement came later, when they were in the air, and her brain screeched that they were too high, too fast, that they would fall to the ground and crumple and the beautiful creature would be injured. But then they landed lightly, as if the horse were walking rather than galloping at breakneck speed.

The horses were not supernatural, despite Anne's nickname. Anne was convinced that their skeletons were as different from Arabians as Arabians were from other horses; they did have short, strong backs, and long legs. Everything about riding Tulpar was a little different, from where the saddle rested, to the angle of the reins.

After the jumps, she galloped him around the meadow. It was so smooth, once he got up to speed, that she felt she could balance a cup of water on her head and not spill a drop. She still thought like a performer.

Pierrette had to begrudgingly give credit to the Templars for bringing these horses into the modern world, and not only because she loved them as a rider. The other transportation projects that obsessed the Templars were mechanical, such as steamships, locomotives. But horses could go where railway lines and ships could not and these resurrected horses were faster and more practical than the other methods for solo travelers. Velocipedes had their limitations, and though some enthusiasts drove personal steam-driven vehicles, they were slow, smoky, and unreliable. Maybe one day that would change, but until then, horses filled the streets of every city, and fast horses meant that Templars could always get away from Assassins on their trail or reach a destination and carry out a mission before the Assassins could catch them.

She had her suspicions about the way the Russian authorities had caught up to the assassins of the tsar, which Simeon had described as seemingly impossible.

Pierrette could believe these horses could do the impossible. They showed no signs of tiredness when she returned them to the paddock. As she finished walking Tulpar, she glanced to the fence and saw George standing there, watching them. Before she even dismounted, Pierrette caught his expression. Whenever she braced herself for bad news, her first thought was that Simeon had been killed. Why it should be him, rather than anyone else, she couldn't say. Ariel and the Robinsons were her family too, in a different way. But Simeon was her teacher, and her dearest friend.

In his last letter, from Russia, he wrote that the Brotherhood wasn't sharing information with him. "Not that I blame them," he wrote. "But you can be sure I will have no more conversations with Templars longer than it takes for them to say their final words."

She told Spider to remove the tack and turn out the horses in the paddock to drink and roam, while she pulled off her gloves and shook George's hand in greeting.

"Even your descriptions didn't prepare me for those horses," George said. He was dressed for traveling, holding a valise.

"They have to be seen to be believed," Pierrette said. "Will you come with me into the barn? I have a water flask there. And you can tell me as we go what the terrible news is."

He paused. "Terrible news?"

"You look worried."

"I know you have enough to occupy you here, Pierrette, and so I have not asked you to take on any assignments."

"I'm still a member of the Brotherhood," she said. "So is Simeon, for that matter. He thinks nobody trusts him anymore."

"Nobody does," George said bluntly. "I'm surprised you do. His judgment with that affair–"

"She had *defected*," Pierrette said, as vehemently defensive of Simeon when others criticized him as she was critical of him in her own thoughts. "She had come to our side. And she was not the first Templar to do so. We all agreed with that assessment."

"And yet you never trusted her."

She snorted. "She once had me shackled and beaten. I think it is fair to say that I had no desire to have a cup of tea with her. But I trusted Simeon, and I still do."

They came into a barn, a small building with stalls below, a litter of piglets in one corner, and a hayloft above. Pierrette drank deeply and hoped the horses were doing the same. It had been a long ride.

"That is your choice," George said. "But the fact remains that the Assassins in Zurich had to hurriedly relocate, moving Irene Egli out of her family home, and that at least one Assassin in France found a gang of Templars waiting for him when he carried out a planned assassination. He barely escaped with his life, no thanks to that treacherous countess."

George was right, of course. The fact that Konstanze hadn't been able to do more damage was largely thanks to the fact that the Brotherhood tended to be decentralized, with information shared as needed. She never had access to everyone's plans, only what was talked about in her presence. Even so, Pierrette wondered sometimes why Konstanze hadn't done even more with the information she did have. A twisted remnant of whatever feeling she'd had for Simeon? Or was the countess simply obsessed with her own projects? Pierrette had never felt entirely confident that the countess hadn't made a copy of Ada's notebook, and Simeon had reported that the countess's friend had referred to plans, notes, and dreams.

Pierrette sighed, feeling exhausted, in more ways than one.

George, seeing her expression, stopped his rant and spoke more gently. "Anyway, that's not what I wanted to ask you about. I've got a job that needs doing in London, and I'm short-handed for it."

She was puzzled. "What about all the recruiting Jacob Frye has done? I thought London was awash in Assassins now."

"And I'll need all of them, in different places. But for this particular role, I want someone whose skills I know and trust. Someone who's an excellent rider."

She sat on a bench just inside the barn door and gestured for him to sit beside her. "All right, you've intrigued me. What do you need me to do?"

"We have reason to believe there's a plot on Queen Victoria's life. What I–"

"No," Pierrette said firmly.

George looked astonished. "No?"

"I refuse. I want nothing to do with it. George, I helped to save Empress Eugenie twice, three times if you count the time I kept Simeon company, and all she's done with the life she was granted is encourage her husband to rule with an iron glove, and go to war against Prussia, a war that resulted in the city of my birth being starved and bombarded. And now she's here in England, living at the seaside, last I heard. Must be lovely. I'm an Assassin, not a bodyguard. I'm not risking my life for these people. No more."

"It's not that simple, Pierrette."

"It's very simple. I serve the ruled, not the rulers."

"The ruled will be the ones to suffer," George said, with more passion than she'd ever heard from him. "Look at Russia. The assassination of the tsar seemed like a blow for freedom, but it didn't change the system. It just gave the new tsar an excuse to stop all reforms, and then there were those damned mobs in Kiev and Warsaw because hatemongers seized the chance to spread the lie that Jews were behind the assassination. I hear the new tsar is considering passing a law restricting Jewish people from owning homes or being educated. It is the ruled who bear the brunt of our decisions–"

"But we can't second-guess these things, George. We can't see the future, and it's dangerous to manipulate it."

"What do you think we do, every time we slide a Hidden Blade into someone's body? We are always manipulating the future. We are always serving the light, and if our actions bring greater darkness, it doesn't matter what our intentions were. We can't act without looking at the evidence before us. We may not see the future, but we can choose to see the present."

Pierrette took a moment to think. A mouse moved somewhere in the loft overhead.

She asked, "And what do you see, then, when you look at Queen Victoria? The great imperialist?"

"An imperialist she may be, but she's worked with the Fryes and with Henry, don't forget."

"You sound like a bureaucrat, George," she said, with a sigh. "You truly believe the world is better off with her in it?"

"Let's say I believe the world could be much worse if she dies tomorrow at the hands of the Templars."

George should have led with that. She did enjoy inconveniencing Templars.

"They've tried to do away with her before," George continued. "I don't know what their game is now, but I suspect they've been working in asylums again, trying to turn the inmates into puppets who can be made to kill, and who will take the blame with no connection to the Order. There's a man who was recently released from an asylum, and one doctor who treated him has Templar connections. He's written a letter to his sister, saying he's going to kill the queen tomorrow."

"Seems like a good day for Her Majesty to stay in a guarded room, then."

"She's stubborn."

Pierrette, who was also stubborn, took this as answer enough. "All right. So are we taking out the man with the gun, then?"

"If we can find him. I have someone on that. But if that fails, I want people near the queen at all times. You'll be in Windsor. And you'll need to wear this." He opened the valise and lifted out a pile of folded clothing in black and white, and a black cap with a silver band.

"I'm regretting this already," Pierrette said.

CHAPTER TWENTY-EIGHT

The white pants and black velvet jacket fitted her well, and with her hair tucked under the black cap, she supposed she wouldn't draw many looks. All eyes would be on the queen in her carriage, anyway, not the person riding postillion. It was a carriage without a driver or coachman, hooked directly up to two horses. Pierrette took her position on the left-most of the two sedate grays. The horse seemed unbothered by her presence, and she silently apologized to him in advance for anything rash she might have to do. The first time she'd saved a monarch, she'd ridden a horse up a construction ramp during a bombing. This time, she hoped that the new Enfield revolver at her side would be all that was necessary. She would have liked one of her own guns, but George said this one would be inconspicuous.

The carriage was waiting at Windsor Royal Station, a short drive from the castle. When the train arrived, the queen would walk a few steps from train to enclosed carriage – that would be the moment of greatest danger, even though the crowd was kept outside the covered yard, where the carriage stood. Riding on the open seat at the back of the carriage were two footmen; they were not Assassins, but George said they passed inspection.

There was another gray horse carrying an outrider in the same black and white livery, a few yards ahead of the carriage horses.

A small crowd had already gathered outside the covered yard, although George had tried to keep the queen's movements secret. Perhaps three dozen people. Pierrette scanned them for the signs of someone planning to kill. A woman with spectacles. Two girls, holding flowers. A man in a battered hat. Two students with umbrellas. Something caught her eye... something wasn't right. But she couldn't pin down what it was.

She forced herself to relax, to start fresh. But then...

The horse in front of her: the angle of the tail, the markings. It was not just any gray. It was *Delilah*.

And the rider on her back was Spider.

Pierrette contained her reaction, but the horse felt her stiffen. An excellent beast. But an ordinary one, unlike the unbelievable creature in front of him. What was Spider thinking? Surely Anne, who was as eager as the Assassins were to keep the Pegasi secret, would not have allowed him to take Delilah here. And even if she could be induced to make such an extraordinary decision, she'd never do so without talking to Pierrette. He'd stolen that mare, and put her in danger.

He'd put *himself* in danger, for that matter. Spider had just turned fourteen. He was not trained for this, even on an ordinary day. And today might be an extraordinary day.

She felt the approach of the train before she heard it, and her mount felt it too. His ears twitched, and he changed the angle of his neck a little, as though he knew he was about to start his work. Pierrette did not relish the possibility of shooting in the midst of a crowd, but at this range, the likelihood of the shot going awry was small. This was a reason to use a blade.

Her gaze swept up onto the rooftop of the station outside. Up to the rafters inside the covered yard. Nothing and nobody.

The train stopped behind the carriage and to the left, inside the covered yard and cut off from the crowd. Pierrette kept her head steady, trying to stay in character, while her eyes followed the small, black-clad woman as she was helped off the train. Just a few steps to the carriage, and then she would be behind whatever protection the door and window offered. Most royal carriages were reinforced. That hadn't saved the tsar in the end, but others were injured that day too, including a fourteen year-old delivery boy.

The same age as Spider.

God, she would give him a tongue-lashing for this.

The queen was almost at the carriage. If there was a gunman inside the covered yard, he'd have shot already. So they were on to the next phase: the drive from here to the castle door. Six minutes, most of it inside the castle precinct. A few minutes of gawkers on the pavement and checking the rooftops. If Spider had truly wanted to help, she could have used him up there, to watch and whistle if he saw anything. It would have been far safer and would not have involved horse theft from their friend and host.

Not that she'd considered asking him to do anything at all. She hadn't even told him where she was going today. He must have finished sooner than she realized with the horses yesterday and been in the barn listening to her conversation with George. Her face burned. The troupe had not raised him to be a sneak.

Some part of her objected to calling this behavior as stealth for an Assassin and sneaking for a boy – nearly a man – as unfair, but she told that part of her to stay quiet.

Behind her, the carriage door clicked shut. There was a hum of excitement from the waiting crowd. She told the horse to walk, and it and its fellow obeyed, lifting their legs like the royal horses they were. They rolled out of the covered yard, into the street. Everyone in the crowd craned their neck, excitedly.

Except for the man in the battered hat.

She reached for her gun as he took his out from behind his jacket and aimed straight at the carriage.

She aimed from her hip. It would be a matter of inches – he was behind the woman in spectacles and a man in a top hat. The man and woman in front of him suddenly saw his outstretched arm between them, and the gun in it.

Someone shouted. People reached for him, but he stepped once, twice, closer to the carriage, and into the open.

She tightened her finger on the trigger.

Delilah reared, twisted to her left, and leaped.

A shot rang out.

It seemed impossible she would clear the crowd, but Delilah was an impossible horse. She went over all their heads, then stopped short at the brick wall of the station. Everyone fell to their knees, their arms over their heads. Even the gunman.

The gunman was knocked down by Delilah, stunned. Other young men tackled him, holding him down. The gun was still in his hand.

Pierrette urged the carriage horses onward. Around the corner, and up to the castle walls, past alarmed onlookers, she stopped and opened the carriage door before the footman.

She had never seen the queen in person, but she'd seen that face on plates, dishtowels, and in the newspaper, often enough. Victoria was now in her sixties, but she looked younger, peering out the window with a puzzled smile.

"What was that?" Queen Victoria asked. "Did a train engine backfire? I hope it didn't frighten the horses too badly."

Then the queen's expression shifted as she saw Pierrette: a woman, and a stranger.

Pierrette ducked out of the way and let the footmen explain. She gritted her teeth through the ten minutes it took to deliver the carriage and then run back down the street, ignoring the shouts of her supposed colleagues. Back to Spider.

When she got to the street, the crowd had grown. Some bobbies had the gunman, and the onlookers gossiped and congratulated the students who'd tackled him.

Spider and Delilah were nowhere to be found.

The first thing Pierrette did when she got back to Crabbet Farm was to use Anne's new Gower-Bell telephone, the first time Pierrette had ever used such a thing. It was a strange contraption, a wooden box the size of a book, stuck on the wall, with two tubes that one stuck to the ears, and a porcelain mouthpiece for speaking into. She told George everything that had happened.

Then she went to the paddock, where she found Spider sitting on a haystack. He leaned back, his arms crossed, his expression smug under his flat cap.

"Where's Delilah?" she demanded.

"Roaming happily. Not a scratch on her. Nor me. But I thought it best to clear out—"

"Oh, you thought it best, did you? Very circumspect after the fact. Never mind that three dozen people saw one of the queen's horses leap from a standing start straight over their heads towards a man with a gun. George will keep it out of the papers, but we can't stop people from talking."

The smugness was replaced with a taut scowl. "We. Who are *we*?"

"I suppose you must have eavesdropped on George telling me about the mission in the barn, when you were pretending to put the horses away."

He protested, "I wasn't eavesdropping. I overheard, that's all. I just want to know…"

"You truly think you can ask me questions, after spying on me, endangering the mission, and the life of the bloody Queen of England—"

"I *saved* the bloody Queen of England!"

"I had it in hand, Spider. I didn't ask for your help."

"Did *you* wait to be asked, that time you stole a horse and rode it into danger to save the emperor and empress?"

It was her turn to scowl. "That wasn't the same. For one thing, I was older. The horse in question was an entirely ordinary one, whose rider was dead by that point. I didn't *plan* it—"

Why was she arguing? There was nothing to persuade him about. He had done wrong, and he knew it. Or perhaps he didn't know it, which was worse.

She pulled out her watch. "I'm due at the house for dinner with Lady Anne. I'm going to tell her about the horse, because she has a right to know, and because she needs to be prepared for any repercussions. Tomorrow, you'll come with me to see her, and you will apologize."

That was the last thing she said to Spider before he went missing.

Four months later, Pierrette leaned on the paddock fence, staring out at Tulpar as he grazed. She didn't want to be here. It reminded her of Spider. She wanted to be back out looking for him, in the docks of Southampton or Liverpool, or the streets of Glasgow or Manchester.

"You seem exhausted," said Gamal, walking up behind her.

Pierrette straightened and put on a smile. Gamal was the reason she'd come back to Crabbet Farm in the first place. He and Safiya had traveled to England to consult with the British Assassins about the possibility of war between their countries. The British fleet was already lying off the coast of Egypt. Communications could soon become difficult.

"Do you remember what I said about the Set animal, that day in the cave?" Gamal asked, staring at Tulpar.

Pierrette suppressed a shudder. She remembered their conversations from the cave tunnels as if from a dream.

She looked at Gamal, gray at the temples now, and thicker about the waist. Safiya walked up to them, slowly, looking out at the green woods with that wondrous insight of hers. Pierrette had missed them. And perhaps it had been long enough since that terrible painted room, now, that the bruise was not too sore.

"I remember you said... let's see. You said that the Set animal might not represent anything real."

"Rather that it might not *look* like something real, but it might symbolize the truth of something real, as the Egyptians of that time saw it. I wonder whether it might have been what you call the Pegasi. And speaking of Pegasus, I wonder whether the representation of horses with wings in other cultures comes from the same lineage. A way of saying 'the horses that are not like other horses.'"

"They certainly are that," Pierrette said.

"Are they guarded well?" Safiya asked.

"George had Assassins in the woods here for weeks after that business with the queen, but the Templars don't seem to have traced the rumors here, from what we can tell."

"Yes," Safiya said. "He told us that the plot against Victoria doesn't seem to have been a Templar one after all. Just a disturbed man with a gun. Which does rather make me wonder why the Brotherhood is so eager to save an imperialist."

There had been reasons to believe the Templar association, including the Templar doctor who might have treated that disturbed man. Templars had arranged assassinations before that ended up hurting innocent people. But she was too tired to argue, and she didn't entirely disagree. She said, "George was concerned about the consequences. It's hard to know what would result from such an assassination."

"Yes," Safiya said. "It's always hard to know."

The queen was alive, but Spider was lost, and privately, Pierrette felt it was a bad trade, though she didn't know how to start talking about it. She felt choked by words she hadn't yet formed in her own mind. An image came to her of Anne's brother, Ada's son Byron, who had gone out to sea as a boy of Spider's age. How damaged he had been when he came home.

If Tillie were alive, she would never stop looking for her son. But Tillie was not alive, so it was Pierrette who would never stop. She had seen Gamal and Safiya; she had shown them the horses. Tomorrow she would take another train. Glasgow, perhaps. Possibly Calais.

They watched the horses in silence for a while, then went back to the house, where Anne was reading a telegram. It brought news that the British fleet was bombarding Alexandria.

CHAPTER TWENTY-NINE

Simeon stood at the top of a hill in Paris, looking down several sets of stairs onto a narrow cobblestone street. The Passage Julien Lacroix was the heart of Belleville, lined with three-story tenements, their balconies hung with washing stiff from the cold. On the cobblestones below were children with hoops and old men playing dice. On the rooftops were his enemies.

He was getting used to never having the element of surprise. These last few years, it felt almost impossible for any Assassin to approach a target with stealth. The Templars seemed to know where they were going and would be waiting for them when they arrived. Just like the day the tsar was assassinated, with the mysterious figure waving him away from danger. The assassins had killed the tsar anyway, but in a way that killed and wounded innocent people, and that resulted in the executions of the conspirators – including Nikolai Rysakov, the young man Simeon had gone there to save.

Simeon knew well enough that several of the Paris Assassins believed he was the reason behind the Templar's uncanny ability to predict their movements – that he was a mole, feeding information to their enemies. He didn't mind taking the blame, as he was sure that Konstanze's study of the Assassin philosophy had helped her develop ways of predicting what they'd do next. And the Templar mastery of transportation helped make sure they could move quickly in response.

That was why Simeon had chosen this day to hunt the thug known only as Centime, one of the worst gang leaders in Belleville. There was a battle between the Terrors, Centime's gang, and a rival gang, down in Père Lachaise Cemetery. Centime himself, who was never on the scene for street fights, would be relatively unprotected. Or so it should have been. But Simeon wasn't surprised to see the shadows up on the rooftops. A few blocks from here, the urban rail line called the Petite Ceinture poked its head up above ground before diving back under; it was easy for the Templars to get a fresh batch of thugs into position here.

Fifteen years ago, this part of Paris had been staunchly pro-Commune; the barricades had lasted here until the end. But the Templars had been building quietly, almost invisibly. Taking a page from how Crawford Starrick had taken over London, they'd started recruiting street gangs. They now had control over Belleville. Centime was one of their lackeys, and Simeon had been tasked with killing him.

This was the sort of assignment he got now, from Michel, who still supported him but seemed unwilling to give him anything really important to do – or any information that would compromise the Brotherhood if the Templars learned about it. Never mind that Simeon had sworn that the next time he saw Konstanze, he would stain a calling card with her blood.

He was not privy to the meetings of the Paris Council, or to the intelligence that came in.

Henri Escoffier, bless him, had done one last thing for Simeon before he'd gone home to Mauritius to spend his final years in peace, although those final years showed no signs of ending soon. Like Amira, who was now a crotchety old lady with a grand house on the outskirts of Cairo still holding literary salons and handing out advice, Henri had defied the odds.

Two years ago, Henri had gone to a months-long conference in Berlin, at which the representatives of fourteen empires carved up Africa among them. Simeon had felt sure Konstanze would be in Berlin for that, given her interest in control over African territory and her hunger for Pieces of Eden. But Henri, who was the best Assassin in the world when it came to finding people, could not find her there.

Maybe she was dead. Or she'd found new and better ways to hide.

At least this thug Centime would not be able to hide from him. Truth be told, Simeon didn't mind that his role in the Brotherhood now was to take petty criminals out of the world. It was simple, clean and satisfying. He no longer worried about the fact that he enjoyed killing them. He was heartily sick of his own nobility and caution. Let it all burn.

And he was not interested in hiding in plain sight. The tenets of his creed were known to his enemies, and they tried to use them against him. Centime was in the habit of drinking and scheming in a one-story tavern near the bottom of Julien Lacroix Street. The tavern had only one entrance, and the alley in front of it had caved in years ago because of an old gypsum mine underneath it. That instability meant there were no new or tall buildings around, either. It was impossible to approach the tavern by any means other than an improvised wood-plank walkway over the caved-in alley, like a drawbridge to a castle.

If there was no use in stealth, Simeon would walk down the middle of the steps, his long coat unbuttoned, his gun in his hand. The children and their mothers saw the gun and scattered, doors and windows closing.

Up on one of the tallest buildings, a shadow moved, and Simeon shot it. He whistled.

> *Farewell and adieu to you, Spanish ladies,*
> *Farewell and adieu to you, ladies of Spain;*
> *For we've received orders for to sail for old England,*
> *But we hope in a short time to see you again.*

When he reached the alley leading off the street, he looked up. A back stairway, made of rusted iron that was swaying despite the air being so still, heavy with the smell of snow that hadn't yet fallen.

They wouldn't hesitate to kill him. Here and now, he was a street thug like any other. Both orders could claim they had nothing to do with anything that happened here today, and Michel – wise, circumspect Michel, who wore spectacles now that seemed to match the lines around his eyes – wouldn't be forced into open war with the new generation of Templars who had moved into Paris, or sprung up from the old guard, most of whom had returned after the Franco-Prussian war.

The only thing protecting Simeon now was his own hand, his own eyes. Action and consequence.

Simeon pulled two smoke bombs out of the satchel on his hip, under his coat. One up and to the right, and one up and to the left. A cloud of smoke, and two muffled yells. His world was suddenly overcast. As he came to the yawning hole in the ground and the plank bridge leading to a small red door, he called out.

"Centime!"

No response.

Simeon shot into the air.

"Centime, come out, you bastard, or I'll set the tavern on fire."

The door creaked open to admit a white handkerchief, and then behind it a mustachioed man who was not Centime.

"He's not here," the man said. "There's nothing for you here now."

Simeon moved quickly, across the plank bridge in three steps, and grabbed the man by the throat. The handkerchief of surrender fluttered down onto the frozen mud. "When did he leave?"

It was death for the man to betray Centime, and death for him not to. Simeon saw the calculations in the man's eyes and then saw those eyes move deliberately to look southward.

He let the man go.

Centime had been there recently, and gone southward.

Back out into Julien Lacroix Street, with the smell from his smoke bombs still settling over him. He could see a church steeple ahead; a good place to climb up and get the lay of the land, if he needed to. But that would take time, and Centime had a head start already.

The scattering was still happening; people were ducking

into side streets, shuttering their windows. The cobblestones in front of him were empty. There was no one – no. That was wrong. There was someone. He was aware of it by instinct first, and he stopped for a moment to let his other senses catch up.

Just beside a lamppost up ahead was one of the iron structures called a *pissotierre,* or sometimes, a *vespasienne.* Public urinals. So common in Paris, he hardly noticed them. This one had curving iron privacy screens on either side of the central column, and at the bottom of one of them were two booted feet.

Simeon strode over and slipped into the urinal opposite. How funny that his enemy should try to hide in plain sight this way. It almost worked, too. What a terrible place to die. It smelled awful.

"You can choose to go left or you can choose to go right," Simeon said. "Decide quickly, though, because I'm going to shoot your feet if you don't."

He had never heard Centime's voice. He'd only seen a photograph of him. A tall, thin man, with a strong jaw and a sharp eye. About ten years younger than Simeon. It seemed everyone was ten years younger that Simeon now.

The voice attempted to sound calm. "I don't care about the Templars, monsieur. Just another gang, and these things change. People change. You want me to join your crew, I can bring a hundred fighters and some good side business. I can start new businesses for you too. I'm a fast learner."

Simeon pulled a long dagger out of his satchel, silently. Left or right?

"Nobody can change," he said.

He went right and grabbed the man's coat.

"And I'm not anyone's teacher."

Simeon stabbed Centime in the heart.

Paris was rebuilding again, polishing itself to a shine. On the Champ de Mars, a monumental iron tower was under construction, and nearby, vast palaces were going up to showcase the arts and sciences. The Exposition Universelle would even include a fake "Street of Cairo", with Egyptians in costume. Simeon had no desire to see such a thing, but he did envy the city its ability to shine on command.

Simeon did not shine. He did what Michel asked of him, but Michel asked little of him. He spent time with the workers of Montmartre, helping the Communards returning from exile. Georges Clemenceau had started a newspaper, and Simeon would tell him what was happening that he ought to know about, from the latest engine designs to the latest science fiction novels.

One day in the early spring, Simeon heard gravel hit the window of his room in Montmartre. He approached from the side, cautiously, but it was only Fabrice Sabourin, grinning up at him. He had short hair now and was stronger and better fed than he'd once been. The old traces of grief were invisible, although Simeon knew that the years he had been in Brussels and Switzerland were years that Fabrice, in Paris, had wandered in a wilderness of his own. He still couldn't believe time had marched them both into 1889. Michel had kept a patient eye on him. And now, Fabrice was grinning up at him as though they were not two men who had lost themselves along the way.

"Come, take a walk with me!"

It was a cold day, and Simeon pulled his coat tight and cupped his gloved hands over his face as they strolled up toward the hill where the enormous new basilica was still, always, under construction. An apology to God for whatever sins had led to France's misfortunes.

"I hear Michel finally inducted you into the Brotherhood," Simeon said. "I always knew you would make a wonderful Assassin."

"I wasn't sure whether he had told you."

"He does tell me some things," Simeon said teasingly. Then he glanced to the side and saw that Fabrice's face was serious, that he was trying to determine how to respond. "Wait, is there something he hasn't told me? Is that why you're here?"

Fabrice looked uncomfortable. "Konstanze von Visler is in Paris."

Simeon stopped walking. "Where?" he demanded.

"We don't know exactly, but we had a reliable sighting of her at the Gare de l'Est. Her ironworking company is supplying some of the material for Gustav Eiffel's new tower, you know. So we've been wondering if she might make an appearance."

"The Gare de l'Est. Where did she go from there?"

"We don't need to know where she is, because we have a solid idea of where she will be. Some Templars have arranged a private viewing of the Gallery of Machines tonight."

The Gallery of Machines was a vast building, part of the Exposition complex, that would show off new inventions. Just the sort of thing Konstanze would love, and a private viewing would appeal to her.

"I didn't know that was ready yet," Simeon said.

"It isn't, but there are several machines there already, and that seems likely to be relevant to her interests, as I understand it."

Simeon thought furiously. It was indeed. It was too obvious, in fact. Too easy.

"Will there be Assassins waiting for her at this viewing?"

"Yes. I'll be one of them. We have orders to take her out. She's dangerous, Michel says."

"An understatement. She has to die. Immediately."

"Simeon, I don't think it's a good idea for you–"

"Oh, don't worry, I won't interfere," Simeon said, forcing a smile. "I understand why Michel didn't want me there. I'm a wild factor, aren't I? But I appreciate you telling me, Fabrice."

He was convinced that this was a trap, or a feint. Konstanze would not be where the Assassins expected her to be. He knew her too well.

He spent the next several hours talking to the cab drivers he knew at the Gare de l'Est, and to porters at the Grand Hotel, showing them the photograph from 1874 he had in his breast pocket. By the time Konstanze von Visler was expected to be at the Gallery of Machines, with the Assassins waiting for her, he was climbing the rails and columns of her hotel, about to break into her room.

Luckily, this section of the hotel was screened from the street by trees. The tall double casement windows were nearly as big as doors. Simeon pulled a thin saw blade out of his pocket and slid it between the two windows and lifted the latch. The window swung in quietly. He waited. If she was in the room, she knew he was here now. And he was vulnerable, clinging to the side of a hotel on a busy street, trees or no trees.

As swiftly and smoothly as possible, he slipped in, drawing his revolver as he landed. But the room seemed to be empty.

He strode over to the wardrobe and unlatched the door; only clothing inside.

The room was large, with four blue-upholstered chairs around a central table, and a four-poster bed off to one side. A yellow silk scarf lay on the back of one chair; he picked it up and put it to his lips. Her perfume. Guerlain's *Eau de Cologne Impériale*. And there was the glass-and-gold perfume bottle on the dressing table; half full. Her silver hairbrush.

The lock on the writing desk broke easily, but inside that was a purple upholstered document box, and this one wouldn't yield. No matter. He'd take it with him, after he killed her.

Footsteps in the corridor.

It could be a chambermaid. Damn it.

He lunged over to the wardrobe and got inside, pulling the door to a crack. With the document box under his right arm, he aimed the gun with his left.

Not a chambermaid. Whoever it was stood just inside the door as it swung open, and sniffed.

"Simeon?"

The voice of Fabrice Sabourin.

Simeon's heart slowed down, and he pushed the wardrobe open. "What the hell are you doing here?"

"Where is she?" Fabrice demanded.

"What do you mean?"

Fabrice shook his head. "I followed her down the hall – this is her room number – I saw her go into…"

Fabrice dashed back out into the corridor and tried the door of the room next door. Then he backed up and slammed into it, once, twice. It opened, and he ran into the room with Simeon on his heels.

It was a copy of the room Simeon was in, but this one had no signs of Konstanze in it: no silk scarf, no perfume. Just an open window, like the one Simeon had come through.

They ran to the window and saw her – or rather, a woman wearing a black asymmetrical hat and a smart blue dress – drop from the railing down to the street, where she half-stumbled into the arms of a young woman.

Simeon aimed.

"There's a burglar in my room," Konstanze cried excitedly, loudly, pointing upwards. "We must get help!"

Fabrice pulled Simeon back, hissing, "You'd hit either of them or neither of them, from this angle. Come on. We'll grab her."

Simeon broke away. "You go down the stairs. I'm going out the window."

"They're looking–"

"I don't care!"

Fabrice shook his head but ran out into the corridor.

Simeon threw the document case out, where it landed on the awning of a café below. Up onto the ledge of the window, then to the railing. He jumped from there to a tree branch, ignoring the scrapes on his hands and face, which brought him almost on top of Konstanze.

And thank God, the girl had run off somewhere. Getting help or just afraid, no doubt.

Konstanze looked up at him.

It was not Konstanze.

A younger woman, with sleek red hair and a pink nose, screamed when she saw him. But he had heard *her* voice. She'd been wearing that hat – that same dress – no, not quite the same. It couldn't be coincidence.

The redhead looked genuinely astonished and afraid. She might be a Templar accomplice, but she might as easily be a woman who worked in the area. Someone Konstanze had planned to use as a decoy, if her room had been discovered.

Fabrice burst out of the hotel door and looked at the redhead with the same astonishment.

At least Michel was excited about the document case. It was surprisingly heavy, and when they finally forced the lock open, they saw why: there was a wooden box inside, with a pattern of inlaid wood forming the Visler crest, the crossed flail and scythe, but without the Latin motto around it. There didn't seem to be any lid or opening.

"I think it's a puzzle box," Michel said, turning it over in his hands. They were at his desk in the gasworks, always the place he retreated to when things were uncertain. Simeon had told him he'd found the countess by asking around at train stations, which was not a lie, and kept Fabrice out of trouble, and spared Michel from having to decide whether to be angry at Simeon, or apologetic for not telling him his former lover was in Paris.

Fabrice asked, "What's a puzzle box?"

Mary came over, looking at them curiously. She and Michel had married in a small ceremony the year before, and she put her hand on his shoulder now.

"A toy or a trick," Mary said. "You have to press the right part of the box, or move things in a certain order, and then it will open. It might have more than one compartment."

Michel traced the wood with his fingertip. "The pattern looks like a Templar cross."

Mary shrugged. "Play with it. What's that writing around the side?"

He turned the box. "Looks like the alphabet. All in order."

"Is there a J or a W?"

Michel checked. "No! So... Latin, then?"

He found that each of the letters depressed slightly. They tried spelling out several phrases, passwords and puns.

Finally, Simeon said, "Try 'TRITICA REGIT PALEAS.'"

Mary looked sharply at him. "If that's something associated with the countess..."

He realized that despite all the information he'd shared, he'd never shown anyone else the letters with Konstanze's seal. Fabrice had seen it once, many years ago, and not long enough to remember the Latin words.

"It doesn't matter if it doesn't work," he said gruffly.

Michel pressed the letters.

The side of the box popped open, a little drawer with folded papers in it. Mary gave Simeon a congratulatory, or apologetic, clap on the shoulder.

Michel shuffled through the papers, written in Konstanze's handwriting, dark blue ink on pale blue paper. "There are numbers, lists, notes. I don't know. We'll have to study this. One of her many inventions, no doubt. Wait, here's a page with other handwriting, and a bit of ciphered writing."

He handed it to Mary, who took it back to her desk. Ten minutes later, she returned, her face pale.

Simeon took the paper from her and read in German:

My dear Konstanze, you have been so patient with all of us, so unshakable in your conviction that the Engine of History could be realized, and you are proven right in the end. It is an astonishing design. I have made few adjustments. My calculations suggest this tower will amplify the power in the Piece of Eden sufficiently to affect the furthest reaches of this continent. The Assassins will not even know that they are vanquished, but we will have the satisfaction of knowing. Final victory is at hand, if we are bold enough to seize it. I await news of the activation eagerly.

F

"Who's F?" Simeon asked, his voice unsteady.

"No idea," Michel said.

Mary handed him the other paper, the original she'd used for the decoding. "Turn it over," she whispered.

On the other side was a sketch of what was, unmistakably, Gustav Eiffel's tower, currently under construction on the Champ de Mars.

CHAPTER THIRTY

Ariel Fine died silently and suddenly at age sixty-eight, three hours after eating a Sunday roast beef dinner with Jim.

Pierrette happened to be in London at the time, modeling for a painter to help finance her continued search for Spider. Now that she was in her fifties, painters were no longer interested in her ability to hang off a trapeze (although she still could, thank you very much) or stand on the back of a moving horse. And she didn't know many painters anymore; Gabriel had died several years back, and she had lost touch with most of the others long before that.

But she eventually found a young man who was willing to pay her to portray an ancient prophetess. Ah well. She was used to wearing a hood.

Ariel had been living in London as well, as it was still early spring, and the troupe was not yet out on the road. Jim said their last words were about what the troupe would need at rehearsal the following day; Ariel had lived and breathed the circus for as long as Pierrette had known them, which was a long time.

All the same, she had never asked where they had grown up. It was, apparently, in a little village an easy half-day's drive from London, where there was a small, old church on a hill, and a yew tree over the grave where Ariel would spend eternity. Jim stood silently at that graveside for a long time, and Pierrette waited a little distance away. Hugh and Nell Robinson stood on either side of her, holding her hands. It was chilly, even for England in early March.

"There's none of us left in the Aurora troupe now who were there at the beginning," Nell said. "But the troupe still has shows booked. Leo would have liked that. His wife's name, in fresh paint."

"What will Jim do?" Pierrette asked.

"I expect he'll stay with the troupe. He'd hate to leave his horses. But it may be too painful. Grief is difficult to predict."

Pierrette turned from the figure by the grave, giving him privacy in these last moments. There was a scattering of daffodils on the hill. The world was terrible and lovely.

Then she saw another figure, at the door of the old stone church, looking up at the grave too. She hardly dared to believe it. She'd looked for Spider in every crowd in six countries, in pubs, train stations, and factories. She'd thought, *perhaps, maybe*, more than once. She'd always been wrong. This time, she knew immediately that she was right.

Letting go of the Robinsons' hands, she walked down the hill as fast as her good shoes would take her and wrapped her arms around him.

He didn't object, but he didn't move. She stepped back to study him.

Spider was now a man of twenty-one. Still skinny and

wiry, with the same floppy blond hair. Clean-shaven, hollow-cheeked. Bright blue eyes. He reminded her of Tillie, and he looked like a stranger.

"How did you know?" she whispered.

"I saw the notice in a newspaper. Was stuffing it into my boot at the time." He grinned briefly.

That's when she noticed the worn overcoat.

"You look like you've been living an honest life," she said. It was a phrase Leo Wallin used to say, whenever Pierrette would complain about having to wear old dresses and patched coats. Spider had never known his grandfather, the man who had taken Pierrette in when she had no one else. He had barely known his mother, and Pierrette bore the guilt of that. She should have trained Tillie more carefully. She should have been there.

Spider looked uncomfortable. "Not always so honest, I'm sorry to say."

"None of that matters now. You're here. God, I wish Ariel could have... well, Ariel would be glad to know you're safe. Come and have a meal with us. I'm buying."

He shuffled. "I only came to pay my respects. I don't ask anything from any of you."

"And I have no right to ask anything of you, but I will anyway. I'll ask you to come and raise a glass to Ariel's memory. I don't want to lose you again, Spider. I'm here. I'm not going anywhere."

He nodded, looking uncertain.

They were about to walk up toward their friends when a young Assassin Pierrette recognized approached them. Angelica was one of Jacob Frye's recruits, and not that young, really, but everyone seemed young to Pierrette these days. Evie had introduced her last year, when she and her brother were both in London on business.

Angelica nodded in greeting. "I'm sorry to disturb you, but I was asked to find you without delay, Miss Arnaud. You've had a telegram."

She passed it to Pierrette, who read:

> *K is here great danger come at once I need you*
> *S*

The letter swam in front of Pierrette's eyes. She couldn't ignore Simeon's summons, not even now. She'd heard little from him since his return to Paris, but Michel kept her apprised, describing Simeon as "all right" in every letter. Carrying on. But not doing well, not even now, more than a decade after that monstrous woman had betrayed him.

The monstrous woman that she wanted to kill with her bare hands.

No, she couldn't ignore this from Simeon. But if she left Spider again, vanishing from his life, would she ever get him back? He didn't seem much more than all right himself. His face was sad, and his clothes were rags.

What could she do? What was the right answer?

"Bad news?" Spider asked, cautiously.

"Urgent news. An old friend needs my help." She decided, set her jaw and looked him in the eye, noting she had to look up to do it, now. "Spider, do you have anything keeping you in England, for the next little while? A job, a sweetheart?"

"Nothing, I'm sorry to say."

"Good. What I mean is that I must go to Paris, and I'd like you come with me. I may be busy while I'm there, but I'll get you a comfortable room of your own and some money for food and you can spend your days as you like. But every moment I can, I'll join you. We'll go to Notre Dame and the Pantheon and I'll show you the theatres where I used to perform with your mother when she was a child. I want us to get to know each other, and I don't want any more time to pass before we do."

He listened to all this with a slow smile.

"Your business in Paris. Is this another mission to save someone's life through daring feats?"

He'd been so eager to help with the rescue of Queen Victoria. And he'd done it. And she'd been so angry that she wanted to keep him out of her work. That was why he'd left; that was why she'd lost him.

Pierrette wasn't sure what to say. Angelica looked at her feet, politely.

Finally, Pierrette said, "There are many things I couldn't tell you when you were a child. Things I can't tell you even now. I should have explained that better, back then."

He held up a hand. "I was a child. But one thing hasn't changed. I want to learn from you, and not just tricks. I want to use what I learn to protect my friends and make a difference in the world. If you can't tell me anything about it, I understand. But I'd like to help, in any way I can. To start to repay some of what I owe."

He looked up the hill, toward the grave he had not approached.

She felt the tears that had been threatening throughout

the service for Ariel come again to the fore, and she blinked them away. "You owe me nothing, and I can't ask you to come without warning you it may be dangerous. But I would be grateful for your company. And your help."

CHAPTER THIRTY-ONE

Pierrette walked up a street in Montmartre in late afternoon, a small suitcase in her hand and Spider at her side. She had the address of the safe house, but there was no doubt about which one it was. Simeon stood in front of the door, his hands in his pockets, waiting.

Then he turned, and saw her, and relief washed over his face.

She put the suitcase down, ran to him and put her arms around him. It surprised her as much as him, but just seeing him, she could sense all the pain he never talked about, the pain he thought he had to carry alone.

"Who's the stranger?" he asked, once she'd released him.

"Spider. Tillie Wallin's son. He's circus-trained, good in a tight spot, and I trust him. Now, tell me, where is the monster and how quickly can I kill her?"

He snorted with a little half-smile. "At the moment, I'm not sure, but she's in Paris. I managed to take some papers out of her hotel room." The half-smile vanished as he continued, "There are drawings and notes that suggest the Eiffel Tower – you know, the big metal thing they're building for the Exhibition – is a Templar machine of some kind. This Engine of History we keep hearing about. We have no idea what it will do, but we believe it's a weapon, possibly with a Piece of Eden to power it. So, we're destroying it."

"When?"

"Tonight."

She whistled. "No time to waste, then. Tell me what you need me to do."

He hesitated. "There's something else you should know."

"What is it? What's so terrible?"

"The other papers in the notebook, the calculations and tables. Once I got a good look at them, I recognized them. Do you remember the paper I tore out of Ada's notebook, all those years ago? The one I sent you?"

She didn't like where this was heading. The paper was folded into a tiny square in the locket around her neck, where she always kept it. A reminder of her worst mistakes, and not to make them again.

She opened the paper, all creased and yellow. Three columns of numbers that meant nothing to her.

Simeon winced. Then he pulled a stack of papers out of his pocket, flipped through them, and showed one to her.

It was the same three columns, and many of the same numbers. Some of the notations around it were different, but there was no doubt that one was inspired by the other.

"That snake! She made a copy before she let you burn it. I knew it was too good to be true."

"And I didn't."

"Come on," she said, taking him by the arm. "We're not

going to give her another chance to defile Ada's memory. It ends tonight."

Michel was already in the sitting room of the safe house, with Mary Fitzpatrick and Fabrice Sabourin. Spider went up to the bedroom, and Simeon took the chance to pull Pierrette aside in the hallway, next to a telephone box.

"Just keep that young bloke out of the way, will you?" Simeon said. "We don't want any casualties or distractions."

"He's here to help," Pierrette objected. "He may not be an Assassin, but this is hardly standard Assassin work, is it? Don't you remember the last time my circus friends got you out of a jam?"

Simeon seemed to have no answer to that. Later, Michel agreed to her logic too, saying they could use another pair of hands. So she brought Spider into the sitting room and introduced him briefly. Michel and Mary asked him a few questions, shook his hand, then returned to their maps and plans, plotting the destruction of the Eiffel Tower.

Michel had started out absolutely set against it, he explained. The repercussions could be terrible, for the Brotherhood, for the government of France, for the world. Even if it didn't lead to the discovery of the Brotherhood, it would be blamed on anarchists or communists or, as had happened in Russia, on Jewish people. It was the opposite of working in the darkness, Michel said. And he was right.

But the likelihood that Konstanze von Visler was in possession of some unknown Piece of Eden was high, given her absence from Europe and her infatuation with the objects. Her company was definitely involved with the construction of the tower, albeit in a hidden fashion, at arm's length. The countess had been working on something called the Engine of History, some terrible weapon that would give the Templars the ultimate control they craved. And here was an unprecedented structure going up in the middle of Paris.

Michel couldn't risk destroying the tower, yet he also couldn't risk taking the time to investigate further. While Simeon had waited for Pierrette to arrive, Michel consulted councils in several cities and others; Simeon didn't know who, exactly. And then Michel told Simeon that he should assemble a team and go ahead, but with a few stipulations: no innocents must be harmed. There must be nothing to link the explosion to the Brotherhood, and in fact, an invented monarchist would leave a confession as his suicide note; he would be angry about the Exhibition celebrating the centenary of the storming of the Bastille. Michel hoped this false trail would protect the Brotherhood and prevent authoritarian state backlash.

And despite Simeon's grumbling, he had to admit that Spider was smart, willing and eager. He noticed things, like the fact that Fabrice seemed bothered by the banging of a shutter in another room, which Spider went to tie down. It was his idea to have the Assassins pose as workmen on the construction site, because, as he put it, nobody pays attention to workers' faces. Pierrette suspected he had been earning his living as a thief, in the years since he'd run away from Crabbet Farm. But who was an Assassin to judge? If he'd had to make difficult choices, it was because he hadn't had the mentor he deserved.

Michel had some allies who helped him make the calculations to bring down the tower. Nothing like it had ever been built; the city had been full of arguments about whether the wind would knock it down. The plan was to weaken all four legs enough that the tower would crumple. If long pieces of it fell, the only structures close enough to be damaged were the exhibition galleries, which were not yet open, and should be empty of workers at night.

The tower site would be empty in the late evening. Michel and Fabrice, pretending to be workmen, would lay the wire. If a guard asked why they were working after dark, they'd start complaining about Monsieur Eiffel's last-minute demands, about some demonstration the following day that they hadn't been told about in time. There were many meters and devices being installed, to demonstrate the tower's usefulness to the public, so they hoped the guards would be persuaded. If not, they would dispatch the guards as quietly as possible.

A few hours later, at two in the morning when even Paris was relatively quiet, Simeon would attach four charges of dynamite and the latest blasting cap design, one to each leg of the tower, near the surface and attached to the detonation wires. The tower itself would not be illuminated until inauguration day, so it should be easy to find patches of darkness away from any streetlights, and avoid the guards. He would then go to the hiding place in the nearby streets where, at three o'clock, Fabrice and Mary would each operate one blasting machine. These were metal boxes with a T-shaped handle on top, each of which would detonate two of the charges.

It had all come a long way from the first stick of dynamite Pierrette had ever seen, in that cane-bomb in Cairo.

The unpredictable factor in their plan was the Templars, who would surely keep an eye on the tower, perhaps even at two o'clock in the morning. So while Simeon, Fabrice and

Mary were doing their work, Pierrette and Spider would roam the area. Pierrette's task was to remove any Templar obstacles, while Spider would shoo any civilians away. He was also told to create a diversion if he saw a policeman, something he cheerfully said he had a lot of practice doing.

During the time they spent talking and making plans, the sun set. After a quick meal, Fabrice and Michel went off to take care of laying the wires. Mary went to get the dynamite from Jean-Baptiste Barbeau, their explosives expert. Spider went up to have a rest, probably sensing that Pierrette and Simeon were overdue a private chat.

It was their first meeting in years. She had assured him by letter that nobody could fault him for his decisions with Konstanze, that he had consulted with the Brotherhood and always done what seemed best to him. But she never said that she forgave him. And she wasn't sure she had that in her to say. She had been suspicious all along. She had kept that damn notebook sewn into her clothing for years, literally carried the weight of it to keep it safe. She had done the hard work to prove to Simeon that she deserved a chance to be taught the history and philosophy of the Assassins.

And Konstanze had proven nothing, had been given the benefit of faith, merely because the possibility of having such a powerful defector on side had dazzled them all. And because Simeon had fallen in love. Which was not something Pierrette had ever done as it held little interest for her. She loved her friends and her family, and her few brief affairs had been distractions at best.

But she knew Simeon had loved Konstanze, probably from

the moment they met, though he wouldn't have admitted it even to himself. She knew that for a part of his life, he had found the sublime connection and purpose he'd always sought. And that woman had plunged a knife into his heart.

Pierrette sat next to Simeon on the settee, tucked up her legs beneath her, an old habit. These days, she felt a twinge in her hip when she sat with her feet on the ground. Simeon was showing his age, too; his stubbly beard was gray and his hair a little thin at the forehead.

"We ought to get a medal for surviving this long," she said. "The Old Assassins Award."

He winced, and she realized he was thinking of the Assassins of the generation before them, the ones he felt he'd let down. Henri Escoffier and Irene Egli, having to move their headquarters in the middle of the night. "They might want to wait one more day before casting the trophy."

"Don't you think we'll pull it off?"

He shrugged. "If we do, that only disrupts their plans. And it leaves one very dangerous loose end."

"We'll find her together, Simeon. You and me. We both have reasons to add her bloodstain to our collections. I'm here now, and I'm not going anywhere until this is finished."

He nodded. "I'm glad you came. We always have been better together."

She pulled a handkerchief out of her pocket; it had the initials K.V. embroidered on it in white thread. "Here. Carry this. For luck."

Simeon went off to meet Mary at the arranged time outside his flat, where he'd take charge of the dynamite. The house was quiet, like the calm before the storm. Pierrette would have to wake Spider soon so they could take up their positions as lookouts.

Pierrette had barely had a chance to show Spider to the Robinsons and Jim before bundling him off to Paris for reasons she didn't explain, and she wasn't sure whether any of them would think to tell Anne.

The safe house had a telephone, a big wooden box on the wall with two bells, a receiver and a speaking tube. Michel had put it in a month ago, and other than the occasional test, they hadn't had a reason to use it.

There was international service between France and England now, and after a couple of attempts, Pierrette contacted the butler, and then Anne. It was difficult to hear Anne's voice under the crackle.

Still, she sounded relieved to hear that Spider had been found.

"He wishes to apologize as soon as he can," Pierrette said.

"Oh, no need for that. I'm just so glad he's with you! And are you all right?"

"Never better. There's something else I want to tell you. Your mother's papers. We've found a part that survives. Some calculations. I can't make head or tail of them, but we're going to put a stop to her plans, and then we'll have someone look at the figures."

"Not the same thing as the bomb, then? Is it something to do with electricity?"

"I couldn't say, but no, I don't think so. I had the whole thing nearly memorized at one time, but it's been so many years. Do you know what it reminds me of most?"

Pierrette paused, realizing she'd stumbled into a potentially hurtful area. It had reminded her of the tables Ada had made to help her place bets in the races, making predictions about how each horse would do, based on their past performance. But Ada's predictions had always come out wrong, and she'd spent the last years of her life in miserable debts to terrible men.

"Yes?"

"The phone – I can't hear. We're all right. I'll send a wire in a day or two."

She ended the call and stood for a moment, her cheeks flushed, thinking.

Then she went to the locked drawer where they were keeping the puzzle-box papers, and lay down on the settee to read them over again. Columns of numbers, with random words and symbols around them. Calculations. A table with numbers in every cell, values that made no sense, with letters of the alphabet beside them.

She was, suddenly, certain. There was a familiarity in all this, and she realized why at last. The calculations *were* the tables that Ada had used for predicting the races. And Pierrette had always suspected there was nothing wrong with those predictions after all, that the races had been rigged.

Forcing herself to slow down, to *think*, she paced. Why would Konstanze want Ada's racetrack calculating tables? As far as she knew, the countess had no need to make money at the track or at card tables; her businesses supplied half the railroads of Europe.

Konstanze had wanted a way to predict what would happen – not what horses would do, but what people would do. She had asked Simeon to teach her the history of the Brotherhood, to understand how the Assassins made decisions. She wanted to control the world, not through some Piece of Eden but through science. Honestly, the Engine of History didn't have to be a device at all.

It might be a method of calculating, of making predictions. Complex predictions. If the Templars could predict where the Assassins would go and what they would do, they could win every encounter – especially if they had faster horses, faster locomotives, faster steamships, private telegraphs. They could appear anywhere they wanted, and Ada's calculations would tell them precisely where and when to appear.

If her new theory was right, the Engine of History might already be complete.

And in which case, the tower itself was a trap. Her heart leapt with how terribly the Assassins had been manipulated, how they had all become predictable.

Simeon did not have a telephone. But his flat, where he was meeting Mary with the cart, was not far. She could run there but by the time she arrived, he might already be on his way to the tower. She needed to move quickly. The house had one of the new safety bicycles: two wheels the same size, and it rode smoothly, Mary had said.

Pierrette ran up the stairs, ready to bang on the bedroom door, but it was open. Spider was sitting up, reading.

"Is it time to go?"

"It would be," she said breathlessly, "but the whole thing's off. I have to get to Simeon and tell him. Go down to the tower as we planned, and tell Fabrice and Michel that I said it's a trap. We're being set up."

Spider leapt to his feet and Pierrette ran downstairs.

All her experience riding bicycles had been with the Aurora

troupe, although she'd never performed on one – it had mostly been to make Spider laugh. But she rode well enough to get the thing rolling out of the back shed, down the laneway and out into the dark street.

And she nearly fell off when she saw Konstanze suddenly standing in front of her, a gun aimed at her chest.

Pierrette's throwing knife fell out of her hand as Konstanze's shot hit her right hip, and then she did fall off the bicycle. The right side of her body burned, her legs were scraped and tangled, and she'd hit her head on the way down. Konstanze was a bit blurred as she came closer.

"Should I stain something with your blood?" she asked. "I am not sentimental enough. Perhaps that's why I never made a convincing Assassin. But I am very good at gaining control of whatever I can. Including telephones. I knew I was right to stay close to you."

She'd listened in on her conversation with Anne, through the wires somehow. Of course. How else could she be here? Pierrette had been *predictable*.

Pierrette croaked, "You want us to blow up the tower. Why?"

Konstanze's answer was to point the gun at her face. "Because this is how we set the Engine of History in motion."

When the shot came, Pierrette was surprised to still be aware of the world, of the ringing in her ears. Of the pain. At the least, there should have been a release from pain. Of the noise.

But another shot hit the pavement near her, and she became aware that the presence standing over her had changed. Konstanze had left and Spider was there, his face worried. Holding a gun. Time moved strangely, like she was underwater.

She was wet, sweating. And the roaring in her ears wasn't water. It was her own breath, coming hard.

That last shot hadn't come from Konstanze's gun, but from Spider's, no doubt chasing Konstanze off. Pierrette hadn't even known he had one.

"Can I carry you?" Spider asked. "We'll get you to the hospital. She's run off; I didn't get her, more's the pity."

She shook her head. "Warn Simeon. The others. Tell them. Don't do it."

Spider, not paying attention, slid his arms beneath her. She winced with the pain.

She gathered her strength. "You can do this for me, Spider. Do what I ask. Please. Tell Simeon the engine is not the tower. It's predictions. Ada's tables. They know what will happen if we blow up the tower. It will be bad for the Brotherhood. The Templars want us to do it."

His face was tortured, but the gunshots had already drawn the police. Pierrette could hear them, the rapid footsteps, the officious yelling.

"Go," she whispered to Spider, who finally listened.

CHAPTER THIRTY-TWO

Simeon was transporting the dynamite in a night soil cart, and several of the barrels were actually full of the contents of people's cesspits, in case of inspection. Much of Paris wasn't yet on the sewer system, giving Simeon an excellent excuse to be driving through the streets in the small hours.

He put on a smelly and battered coat and hat, and drove the cart south through quiet streets, crossed the Seine under the streetlamps. A few people a little the worse for wine touched their caps and yelled greetings at him as he passed, but otherwise he saw no one.

When he reached the shadow of the tower, he drove the cart into an alley, and shifted the dynamite charges to a pack on his back.

It was easy to approach the tower without spending much time in the open, thanks to the rows of buildings under construction to host the Great Exhibition. The tower itself was still under construction, too: by day, the area rang with the sound of hammers on metal, and the stench of coal smoke hung in the air. The tower was almost complete; the highest platform and railing encircled the top, like the band of a crown, but above that was ragged metal pointing at the sky.

Everything was ready.

But Simeon was nervous, all the same. Konstanze knew they had the puzzle box, so she had to assume they had the papers. She must have someone watching the tower. He hoped she assumed they would be too noble and circumspect to use explosives in the heart of Paris. A prediction that had nearly been true.

At the edge of the exhibition area, the base of the tower yawned, the four pillars curving upward. There were several huts for the workers, dark now, and a lighted guard hut beyond.

He tilted his pocket watch to catch enough moonlight to read it: ten minutes to three o'clock. A long ten minutes, while he lounged against the corner of the exhibition hall, waiting.

At last: a distant whistle. Fabrice carrying out the diversion.

The guard took his lantern and loped off toward the whistle.

Simeon dashed forward, staying out of the moonlight. He tied each charge to a girder near the ground and connected the wires to the blasting caps. The guard returned just as he had finished the fourth leg, and there was nowhere to dash, so Simeon went up. Grabbed a girder, put his foot onto it, grabbed the next one, then froze as the guard stood in his hut and swept his lantern around.

The cold iron bit into Simeon's palms. He'd removed his gloves to have more dexterity while setting the charges. He was holding on to a concave curve that had not been designed for the comfort of a man trying to hang off it without making any noise or movement.

I'm too old for this.

When the guard had retreated to his hut door, Simeon moved around to the far side of the pillar to drop down, when he paused.

The silhouette of a woman, strolling through the darkness as though it were Sunday at the park. The silhouette of *the* woman. He was sure of it. But Konstanze wasn't alone. She was holding hands with someone shorter than her. When they came into the glow of the guard's lantern, he caught sight of long brown ringlets resting on a pack strapped to her back.

A girl, no older than twelve, at a guess. At three o'clock in the morning.

An innocent.

She looked familiar, and then he remembered the girl who had played the part of the alarmed stranger when Konstanze climbed out of the hotel.

The guard was clearly on Konstanze's side or on her payroll, because after a brief conversation, he handed them a second lantern and gestured toward the nearest pillar. Konstanze and the girl started climbing a staircase inside the pillar across from him. He craned his neck and looked up. There was a platform on the first level; he could intercept them there.

Climbing the tower, once he got going, was a delight; there always seemed to be a handhold or foothold where he needed it, and the shape of the thing guided him so smoothly that he never had to stop and rethink his path. It was hard on his hands, though.

He pulled himself up to a railing in time to see Konstanze and the girl walking across a platform within the tower. Konstanze had a pack on her shoulders, just as he did. What were they carrying up to the top?

Damn it. At four o'clock, Fabrice and Mary would press down the T-bars on the blasting machines, whether or not Simeon was there. They'd settled on that, in case he was taken after laying the charges, or couldn't get to his colleagues without being seen. They only had an hour before this tower would fall, taking anyone inside with it.

There was a gun in his belt, but a shot might draw the police and jeopardize the operation. Besides, shooting toward a girl in a cage full of iron where the bullet might ricochet in any direction seemed like a recipe for regret. Damn Konstanze. She had always been ruthless, but it was hard to believe that even she would deliberately use a child as a human shield. Perhaps there was some other reason the girl was here. Some Templars did take young protégés; Konstanze had been involved in the Order's work from a young age herself. This could be a niece or cousin, just as an aunt had raised Konstanze. She'd never mentioned such a relationship, but the girl wouldn't have been born when Simeon had been with Konstanze. He knew nothing about her life now.

He was close enough now to hear their conversation. Konstanze spoke to the girl, "Just wait until we get to the top. I really believe this is my best design yet. The culmination of a lifetime of work. It changes everything. And I'm so glad you're here with me to see it, my dear."

They went up a short spiral staircase, toward a second platform.

Simeon stopped thinking and acted. He crawled upward as quickly as he could and jumped onto the second platform, the sound of his boots hitting the iron ringing out.

Konstanze and the girl turned.

"What a delightful surprise," Konstanze said drily, her expression totally blank. He kept his own steady. If she wasn't going to show the slightest joy or pain upon seeing him, then neither would he. He had years of practice at keeping the surface of the sea completely calm, no matter what was going on beneath.

But unlike Konstanze, he had no interest in banter and games.

"Get off the tower," he said. "It's not safe here at night, in the darkness. You should know better than to bring a girl up here."

"Oh, but this girl is very good with heights." She put her hand on the girl's shoulder, a tight grip. "Allow me to introduce you. Simeon, this is Gisela, your daughter. Say hello to your father, Gisela."

"Hello," the girl said.

The word *daughter* registered slowly, like a sound underwater, echoing in his brain before he grasped its meaning. What a horrible game for Konstanze to play, on him but worst of all, on the girl. Could it really be? She was the right age, if Konstanze had been pregnant when he left. When she'd held a gun on him.

All these years, he'd had a daughter. A dozen years of her life, missed, when he was stalking thugs and chasing after misguided radicals.

Of course, Konstanze could be lying. It could be any other man's daughter. It could be a trick.

It didn't matter anyway, in this moment, who her father was. She was an innocent, and she was in the way. He shut himself down and acted.

Pulling a knife out of his boot, he shouted, "Step away from her. You're putting the girl in danger."

"You're the one holding the knife, Simeon. But if you'd like to murder me in front of my child, by all means, I'll make it easy for you. Go on up, Gisela. Don't worry. Remember your training."

The girl hesitated, holding his gaze one moment, curiosity in her eyes. Then she walked toward a corkscrew staircase that stretched right up the tower toward the summit. She went up one turn of the staircase and then looked out at them over the railing. Simeon couldn't read her expression at this distance.

He wished he had Pierrette's skill with knives. And he wished that he could bring himself to kill Konstanze here and now, despite the girl looking on. But with a small grunt of frustration, he threw the knife at Konstanze's leg instead.

She stumbled back, her hand to her thigh. Her voice was raspy as she fell to her knees. "You really did it."

An injury; enough to slow her down, perhaps. But not enough to stop her shooting him, if she chose. He moved quickly, pulling himself up to a girder and running across it toward the staircase, above Konstanze. He'd get the girl, carry her down, and Fabrice and Mary would blow the tower.

And then he would go to bed and never get up again.

"Run, darling!" Konstanze called from below. "Remember what you've learned."

Gisela started running up the stairs, her gloved hand light on the railing, her boots beating the iron steps. Simeon jumped to the staircase and then pulled himself from one loop of the spiral to the one above, using the railing. He gained a little ground, but his shoulders were screaming at him, and what they screamed was: *old man.*

At the next loop, he pulled himself inside the staircase

and ran up the steps after her. A half-dozen steps were all that separated them, but the gap never closed. He could hear Konstanze behind him now; the wound in her leg was slowing her. His breath was coming like the tide by the time they reached the top.

A wide circle of iron, a platform with the railing already around it. But in the center, the summit was not complete. Simeon could see iron bars ending abruptly at all angles, poking out like a weird bouquet.

Something like a miniature railway track ran all around the platform. Two giant spotlights were set on trolleys on the track, but they were dark; they were intended to light up on inauguration day and spotlight Exhibition buildings. They were the only electrical lights on the tower, in addition to a beacon at the as-yet-unfinished summit. The rest of the tower would be lit by gas when the day arrived. But now it was dark, illuminated only by the moonlight.

Gisela ran to the edge of the platform, stopping at the railing.

He ran toward her. Paris was laid out below them, a pattern of lights. He hadn't seen the world from this height since his balloon ride. The city seemed like a single glowing organism in the darkness, waiting to receive him, if he just let one foot slip into the air.

Gisela was up against the rail that encircled the platform. All he had to do was get the girl and guide her down the stairs. That might mean killing Konstanze in front of her.

He should have done it years ago. The Brotherhood taught that there was a cost to *not* killing people, and here was a painful demonstration just for him. And for the world, if he failed. He had no doubt now that this tower meant something to Konstanze: *It changes everything,* she'd said. There must be a Piece of Eden up here; or perhaps she had brought it with her.

Konstanze was still on the staircase below. He paused at the top, drew his gun. Would the shot carry down to the world below? It seemed to be almost another planet. He could just see pieces of her, as she climbed; he waited for a clear shot. In the meantime, there was nowhere for Gisela to go.

It was so quiet up here; the city slept in total silence.

Konstanze spoke calmly, almost sadly. "It's time to use your toy, darling."

Simeon whirled. Gisela held out something toward Simeon; it looked like a ball in her upturned palm. He'd made the fundamental mistake of turning his back on an enemy. He hadn't thought of her as anything other than an innocent pawn.

He was dizzy. The world tilted like the deck of a sinking ship, and he grabbed onto the nearest piece of iron to keep from falling into death. There was something horrible about this height, something unnatural. The tower was a monster standing over the city, a giant nearly ready to wake up and take control. From here, a signal could blanket Europe like a storm cloud. Soon every city in the world would have an iron henchman ready to serve the will of the Templars, to keep the minds of the people in check. Because that was what the Pieces of Eden did, wasn't it? They manipulated body and mind. They took away people's control.

But Simeon knew what he wanted. It was perfectly clear, what needed to be done. The tower could not stand. It was too dangerous, and the lives of three people were nothing. Standing steadily now, he watched himself as if from a distance, as if he was not choosing any more, only acting. It was a blessed relief.

No more doubt. At four o'clock, one push of the plunger and his pain would be over, and the world would be safe. He didn't have to do anything.

A figure out of the darkness leaped from the railing behind Gisela and knocked her down.

The ball in her hand rolled onto the platform.

And suddenly, Simeon's mind was his own again.

Gisela was down on the iron platform, wrestling with Spider. Spider! He must have been right behind them, and climbed up this part of the tower from the outside to knock Gisela down and stop her from using her ball – no. The Apple of Eden. The Apple of Eden that Konstanze had taken from Oscar Kane, decades before. An ancient device that could control minds.

Spider drew a knife and held it to Gisela's neck. Panting, he said to Simeon, "Pierrette sent me. The Templars want us to blow up the tower. She said something like, 'The engine is not the tower'. I don't know if that makes sense. She said, 'It's predictions. Ada's tables. They know what will happen'. Something about it being bad for the Brotherhood, if the tower fell."

Ada's tables. Predictions.

The Templars with their fast trains and fast horses, moving pieces into position, knowing exactly where those positions should be. Studying the past to predict the future. If the Templars could make the Assassins do something terrible, something public, bring them out into the light of scrutiny, the Brotherhood would find itself a public enemy across Europe. Chaos, fear and unrest would give governments the excuse to impose tyrannical laws, paving the way for Templar control. Michel had known there were risks in blowing up the tower, and he'd taken precautions, to pin the explosion on an invented scapegoat. But the Templars must have known that Michel's precautions would fail.

The Templars were playing a long game, and they were confident of the outcome. To stoke the fear of international terrorism and shore up support for powerful empires. Konstanze had never truly lost faith in Ada's ideas, and Simeon should have done the same.

The engine is not the tower.

The letter Mary had deciphered. The sketch of the tower on the back. Red herrings to lead them here, thinking there was some sort of Piece of Eden bound up in this strange metal monster. But the engine was a column of numbers somewhere, telling the Templars the likelihood of any outcome. Telling them where to find their enemies, so they could arrive there first. Telling them what the Assassins would do, based on the information they had about how Assassins thought and acted: information Simeon had supplied.

Konstanze had never given up on the Engine of History. She had summoned him to her castle because she needed information to feed into her columns. Her pet project that her colleagues thought would never work. She was going to prove them wrong. She was going to make the Assassins destroy themselves, starting with an act of terrorism in the heart of Europe.

Konstanze was nearly at the top of the stairs now, her gaze on him. He pulled Pierrette's handkerchief out of a pocket and threw it onto the platform floor, a challenge and a warning. Konstanze would know what that meant; she would know he was serious.

He leaped on her, his Hidden Blade half an inch from her throat when she twisted away from him. She clawed his cheek, and her good knee came up to his solar plexus, but her wounded leg was weak and he pushed on it, and she buckled. They danced on a network of girders between the staircase and the ring of the platform, until he shoved her right up against a piece of iron studded with rivets and watched the blood trickle out the side of her neck.

Simeon's Hidden Blade snicked out of its gauntlet, aimed at Konstanze's throat.

The blade went wide, slicing into the tendons joining her neck to her shoulder instead. Someone had pushed him from behind, and he tumbled over the edge of a girder, grabbed on, his legs dangling nine hundred feet over Paris. He heard Konstanze scream from the pain of the wound he'd just given her.

He was dimly aware, as his shoulders started to come apart and his fingers started to slip, that Gisela knelt on the platform, using Pierrette's handkerchief to staunch the wound on her mother's neck. She'd got out of Spider's grip.

Spider crawled onto the girder above Simeon and reached one arm down to grasp Simeon's by the shoulder, which gave Simeon enough strength to get his other arm around the girder and pull himself up, barely managing to do this without overbalancing them both. They crawled over to the platform, but Konstanze and Gisela were not where they had left them. They were standing by the railing, holding hands, looking out over the city. Konstanze did not turn around, but said in a weak voice to him, "I wanted to know whether you'd do it."

She and Gisela stepped up onto the thin railing, as the packs on their backs opened into vast wings of leather and metal, as complex as the wings of flying creatures, but not quite like any Simeon had ever seen. Before Simeon could register what he was seeing, mother and daughter stepped into the air.

He and Spider rushed over to the side. The two figures were gliding in a spiral slowly downward.

"Where is the Apple?" Simeon demanded, looking at Spider.

Spider's face was blank, then understanding dawned. "The ball? It rolled over there." They both looked in the direction Spider pointed, but the platform was empty. "The girl must have grabbed it. Taken it with her."

Simeon gripped the railing, watching, frustration building that he had no way to alert the Assassins on the ground to Konstanze's location, to the girl who held an Apple of Eden. From above, they looked like massive birds out of some legend, not like humans at all. But they were humans: the woman he had loved, and the child he'd never known, getting smaller as the distance grew between them.

Then the figure on the left started moving strangely, one wing folding like an injured insect. Konstanze was badly injured; the wings must have been agony, and she couldn't operate them. She fell too fast.

In the moonlight, Konstanze crashed to the ground.

The time it took for Gisela to drift down beside her mother's body must have been a lifetime. Simeon felt no victory, no closure, just bile in his mouth, thinking of his daughter, of this child, on the street below.

He numbed himself as best he could and turned to Spider. "Will Pierrette tell them to call off the detonation?"

Spider said nothing for a moment. Then, in an odd, strangled

voice: "Pierrette is at the hospital. That woman shot her. She
sent me here. I don't think the others know. I wasn't sure where
to find them, thought I could tell you first–"

Simeon looked at his watch and swore. The plan was that
at four o'clock, if Simeon hadn't shown up yet, they would
assume he'd been taken, and detonate, in the hopes that he'd
been able to set the charges first. He had to tell Fabrice and
Mary to stop.

But it was ten minutes to four.

Impossible to get down all those stairs in time.

He wasn't sure he had ever had enough faith to survive a leap
from this height, even when his body and heart were younger.
In any case, if he leaped, he couldn't take Spider with him, and
Spider was not a trained Assassin. Simeon didn't want to live
if it meant facing Pierrette and telling her he'd left Tillie's son
to die.

He looked around, trying to think, to take every fact in and
see how he could use it.

"The moonlight," he said. "If we had a mirror, we could
signal. But what kind of mirror would be bright enough up
here?"

"Look at this!" Spider ran a few feet and crouched by the
two giant spotlight casings on their track. Their glass lenses
pointing downward, toward the city. "We can use these to
signal. Can't we?"

Simeon had caught sight of the steam engines in the pillars
below; for operating the lifts that would go in eventually, he
assumed, but they probably powered the lights, too. "We can't
make it down to the engine in time."

"No, look, there's a battery array here. Perhaps it's a backup, or they were testing it. Should I try it? I'm good with wires and things."

"By all means," Simeon said, running over.

He was nearly blinded when the thing came on, as powerful as a lighthouse beacon, a circle of cold white light.

A few minutes, before the tower fell, and he and Spider with it, into a fireball. A few moments left to live, unless he could think of a message that Fabrice and Mary would be sure to understand, and one that they would believe came from him.

He pulled off his coat and clambered up on top of the spotlight, which creaked and yawed alarmingly. He tried not to think about how terribly distant the world was. He thought only about dropping his coat in front of the lens, and then smoothly pulling it aside at intervals, long and short, spelling out the message in Morse:

S-T-O-P-N-O-G-O-D-S-N-O-M-A-S-T-E-R-S-S-T-O-P

He spelled it out continuously, his legs cramping, his body cold, until Spider said, "Simeon. It's three minutes past four."

There was no sign of Gisela or of Konstanze on the streets below. Simeon and Spider managed to get the charges disconnected and off the tower, and they told Fabrice and Mary the basic facts of what they'd learned. By that time, Michel had reached them too, and being Michel, he already knew where Pierrette had gone: the Lariboisière hospital, not far from Montmartre. The doctors said she would live, but the bones had shattered in her hip, and she would be many weeks in recovery.

There was much more to discuss but it would have to wait. Simeon wanted to get to Pierrette. He and Spider "borrowed" a carriage and drove north.

The night soil men had finished their business (although Simeon's abandoned cart would no doubt mean a bad day for someone). Now, the bakers and shoeshine boys were busy. The sun was not over the buildings yet, but the sky was waking up.

It seemed to bring a sense of reality with it. Konstanze von Visler was gone from the world. He felt a sick sense of vertigo. The weight of guilt and anger lifted from him. The woman who had haunted him for the last twelve years, who had been a constant worry before that, who had kidnapped and hurt his dearest friend…

He choked it back. He remembered her eyes, looking at him in that train car, studying him in his room in Brussels, in their cabin in the mountains.

Simeon was glad Spider drove the carriage. Konstanze was brilliant, and passionate, and loved the world. She loved it the way she had no doubt loved her daughter, the way a potter loves the clay, the way an Assassin loves the blade.

But he had loved her genuinely, once. Maybe always.

They drove slowly through a group of factory men in flat caps, walking to work.

"I saw it, and so did my wife," said one of them. "No gods, no masters. Just like we used to say in '71. During the Commune."

"Hush," said a man beside him. "You don't want anyone hearing you talk about that."

"Why not? It might do some people good to hear it." The man drew a breath, and yelled, "No gods, no masters!"

The city was quiet, and then, from a distant window, came the response. "No gods, no masters!"

Something swelled in Simeon's chest, and he felt the way he did at the opera, when the overture began. Good changes were possible. The work he had done, the work they had all done, was not for nothing. Governments came and went but the people remembered their power. Not even the Templars could predict the consequences of that power, not with all the numbers in the world. He had lost so much, but not everything. Michel, Mary and Fabrice were alive and they would keep working for the creed they shared.

And Pierrette would live. She had spent so many years protecting Ada's legacy and keeping harm out of the world. She would never give up. As long as she needed friends at her side, Simeon would not give up either.

Neither would he give up on the girl somewhere out there frightened and grieving now, who would no doubt believe her father was her mortal enemy. The girl raised to be a Templar. The girl who held minds in her hand.

They came to the hospital gates. As he opened the carriage door, he realized he was exhausted, and an old leg wound was acting up. He let Spider take his arm.

It went up around them as they walked, old men muttering it, young women shouting it. *No gods, no masters.*

Simeon's eyes burned. Freedom was not a fight to be won or lost. Freedom *was* the fight. And he was still standing.

ACKNOWLEDGMENTS

The community of Assassin's Creed players, readers, bloggers, podcasters, artists and fans have been so welcoming since the publication of *The Magus Conspiracy*, and that reception really buoyed me during the writing of the sequel.

My thanks to my editor, Gwendolyn Nix, whose wise feedback helped this book become what it needed to be. And to everyone at Aconyte Books for their hard work, including Marc Gascoigne, Joe Riley, Nick Tyler, Ashley Stephens, and Amanda Treseler. Thanks as well to Anjuli Smith and also to everyone at Wunderkind PR, including Elena Stokes, Brianna Robinson and Lisa Giampietro. And thanks to Bastien Jez for the glorious cover artwork. And of course, I'm so grateful to Ubisoft for their support of this series and for creating this world to play in.

I've relied a lot on the work of historians, documentarians and non-fiction writers, and on the writing left to us from witnesses to the Franco-Prussian war and the other events in the novel.

My partner Brent and my son Xavier have been unfailingly patient and supportive during the writing of this book. And finally, my agent, Jennie Goloboy, has all my gratitude, as ever, for her hard work, vision and encouragement.

About the Author

KATE HEARTFIELD writes novels, novellas, stories and games. Her most recent novels are *The Valkyrie* (2023) and *Assassin's Creed: The Magus Conspiracy* (2022). Her works also include the *Sunday Times* bestseller *The Embroidered Book* (2022), and the Alice Payne time travel novellas (2018/2019). She also writes interactive fiction, including *The Road to Canterbury* and *The Magician's Workshop*, both published by Choice of Games. Kate's work has been shortlisted for several awards, including the Nebula and Locus awards. A former newspaper journalist, she is now a freelance editor and writer, and she teaches journalism and creative writing. Kate lives in Ottawa, Canada.

heartfieldfiction.com
twitter.com/kateheartfield

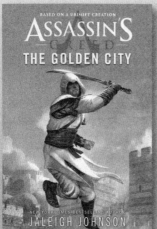